THE BRU INITIATIVE

(or what men do together)

Martyn H. Taylor

ISBN: 9798796352779

I cannot teach anyone anything. I can only make them think. - Socrates

Chapter One

MARCUS'S COMING OF AGE

September, 1977.

"Okay, Marcus," said Luigi, "get prepared... you know what to do. You've seen it all before." Marcus was expecting these words, or something similar, but the reality of what was to come momentarily froze him to the spot.

"Next door and change down to just your jeans," instructed his trainer, waving a hand to indicate the room Marcus should go to.

It only took a few minutes for him to get fully undressed and then put on his jeans, and come out again. He felt nervous and vulnerable as he ran his hand along his smooth chest. The wooden floor seemed cold underfoot as Marcus took another step towards his fate.

Everyone was now in place around the perimeter of the room. Marcus was aware that he had become the centre of everyone's attention. All eyes were now fixed on him and his actions.

He knew he would be judged by what would happen in the next twenty minutes or so. This could be the last time he would have to prove himself, he thought. One of the main lights in the gym had been switched off but the room glowed in an eerie way from one corner. Several lighted candles had been placed on a large metal folding table. Marcus looked over to the middle of the room to focus on the padded sports bench that had been carefully positioned allowing equal space for people to move around freely.

Luigi walked over to Marcus and tied his hands behind his back with a blue chord saved from an old dressing gown, long since thrown away. Marcus then moved over to the bench, which was low enough for him to sit on. He moved his weight across and was now lying down, staring at the high ceiling. One of the other men in the room positioned Marcus's legs so that his ankles could slip into ties at the end. The tethered young captive

1

prepared himself for what was coming next by taking a slow, deep breath.

"Well, folks, Marcus's time with us is drawing to a close. He has already fought his last fight for us and must move on," said Luigi, addressing the dozen or so onlookers.

Luigi looked directly at Marcus. Would he lie back stoically and accept what was coming or pretend to put up a bit of a mock fight. As Marcus did not much like the limelight he decided on the former course of action. He took another deep breath and waited for the pain.

Dean was the first boxer in the gym to bring his candle over. He, like most of the others, was dressed in a grey tracksuit and a dull orange gym logoed T-shirt. Leaning over and slowly, deliberately moving his wrist he let all his candle wax fall onto Marcus's unprotected chest.

The dripping wax momentarily burned, but Marcus could stand it. All the others were near him now, crowding in on both sides of the bench to get a closer view. Some tipped their wax silently others wished him luck in whatever he did with his life after leaving the Tyneside gym.

"Ah, that hurt … bastard … who was that," Marcus growled. With a chuckle Simon turned away to get another candle. As Marcus looked down at his chest, he could see the winter patterns the white wax was forming as it dried hard. Almost everyone had delivered their wax and were now standing back, talking or laughing, or just looking over at their victim.

"Howay the Magpies," someone shouted from the back of the group, followed by muffled laughter. Marcus was aware that, unlike most of his comrades, he had little interest in football. Simon came back with his second delivery of hot wax. Marcus wondered when the ritualised humiliation would end.

"All of you … all of you," said Luigi raising his voice, "back to what you were previously doing. I know most of you were about to go home." Marcus began to relax. He was sure it was just he and Ali in the room, but Stefan walked in carrying a lighted candle in each hand. "Give it to him," said Ali, grinning, "You can do what you like with him. I'll be in the back packing away the equipment."

2

"I haven't done *my* bit," said Stefan. Marcus tensed again on hearing these words. Stefan was leaning over Marcus, picking the wax from his young victim's chest. Looking down, it reminded him of little streams of frozen ice. Most of his upper chest was pink from the ordeal.

"Are you a man or a mouse," asked Stefan, running his hand over Marcus's chest. Marcus did not reply. "Well, we'll find out then," Stefan said, in a menacing tone. Marcus knew Stefan to be a tough, brutal fighter who liked to get his opponents bloodied. He braced himself to be Stefan's trapped mouse.

For a full ten minutes Stefan subjected Marcus to what he referred to as a 'mild torture' session. He had heard Stefan use the term after giving another boxer a thrashing in the ring. When Stefan was confident of a win, he would wear his opponent down round after round until going in hard towards the end. The boxing public loved it, as did the trainers and managers, who gained from the financial spin off. They would be confident that audiences got more for their money, so were likely to return again. Stefan was a favourite and could do no wrong, and he knew it.

Stefan pulled Marcus up by his short, mousy hair. Once in a sitting position his wrists were untied.

"Lay back and put your arms out," demanded Stefan. Marcus was in no place to defy him. Stefan had soon tied both of his victim's wrists to the bench. He did the same with his prey's ankles. Marcus's chest was exposed and he could only wriggle and arch his abdomen. "That's more like it," said Stefan, as he came across with more lighted candles. He paused and let each load of hot wax drip onto Marcus's nipples.

After another few minutes or so Stefan withdrew; he had had his fun and was becoming bored. He untied the chords that had held Marcus to the bench. As Marcus moved to a standing position Stefan reminded him that the jeans he was wearing belonged to the gym. Stefan put out his hand to receive them. A naked Marcus walked back to the changing room.

"Nice arse," shouted Stefan. Marcus felt embarrassed, but not defeated.

--o--

The next morning found Marcus in bed, daydreaming. He glanced to the right to see that it was nearly ten o'clock. He looked over at the red and white calendar hanging on his bedroom wall. Tomorrow would be the night of the autumn equinox. It always seemed that the summer would never return after that date. Marcus got up and out of bed and flicked the calendar to the next month. He would be twenty-one years old on 10th. It was unlikely that he would celebrate his birthday in any meaningful way.

After all, Marcus never did anything special for his 'coming of age' on his eighteenth so why would twenty-one be any different, he pondered. 10th October would mark something else. On that day Marcus's boxing management contract would officially come to an end.

Marcus was feeling subdued and dejected and returned to his bed. As he looked back over the years, he suddenly felt quite sad. He took a deep breath. This feeling soon passed like a solitary dark cloud moving quickly across the sun on an otherwise bright day.

Marcus had been given the usual 'send-off' the evening before and now he was moving into another era. Looking back, he concluded that he did have some good times participating in the inter-school bouts, the training, and the more frequent contests since leaving his school.

The training had left him quite fit – he could see that without looking in a full-length mirror – but some of the physical punishments for getting things wrong were harsh by 1970's standards, and probably more suited to a borstal environment fifty years earlier, he thought. He hated having his photograph taken, which seemed a regular part of his life as a boxer, and yet another imposed ritual.

The many past punishments made Marcus's parting from his contract look relatively tame. He guessed trainers wanted to make the point that it is no good doing things in the 'wrong' way. Marcus found himself looking back to the last weeks of his schooling to when he was brought into the Head's dingy, dark little office, with its numerous shelves of books, and told he had to sign a boxing management contract. He had not even reached the age of seventeen. Marcus had been forced to box but somehow, on some base level, had agreed to all of it.

When someone takes on a boxing management contract they must have faith in their trainers, Marcus pondered. He was convincing himself that the last few years had not all been a waste. Boxers either do what their mentor wants, or not – the choice is always theirs. Choose the latter and you will soon be dropped into oblivion, Marcus concluded.

He continued to let his mind wander and his attention was soon drawn to a small quartz skull that sat on his window ledge. It was in its usual place, half obscured by a curtain. Marcus was shocked not to remember when and how he obtained the head. His mind continued its wanderings. What was the point in getting up now, he thought? He had been an awkward teenager when he was first involved in boxing but it was all now about to come to an end – like everything in life. Boxing got him away from cheap cider and sniffing glue.

Boxing gave him confidence and determination and had built up the body of a weedy, shy individual who had been afraid of boys his own age. If he was honest with himself, Marcus was still just as shy inside but going into a boxing ring meant he was perceived as strong. Marcus found himself going back in time to when he was a young boy; when he had seaside holidays with his parents on the harsh North Sea coast with its beautiful blue seas. He found South Shields fascinating but could not get away from the feeling that he was just there as an onlooker.

It was as if his parents delivered him to the seaside and he just watched as someone who was alone but not lonely. He recalled the times when, every day, he looked at other people and wondered if any of them felt the same way. He remembered that at the time he concluded they did not.

Years on, the main regret Marcus was now left with was that he did not make any money from entertaining the public and his, sometimes sadistic, teachers, trainers and managers. Others obviously did. Was his fate to be a perpetual observer, he wondered. It occurred to him that maybe his destiny was somewhere outside his familiar north-east.

Smiling inwardly, Marcus's thoughts jumped to the previous evening. He hoped that he had entertained Luigi and the other boxers at the gym. If he had not it was too late. With a sigh, Marcus thought that he would probably never step into the ring again.

The unmistakable bang of the front door closing hard shot Marcus back to the here and now. He had assumed that he was alone in the house. Peering out of the window he spied Stefan's distinctive white, early model Ford Transit van, with its extra chrome. It was parked outside. Marcus was now expecting a visit, and quickly grabbed a green woollen jumper to put on.

Heavy footsteps were pounding up the stairs getting ever louder. Stefan was soon outside Marcus's door. He knocked, but then came straight inside the bedroom. Marcus braced himself.

"How are you, Marcus," asked Stefan. Marcus replied that he was feeling good. Stefan wanted to know if any of the candle wax from the evening before had marked his chest. Marcus replied that it had not. He slipped his jumper off to prove the point but did not know why he was pandering to his visitor's agenda.

"Well then, I can see I should have been a bit rougher with you," he said, pausing. "Anyway, Luigi has sent me." Marcus braced himself for a second hit.

"He wants you out of here before your birthday," he continued. A wave of shock rippled through Marcus, but he tried to hide it from his gym buddy. Stefan might have said more before leaving, but Marcus did not hear any further words.

He knew it was time to move on.

Chapter Two

BUILD UP TO LOWGATE

April, 1980.

Marcus looked out of the office window where he worked as a Finance Assistant. It was very dirty. The window cleaners hardly ever came to this grey, brutal looking office block. Marcus considered it a blight on the landscape, but sadly there were similarly brutal looking buildings in that part of the city. If he stood up, and moved closer to one of the big, square windows, he could glimpse Victorian buildings nearby. He marvelled at some of the detail the architects put into the brickwork. 'One day,' he thought to himself, he would own an old house.

Every time it rained the windows on his utilitarian office block would appear cleaner, but it was an illusion. Now, a tiny spider was attempting to spin a fine web in one corner of a large pane of glass. The constant wind at the eighth floor was making it difficult, but the spider was not in the mood to give up.

In the street below people were hurrying about their business. It was one of those typically English spring days: a little bit of sun, a little bit of wind, then a little bit of rain. Most of Marcus's work colleagues were out of the office leaving only him and his boss, Roger, to answer the phones and deal with the correspondence.

Marcus had learned the insurance business over the past eighteen months. He had received a lot of training in the post, and his boss was particularly helpful in passing on his knowledge. It did not seem to matter to people in the office that Marcus had a difficult upbringing. It was his job to check the paperwork before authorising a payment to claimants. He liked the work, which gave him a regular income, but he liked his work colleagues more.

"Marcus, stop daydreaming," said Roger, "Look … check this out. Have you seen this news thing from the trade union that is doing the rounds?" He was becoming ever animated. Marcus

7

glanced across to his boss, who was waving a bit of light blue, printed paper to catch his work colleague's attention.

"No, what is it," Marcus replied, getting up from his desk and slowly walking over.

Roger was a few years older than Marcus and was the sort who would get excited by anything to do with sports. He was an active member of a local cricket team and played football in a Sunday league. He saw himself as a bit of an expert on most sports apart from motor racing, which he could not stand.

'A fraction of a second here, a fraction of a second there, I cannot see the point of it all' he often could be heard telling anyone who was hapless enough to mention the subject. Roger was not a bad person, and people always thought he would act as an inspiration to his two young children at a time when some politicians were starting to talk of strange things like selling off school playing fields to build luxury flats.

Sitting behind his old oak desk Roger explained enthusiastically how Optimus was planning to arrange a boxing tournament, if they could get enough trained volunteers.

"I'm surprised our union would want to get involved with boxing," said Marcus, "I can imagine football, even rugby, but not boxing."

"Well, that's what it says... take a good look for yourself," responded Roger. Marcus asked Roger if he was thinking of entering himself on behalf of the section.

"No, but you could do it," he said with an excited tone of voice. Marcus recalled having a long conversation with Roger the previous Christmas Eve about his earlier boxing career. He wondered, in hindsight, if he had disclosed too much.

Most of the office had gone to the 'Kings Arms' before staggering on to their bus or train to get back home. Roger and Marcus, quite drunk by the end of that day, had stayed on until closing time to try to put the world to rights. Obviously, Roger had remembered that Marcus had a former life as a boxer.

"Think about it," said Roger, looking for an instant 'yes.' His loyal employee agreed not to dismiss it out of hand.

After all, Marcus pondered, his boxing career supposedly ended when he was twenty-one years old and his school instigated contract expired. It had been a tough, if not brutal, period of his earlier life; one which he wanted to let go of.

Thinking about it put Marcus back to the time of him leaving his old gym and the send-off Ali had arranged for him. The newssheet was now in front of him, on his desk, and seeing it broke his chain of thought.

It looked quite easy to register an interest in taking part in the union contest. All anyone had to do was 'phone the office and give their name and address, union number and where they worked, plus a daytime contact number. After much pestering from Roger, Marcus told the Optimus official that he was prepared to represent the section where he worked.

"Excellent," remarked Roger after Marcus had told him what he had just done.

"When's the contest," he wanted to know.

"They set the date for June 16th and are hoping to use the Council's Lowgate Hall. That's all I know at the moment," replied Marcus.

Marcus had some doubts; he had not boxed in over two years so needed to catch up with some serious training. He took a piece of pale pink wasted paper that had been printed on one side and started jotting notes.

Running, weights, punch bag. Paul still had a punch bag in his garage Marcus thought, and he had weights at home. The running was easy to arrange. Marcus just had to plan a route and made sure he stuck to a strict regime.

--o--

Everything was progressing well. Paul had allowed Marcus the use of his punch bag. Marcus was using his own weights and had the enthusiasm to go running each evening after work. On some days he was even running in the morning before setting off for the office.

At the end of each week Marcus was looking in a full-length mirror to gauge his muscle tone. He realised he would be boxing bare-chested, just like his school days, and image was half the battle. Marcus knew from his youth that the paying public wanted to see boxers that looked as if they had trained hard all year.

Even Roger was keen to get involved. He suggested that after work they both do at least forty-five minutes jogging around one of the local parks. It was only five minutes from the office and was almost large enough to get lost in.

A majestic oak tree, with its damaged bark, became a marker for turning back. However, both Roger and Marcus liked the point where they could jog past a double row of weather-beaten palm trees as, for a brief few minutes, they could pretend they were in some far off, exotic land before returning to the office.

The two joggers were fortunate in that their building had a shower area on the second floor and Roger had made sure he had a key to the room so that they could use the shower after they got back from the runs.

The austere room only allowed one person to shower at a time, although there was plenty of space to change down in and store clothing away from any moisture. Roger and Marcus usually worked it so that the boss would get changed and use the shower first.

Roger was a real water baby and loved trying to get the hot and cold mix just right. 'I think I've got it just perfect for you,' he used to say. Marcus realised that this was his signal for him to come out. It was easier if he was undressed at that stage.

Marcus always handed Roger a fresh towel as he stepped out of the shower and quickly manoeuvred himself in. Unlike Roger, he hated getting his hair wet so would only place his head under the shower for a few seconds. To come out with dry hair, Marcus thought, would look a bit strange and would lead to some very awkward questions.

Yes, it seemed, everything was on track for the bout. Marcus was sitting in the office feeling smug about his progress when the 'phone rang.

"Can I speak to Marcus Ingram," said a woman at the other end.

"Marcus Ingram speaking," he replied formally. The woman on the 'phone sounded apologetic as she explained that she was an Optimus union official, and then went to say that there was a problem with the contest.

Apparently, an official at the Council had objected to their civic halls being used for boxing. All was not lost, said the caller, as this same official wanted to meet one of the boxers to put his mind at rest. "Your name was picked at random from the list. Can you meet him," she wanted to know. "Yes, I'll meet with him," Marcus replied without thinking, "Just give me the details."

--o--

All Marcus knew was that he was meeting someone called Malcolm Bauer. It had been arranged that the two meet up in a busy pub called the 'Wild Boar,' near to the Council offices after work. Marcus was given a brief description of Malcolm but did not really know what to expect. He decided to get to the pub early.

It only took a few minutes to walk to the pub, which was situated down an alleyway off the main road. The door to the pub was angled prominently on one corner. Marcus approached the old flagstone step and slipped into the smoky den.

The 'Wild Boar,' or 'old bore' as some locals called it, was the dark, dreary haunt of men over sixty who reminisced about the past. Their conversations would be the same every day and were only temporarily suspended when someone else stepped into their space. Every time a new person came in off the street they would stop talking and look round.

Marcus had noticed this on more than one occasion. The regulars formed little social groups of drinkers who talked about what they *didn't* do in the war or how the economy was going downhill. Most did not agree with a woman Prime Minister leading the country. Weirdly, none of them admitted to voting for Margaret Thatcher.

After ordering half a pint of dry cider Marcus took a table near the door so he could join in the custom of looking at people entering the pub. The difference between him and most of the older drinkers was that he did not smoke. He never had, but was tolerant enough of the smokers that often surrounded him.

Marcus looked across the bar at an old clock. Its dark wooden surround and generous size made it look like an antique. It was

11

five minutes slow but it was only Marcus who had made a mental note of that.

"Are you here to meet someone," Marcus enquired after seeing a man vaguely fitting Malcolm's description walking slowly round the pub; he looked strangely out of place. It had taken all his courage to speak, as he hated exposing himself to possible rejection. Marcus wondered how he could have originally missed the stranger in the brown suit and mustard yellow coloured shirt. He must have walked straight past me, he speculated.

"Yes, someone called Marcus Ingram," came the reply.

"That's me, ... hello," Marcus said. Malcolm formally introduced himself but looked quite confused as he shook Marcus's hand.

"And you're the one who is going to box at Lowgate Hall," Malcolm asked?

"Yes, on the sixteenth," Marcus responded. He was pleased that he had enough confidence to deal with Malcolm and his questions. Malcolm went to the bar and ordered a pint of Guinness. It took quite a time to pour, and Malcolm kept looking over towards Marcus in an unnerving way. He carried his drink across and put it on the small round table and sat down opposite Marcus, accidently flinging a stained beer mat on to the floor in the process. Malcolm bent down and retrieved the piece of round cardboard.

An embarrassing pause was broken when Malcolm admitted to being confused. Marcus warmed to his honesty. Malcolm said that he did not expect Marcus to be as slim or as short as he was. Marcus explained that he was around five foot six and a half tall, but took Malcolm's surprise as a compliment; especially as he thought Marcus looked younger than his age of 23 years.

Malcolm went on to explain that colleagues had informed him that boxers were grouped by size and weight. He had been told that Marcus was something like a 'Flyweight.' Malcolm felt pleased that he sounded knowledgeable in a subject he knew virtually nothing about.

"The thing is, Marcus, I absolutely need to satisfy myself that everything is in order before agreeing to Lowgate Hall, or any of our other premises being used for boxing," explained Malcolm,

"After all, boxing is a very primitive sport, if you can call it that, and we have to think of the good image of the Council."

Malcolm was speaking in a very official tone. Marcus's heart sunk as he had assumed that Malcolm was trying to let him down gently and would declare that the contest had been banned. Both were looking at the half empty drinks in front of them.

"Are you saying the contest is off," Marcus wanted to know.

"No, no, I'm not saying that ...," Malcolm responded, his words trailing off as he spoke. After conversing for about ten minutes Malcolm said that he wanted to know what made boxers tick – was Marcus Ingram a typical boxer? He seemed even more confused, and this feeling was now spreading to Marcus.

"How long have you been boxing," enquired Malcolm. Marcus paused before answering but decided to 'come clean,' as he had done with Roger.

Marcus explained that he had done some boxing at school, as a reluctant teenager and then at sixteen had been given a boxing management contract, which lasted until he was twenty-one years old. By then the contract was in the hands of a Tyneside business family.

"Did they offer you a lot of money," Malcolm enquired.

"No, not really," Marcus replied, "I was hoping to make some money out of it but that hasn't happened ... yet." Marcus conceded that he probably would never make any money from boxing. Although he had originally wanted to get into aviation after leaving school, Marcus did a few odd jobs before moving down south.

After studying he then got a more permanent job with a big insurance company based in the city centre. Malcolm had some brief facts to work with but Marcus could see that it did not make a lot of sense to him. His face gave him away; he looked perplexed.

"If you weren't making money by boxing, why did you do it ... did someone force you into it," enquired Malcolm. Marcus explained that, in lots of ways, he *was* forced to box whilst at his school – an approved school. He had taken a gamble in disclosing this to a stranger but felt unburdened inside.

Marcus looked into his drink and then at Malcolm, expecting him to finish his pint and leave. Malcolm took a sip of Guinness and sat back waiting for more information. Marcus, relieved, felt it was safe enough to tell his story.

"I probably wouldn't have ever boxed had I not gone to that school," Marcus disclosed.

"I did a little bit of boxing at fourteen, nothing much, but a year later had a bad experience. Marcus explained that he, and another lad, were both taken by one of the trainers at the school by car to Hadrian's Wall.

"You mean Hadrian's Wall, near Newcastle," enquired Malcolm.

"Yes," recalled Marcus, "The wall was about half an hour's drive away."

Marcus paused and took a deep breath.

"We had to box and we were tricked into believing that the winner would be allowed home from the school for good," he said. Looking back, Marcus remembered that both he and the other lad had wanted 'out.' Marcus explained that they were forced to box bare-knuckled.

After about five minutes of raw combat, he was briefly knocked out, and came to lying on his back on some grass. Dazed, and with his white school shirt removed, his trainer was pouring cold water over his face.

"When I reached out and put my shirt back on it had blood on it … my blood," said Marcus. Malcolm thought that this was a terrible experience for anyone to go through.

"To top it all," said Marcus, "the trainer took a Polaroid photo of me lying there posed, with arms outstretched and unconscious, and gave it to the other lad as a sort of sick trophy."

Marcus said that he was made to feel puny and weak. He said that after that he vowed to build his strength up and not to get knocked out ever again. Marcus noticed that Malcolm looked angry and he half expected the older man to leave at this point.

"Call it a sort of initiation," said Marcus, not thinking of anything else that would make sense. "An initiation," repeated Malcolm slowly.

Marcus was aware that he could be confusing Malcolm further, maybe even angering him, which was not helpful if the tournament was to go ahead.

14

"Yes, you know, when you do something difficult to prove yourself," he explained, "Maybe an initiation into the adult world."

"You mean prove yourself to yourself," Malcolm said wistfully leaning back in his seat. He seemed more relaxed again. Marcus got the impression that Malcolm was quite perceptive and seemed to have clarified a point for them both. Malcolm seemed equally receptive to the concept of a stoic male initiation, and agreed life could be tough. Marcus was pleasantly coming round to the idea that maybe Malcolm had not closed his mind to boxing as a genuine contact sport. However, he could not judge how Malcolm had viewed him coming from an approved school and wondered, initially, if he had 'blown it' with his openness and honesty.

After one long drink, and a forty-minute chat, Malcolm asked if he could come to the bout.

"I can't stop you," Marcus said, rather surprised. He had not expected that. The next day Malcolm made sure he had reserved a seat for himself at Lowgate Hall. It surprised Marcus that Malcolm wanted to accompany him to the fight.

Marcus pondered that maybe the honest approach does work, but deep down he was quite expecting Malcolm to back out at the last minute. Not only had he booked himself a seat in the hall but Malcolm notified the authorities that he would join Marcus for the pre-fight medical.

Out of courtesy, Malcolm let the fighter know what he was planning to do, so the two could meet up at the clinic.

--o--

As both men walked into the medical waiting room Marcus wondered if he was the only person there for a pre-fight assessment. Some parts of the room were screened off, not allowing him to see if anyone else was around. There were a lot of people coming and going adding to the confusion.

Malcolm found a seat, moved it, and sat down. Marcus slipped away and found a place to change down to black boxing shorts and a plain Forest Green T-shirt, returning to where Malcolm was sitting. Malcolm glanced up but remained silent.

Marcus took his place on a varnished wooden bench opposite Malcolm.

The waiting was awful, and Marcus felt tense. He had a fleeting moment of doubt as he wondered why he had been so willing to enter his name for the contest. Perhaps Malcolm picked this up as he tried to engage his younger colleague in trivial conversation.

"When did you last box," he enquired.

"Not sure, ages ago, I think," Marcus replied.

"Did you win," Malcolm continued.

"Not sure," came a sharp reply. Marcus was not in the mood to think, let alone talk.

"Marcus Ingram," a deep, authoritative voice boomed out from behind a screened area. Both Marcus and Malcolm stood up at the same time and were shown to a larger room where the doctor was waiting.

"Are you his trainer," he enquired, peering at Malcolm over his glasses. Startled, Malcolm just muttered 'no' in a low voice. This brought a smile to Marcus's face and broke the tension of the surreal situation. Marcus wondered afterwards why Malcolm just did not blurt out that he was a cynical observer. Marcus tensed again fantasising that if Malcolm were to lay his cards on the table, he might find an ally.

A brief period of silence followed, but to Marcus it seemed to last forever. Perhaps Malcolm was already in two minds about what to do. In any case, the doctor did not react and assumed that if not a trainer, Malcolm was a manager.

"Slip off you T-shirt, boy," said the doctor, as he fumbled to find his blood pressure monitor. Marcus could see that Malcolm was looking at him across the room. As their eyes met Malcolm looked towards the floor. Marcus wondered what was going through his mind as he tossed his T-shirt in Malcolm's direction.

The doctor put the black sleeve around Marcus's right arm and started to pump in some air.

"Yes, your blood pressure is fine," he commented, glancing at the dial. Marcus knew what would come next. Medicals normally went through in the same order. The doctor pressed his stethoscope onto Marcus's chest. It felt cold on the skin; it always did. He now needed to judge Marcus's overall physique.

"Flex, ...and turn, ...bend sideways ...bend backwards, ...bend forwards, and flex again," commanded the doctor, pausing to make notes every so often.

The instructions came at a steady pace. Marcus glanced across to Malcolm, sitting on a small metal framed chair in the corner, and wondered what he was making of all this. He had Marcus's T-shirt on his lap but it seemed he was trying not to be noticed. For a brief moment Marcus thought it would be nice to exchange places with him. Marcus hated being judged like this, but it had to be done.

"Yes, everything seems fine... can't see anything of concern," concluded the doctor, putting his expensive looking pen back on his desk.

"Okay boy, behind the screen and slip off your shorts for the final bit," said the doctor pointing to the left. As Marcus walked over and disappeared behind the blue curtain, his mind flashed back to his last day at the gym. He grounded himself by thinking about the cold floor underfoot.

Marcus knew what he had to do next. His heart was pounding. Even though he had done it many times before he still felt embarrassed presenting himself naked in front of another person. He felt that something unusual would be picked up from such a medical, but it never did. Seeing the hospital type screens in the waiting area took Marcus's thoughts back to school boxing medicals.

The doctor came through and Marcus moved his feet apart and put his hands behind his back and he had done countless times before. He tried to look upwards but was still tense. He tried to put his mind outside his body. However, his mind went back to the first time he had had to present himself in a medical, wondering, in hindsight, if it really was a medical or an excuse to see him naked. Marcus did not need to be given any more instructions. The doctor completed his examination with a nodding acceptance.

That was good enough for Marcus. As the doctor left Marcus on his own, he knew his self-created ordeal was now over. Malcolm and Marcus had a brief chat after coming away from the medical. Malcolm said that he had not realised that fight preparations were so involved.

"It makes me think that my part in all of this is quite small," reflected Malcolm.

"It sounds like you are learning," Marcus replied in a chirpy voice.

"Well, I could see you are more than just the slim twenty-three-year-old office worker I assumed you to be from our first meeting," Malcolm explained.

"Your muscle tone was better than I expected, particularly around your abdomen, Marcus, and that surprised me," he continued. Marcus listened perplexed, aware that he found it difficult to accept compliments of any kind let alone about his physique.

"So, you noticed then," Marcus interjected trying, but failing, to move the subject away from himself and his appearance. Malcolm said that he knew Marcus was 'no Arnold Schwarzenegger,' but he thought that he was 'in proportion,' and looked like a boxer.

"If things look right, they normally were right," said Malcolm, ending the conversation with a reference to London's world famous red Routemaster buses. Marcus now felt better as the limelight was, at last, no longer on him and his looks. Malcolm was keen to get back home. Marcus's head was full of questions but Malcolm was off, heading for the car park.

--o--

The next day found Marcus in the office sitting at his desk, his mind not on the job and looking out of the window. Roger came across asking about the physical examination and how it had gone. Marcus told him it was a routine check but that he had passed.

"I'm just awaiting the paperwork in the post," he explained. Roger was eager to know if Malcolm had attended and if Marcus had been able to 'talk him round.'

"You're telling me he actually went to the medical with you," Roger wanted to check.

"Well, yes, he did," Marcus said, "and I think he was reasonably impressed by it all."

"You don't feel like pulling out do you," enquired Roger. Marcus wondered if Roger was fooling around or putting him to the test.

"Why no, man, I'm doing it for you. I'll go ahead with it if the Council allow the tournament," Marcus concluded.

"Fantastic!" said Roger, "Let me get you a cup of tea."

Later that day news came through that any official opposition to the fight had been lifted. Marcus felt a mixture of relief and anxiety in equal measure. He was to fight someone called Luke Mills in the third bout of the evening. There had been a fair amount of publicity, with a lot of small posters going up near the fight venue. Most of these were head and shoulders shots.

Although the Council's opposition was no longer an issue a small, but vocal, group within the union had produced their own flyers saying boxing was 'a sport too far.' Roger had earlier come across a few activists giving out some of the anti-boxing flyers in the street. He and Marcus hoped their action would not sway the union into cancelling the event at the eleventh hour.

Malcolm was offered a seat in the front row but he had made it known that he would probably end up sitting nearer the back. He had tried to explain his position to Marcus over the 'phone. It was not that he did not want to support Marcus but he was in a quandary as to how much he really wanted to witness. 'Supposing there is a lot of blood, supposing someone got knocked out', Malcolm kept ruminating.

Somehow, he thought that by visibly sitting near the front he would be directly involved, so directly responsible if something bad happened. By the end of the call Marcus wondered if Malcolm would actually attend the fight. The chances of him backing out at the last minute seemed high, Marcus thought. Roger reassuringly made it known that he would be in the audience along with a few of his friends, plus his sister

--o—

Marcus left work at precisely 5.15. He was soon out of the grey, soulless office building, where he had worked for almost two years, and into the organised chaos that made up life in the city centre. Outside was still lively with shoppers heading for the

19

buses and suited workers looking for either a taxi or a good restaurant, or drinking hole.

Marcus thought he would pick up a Wimpy burger, and headed straight for Joseph Street. The traffic was unusually heavy. One of the main junctions had become blocked after the traffic lights stuck on red. Motorists, eager to get out of the city and head home, were allowing their frustrations to get the better of them.

The countryside yearned for Marcus too, but he locked his thoughts deep within himself. He walked on in silence. Several of the side roads were brimming with traffic and the sound of car horns pierced the air.

"Bloody get a move on," shouted an irate van driver when an old, faded white coloured mini refused to move up to within an inch of the vehicle in front of it.

Suddenly a large, feisty-looking woman wearing what resembled a colourful smock got out of her car and started gesturing towards the offending driver. Marcus chuckled to himself inwardly. He thought the mini driver might have been Boudicca reincarnated. He was pleased that he could either take the bus back, or simply walk. On evenings like this, he thought, it is better not to be behind the wheel of a car.

The Wimpy bar had only a few customers inside. They looked like regulars, and Marcus was pleased to get noticed as soon as he reached the counter.

One of the Greek born staff beckoned him to a table near the window. Marcus looked at the wipe clean, plastic-coated menu but knew what he wanted without reviewing all the meals on offer. He glanced outside. It seemed that things were slowly becoming less hectic. A waiter was now standing in front of him ready to take his order.

"Wimpy burger with fries," he said not even looking up, "and a coffee." The waiter read back the order and disappeared. A mug of steaming coffee was on his table within an instant.

As he sipped the hot drink Marcus looked back on the day. He remembered clearly how he told Roger that he did not have any doubts about being entered for the boxing bout – but he knew this was a lie. He had many fears and had considered pulling out while he still could. He wondered if he was simply trying to prove something to his boss.

Marcus's mind was split two ways and he questioned himself endlessly as to why he was so easily persuaded to take up the challenge of the union fight. On the one hand he knew he was fit enough to battle another amateur of similar ability, weight and build. However, he knew he hated being 'centre stage' and under the lights, literally.

His food was now on his table, which allowed him to concentrate on eating. As he carefully cut into his burger, he could see a steady flow of tired looking customers coming into the restaurant. Marcus started to eat quicker. A free second coffee was placed on his table and his plate was soon clean.

He drank most of the second cup of coffee before paying for his meal at the till. As the change was handed over Marcus suddenly had the urge to see a film. He had not been to the cinema in months and had no idea what was billed. The Cruz cinema was only a few streets away and seemed to be calling him.

"One for The Eagle has Landed," said Marcus thrusting a crisp five-pound note into the cashier's hand. She gave him his change and the ticket with what looked like a genuine smile. He paused, taking the ticket from her, and walked towards the door for the stalls.

Marcus stumbled his way into the heart of the cinema and sat down. A drinks commercial was showing on the big screen in front of him. The cinema sound was of sufficient level to drown out all but the loudest of conversations. Marcus relaxed into his seat. People were quieter now and the film was about to start.

Marcus was drawn into the film from the start. The vividness of the colours and the multitude of sounds took him into a fantasy world combining bravery and action with history. Marcus wished that he had been born a generation earlier; the scenes from the Second World War only emphasised that in his young mind.

He could imagine himself in military uniform, perhaps as a fighter pilot, alone in the skies over Kent, shooting down the enemy before landing in the light before dusk. That would be a great life, he thought to himself. His mood suddenly saddened by the reality that it was not ever to be.

The film captivated him and Marcus lost all sense of time. It was dark by the time he left the cinema. He was not in any mood to return home to his small, cramped flat where he lived on his own. Something was drawing him towards the river. It was only a short distance away. As he started walking, he questioned himself.

Why, he thought, was a non-swimmer, someone who hated water, so keen to get near the river? He thought he must be mad. Maybe it was the scene in the film where the German soldier dived into the water to rescue the drowning child. Whatever illogical reason, something connected to the water was calling him ever nearer.

Marcus turned towards the road bridge that took most of the city traffic across the river. There was a steady flow of vehicles but few pedestrians venturing that way. Marcus paused briefly to look at the dark, moving currents below. Fragments of reflected light swirled in the river like a monochrome kaleidoscope.

Dark water had always proved a fascination to Marcus in a strangely morbid, deathly way. He did not know why. A row of pale coloured cabin cruisers moored near the yacht club caught Marcus's attention. That part of the river always had a buzz about it, especially in the summer season when holidaymakers hired craft for a week, or two.

Although not that interested in boats, Marcus felt an energy that was drawing him nearer to the riverbank. As he drew closer the hum of power generators and the sound of music being played on a transistor radio broke the silence of the early night. Marcus strolled along the bank passing several craft. Most boaters were inside, out of the wind, preparing food or listening to music. A few brought portable televisions and were catching up with their regular programmes, despite the poor signal.

A wooden seat caught Marcus's attention and he decided to sit down. It was a good place to act the invisible observer. There was stillness, and it was as if time was standing still. The movement of the tethered boats being gently pulled by the tide fascinated him. He could see that a small dog had appeared on the deck of the boat in front of him. It did not bark but seemed happy enough to wander up and down, pausing to sniff various parts as it patrolled 'Lagu IX.'

22

After a while its owner called it back below decks.

As Marcus sank back into the hard wooden bench, he became aware that he was not alone on the seat. He glanced to his right to see the figure of an older woman. Her face seemed weather-worn in the dimly lit riverside, but she somehow seemed open and worldly wise.

"You don't like water," she said, "but you will go on a boat like these." She looked at the boats without pointing. Marcus was shocked as the first part of her statement was true, although he had no desire to go on the water. Marcus politely confirmed that she was, in part, correct before focussing on the boats again.

"You've come here to make a decision, luv," the woman continued, "but you'll reach the right decision before this time tomorrow." Marcus was intrigued. He knew that he had to either commit to the boxing tournament fully, or just gracefully pull out. A part of him wanted to get up and leave, but curiosity was urging him to stay.

"I don't ask for anything," the woman continued. Marcus wondered if she was reading his mind. Slightly unnerved, he turned to say something but no words came out.

"You'll be helping one of our kind before long... and he deserves a bit of help," the stranger continued. Marcus turned towards her, wanting more of an explanation.

"Your kind," he enquired. She did not answer his question, instead giving a long, deep sigh. Marcus noticed the woman was fiddling with a small bag, which she had on her lap. He could see that she was pulling out little light-coloured wooden squares, looking at them, before placing each carefully back in the bag again. She did this several times without uttering a word.

"Runes," she said, as if reading Marcus's thoughts once more. "They're runes, luv." The wooden pieces made a weird sound in the bag as they knocked into each other. They seemed to be singing a tune all of their own. Marcus could see in the artificial light that the rune squares had designs of them, made up entirely of straight red coloured lines.

"Onward and upward," the old woman muttered. "You've had a lot of unhappiness in your younger years," she continued, "but the worst is over, luv. Don't keep looking back; we can't change our past." Marcus found himself being drawn into a pensive, carefree state of mind, where nothing seemed to matter.

"Knowledge demands a sacrifice; loyalty comes at a price," she ended.

"Thanks," said Marcus to the empty air. He turned to where the rune woman sat, but she was already gone.

Marcus got up from the bench and looked, both ways, along the tow path. The craggy faced visitor was nowhere to be seen. Marcus quickly ran his sight along the line of the moored boats. He was surprised to see little movement. There was still no sign of the weird, old woman.

A swan ran along the bank before lifting off, then splashing into the night water. Marcus walked towards the area where the swan came from hoping to catch a last glimpse of 'rune woman.' He was suspicious of her when she sat next to him but he was now disappointed that he could not ask her anything more, knowing what she had revealed seemed to be correct.

The dull background chatter of people talking, merging with music playing from afar, filled the otherwise peaceful air. The riverside had taken on a strange, over-worldly atmosphere and Marcus was feeling both confused and refreshed by the evening's events. He felt he had stayed long enough and was now in a mood to finally return home. He would jog rather than walk.

If he maintained a steady pace, he would be back in his flat within twenty minutes. Marcus set off with a renewed determination, crunching the gravel along the tow path as he headed in the direction of the bridge and the bright lights of the city centre. He felt alive as he paced himself on his journey home.

The city centre soon gave way to Victorian streets interspersed with more modern developments. Marcus quickly passed the fire station and wondered what it would be like fighting fires and rescuing elderly shoppers from broken down lifts in tired, family-run departmental stores. A grin came over his face and he visualised a cat stuck high in a tree. That is the sort of annoying thing they would do just to be awkward, he concluded.

Marcus had no more time to think of such things as he approached the property he loosely called 'home.' He put the key into the main door where he rented his flat. It was good to get inside as it had been an unusually busy day.

Despite feeling hot, Marcus was soon up the main stairs and through the pale blue door marked with a stencilled '3.' This tiny flat may have been converted from two original rooms, but it was Marcus's special space; a foxhole where he could escape the world. It was also the place where he could get a much-needed drink. Marcus reached out and turned the tap over the tired kitchen sink full on, allowing cold water to fill an old metal camping mug. The water continued gushing over Marcus's hand and he tipped the cup over his head, allowing the cooling water to revive him. The next refill was for drinking.

As he slumped back in a tatty armchair Marcus could not get thoughts of the strange, old 'rune woman' from his mind. If I had not gone to see the film, I would not have met her, thought Marcus. He knew, strangely, that the film had special significance for him and that the two after-work events were linked.

There was something about 'determination' that connected them and in an instant Marcus knew that he had to nurture his own resources and mentally commit to the bout with Luke Mills. Somehow, he knew deep inside himself that by participating in the contest his life would change forever.

Chapter 3

NO ESCAPING THE PAST

The day of the fight was soon upon Marcus, and with it an emotional build-up. Marcus had felt tense for the proceeding twenty-four hours, if not longer. He still had moments when he questioned what he was doing but it was too late, he told himself, to 'bottle out.' He felt a duty, having agreed with everyone, to carry the fight through to its conclusion.

Lowgate Hall had been transformed by the boxing ring, which seemed to take up most of the interior space. There were powerful lights installed on large metal stands to illuminate the structure. Colourful banners were draped around the walls, some carrying the green and purple logo of the union Optimus. Neat rows of identical seats on two sides of the hall completed the scene. Outside, a few hardened protesters were still making their point to anyone who was prepared to listen.

As Marcus stepped into the ring, he tried looking for Malcolm's familiar face in the darkened sea of spectators. It was almost impossible to view anyone past the first few rows because of the way the lighting was set up. The two boxers were now in the ring and on show to the public like modern day gladiators. Apart from their boxing gloves they were dressed only in shorts. Luke wore blue with a red stripe, and Marcus black. This was how Marcus boxed for over six years both at school and at the gym. For a fleeting moment he remembered those trying times. Like a freed slave, Marcus could never get away from his past.

The referee announced the bout and introduced Luke and Marcus to the excited crowd. Marcus knew what he had to do when his name was spoken over the microphone. He took a few steps from the corner and flexed his muscles for the benefit of the curious onlookers. Marcus was not ashamed of his body but he hated the feeling of being put on public display.

He always felt uneasy until the fight got under way. Today was no exception. Marcus felt pleased inside that cynical Malcolm had seen him as a boxer. This gave Marcus some inner confidence to continue and deploy all his old skills. The contestants were beckoned to the middle of the ring and got a brief talk about the rules by the referee. That over, the boxers quickly squared up to each other. Luke came in fast and nimble, and got an early score.

Marcus was thinking 'this guy's good' as he attacked, using a right hook. He became more focussed on the fight and went into autopilot. Marcus was hardly aware of what was really happening; unaware of thought, unaware of time. The bell at the end of the first round brought his attention into clear focus again. Marcus returned to his corner and sat on the three-legged wooden stool provided.

The union had allocated both boxers a ringside helper. Wayne was in Marcus's corner, whispering words of encouragement and telling him he could win.

"Come on Marcus, mate," he said, "You can win this one." The bell rang again and Marcus leapt off his seat and moved to meet Luke in the middle of the ring. This ritual was repeated several more times. Each time Marcus returned to his corner he felt hotter, more battered and wearier.

Luke and Marcus had been in contact for over ten minutes and the crowd were enjoying the entertainment unfolding in front of them. Luke moved around the ring like a young gazelle and was able to dodge and dive some of Marcus's best punches. For a moment Marcus's mind wandered back to the time when he was forced to box in front of sadistic spectators. He suddenly felt himself going down, falling backwards, but managed to bounce off the ropes.

Marcus re-focussed and came back with vengeance, scoring points with an upper cut. The bell sounded the end of the round. The two fighters had been battling for six rounds. As Marcus returned to his corner he felt as if he were in a sauna and was trying to catch his breath by breathing deeply. His body was telling him that he had run a marathon up the side of the steepest part of the Himalayan Mountain range. Marcus wondered if he should have put in more training, and verbalised this.

"No, don't think like that," responded Wayne, "You'll be okay. Just keep going."

He snatched a water bottle off Wayne and took a gulp. Even that tasted warm, he thought, as he tried not to spill too much liquid down his chin. Wayne was fussing around Marcus, towelling his protégé down but the sweat kept appearing. Ever the optimist, Wayne was urging Marcus on.

"Come on Marcus, you can win it," he repeated, like a positive mind mantra.

With the bell sounding again Marcus got up to his feet. He felt much slower now. Marcus could see that Luke had also slowed down compared to the first round.

"Fight on," the referee demanded. The crowd were becoming more vocal, but all the voices seemed to blend into one continuous hum. Luke came at Marcus but was repelled back with some jabs. Luke seemed to turn and stumble but regained his stance.

"Yes!" shouted Wayne from below the ring. As Marcus moved in again, he remembered thinking that his ankles were really aching.

The time-keeper sounded the bell once more and the referee moved in to the middle of the ring, indicating both boxers should follow. He was in between Luke and Marcus now and holding up one arm from each. A draw was announced and the fight was over. Marcus half embraced, and then half fell, into Luke's sweaty torso. Marcus was still catching his breath, but felt relief. He followed Luke under the ropes, out of the ring, and along the corridor to the medical area. Both Luke and Marcus were too tired to speak, but an exchange of glances said 'well done.'

As Marcus came through the door he could see Malcolm inside, sitting on a bench near to the far corner. Marcus noticed that the doctor was seeing to a small cut near to Luke's left eye. Marcus had not noticed that before. This was soon dealt with and the doctor turned to look at Marcus.

"Okay," he said, "just take some water." There was a supply of plastic bags full of ice cubes for the boxers to use. "I'm glad that's over," Marcus commented, half choking on his water. Marcus thought he heard Malcolm make a quip about not talking and drinking at the same time.

Luke's trainer passed his protégé a towel and Malcolm copied without being prompted.

"What did you think of it then," Marcus asked. He was genuinely curious to get a straight answer.

"I'm not at all sure. For one thing it seemed to end sooner than I expected," replied Malcolm.

"So, you wanted it to go on a right to the very end, then," came Marcus's sharp response. He felt that his brain was functioning again.

"You should try it sometime," Marcus said, feeling irritated. Marcus looked at Malcolm but he said nothing more. Malcolm looked deep in thought. Wayne had now entered the room and dispersed an awkward atmosphere.

"Mate, that was pretty impressive," said Wayne in an excited voice. Marcus thanked him for his support.

Wayne was eager to be involved and he began rubbing the sweat off Marcus's chest and arms. Marcus reached for one of the ice bags on the side and pressed it against his forehead.

"Are you alright," Malcolm enquired furtively.

"Yeah, I'll be fine in a moment," Marcus replied. After a few minutes of resting Marcus gradually put on more of his clothing.

"Take it slowly, mate," said Wayne, looking on.

The doctor continued to see all the returning boxers as if it was a human production line of damaged and dazed men coming in from a war zone. There were boxers chatting to their trainers or waiting to see the doctor or just getting ready to leave. The room seemed to be filling up with bodies. Marcus looked for Malcolm, considering it was time to leave, but Malcolm was nowhere to be seen. He had quietly slipped away in the confusion.

Wayne was keen to be seen helping out. By appearance he was a few inches taller than Marcus and stockier without being overweight. He had an excitable personality that made his work colleagues call him a 'drama queen.' Wayne had just turned thirty. His wife never saw much of him, even though they had been married for over ten years, but his heart was in the right place. Everyone who knew him said that.

Wayne was employed as a driver working for Social Services. He liked his work, which gave him the opportunity to talk to the elderly and disabled. Wayne offered to drive Marcus back to his rented accommodation, a basic conversion in a red brick Victorian house. At least Marcus could call it 'home.'

"Well, did you enjoy it," Marcus asked Wayne, as they drew up outside a former grand villa that sat back from the road.

"Yeah, yeah, I enjoyed it. Loads of action," he blurted, becoming very animated, "I had the greatest ringside view and could see how hard you were fighting." Marcus felt relieved that at least one person had appreciated his efforts.

"I was given some of this anti-bruising balm," said Wayne pushing a strange looking blue bottle in front of him. Wayne twisted off the lid and thrust the container under Marcus's nose.

"Man, it's not smelling salts," joked Marcus before inviting Wayne back inside.

The drive back had taken less than twenty minutes despite Wayne taking a wrong turning. Marcus was becoming tired but both were soon inside his small flat. The bedroom seemed cramped. Marcus told Wayne to leave the balm by the side of the bed, and he would use it the next morning. He appreciated the lift back but felt so drained of energy that he just wanted to lie on his own bed and go to sleep.

"No, mate, it's best if you use it straight away," insisted Wayne.

Marcus was in no mood to argue. His adrenaline levels had dropped sharply leaving him drowsy.

"Take this off, mate," said Wayne as he helped his new friend to remove his shirt and then directed him to an old, wooden kitchen stool. He used the balm on Marcus's arms and upper body, carefully rubbing it in like a professional trainer.

"I can't just abandon you and walk away, can I," said Wayne looking at all the patches of bright pink skin, "My job's not over yet."

--o--

The next day, after leaving work, Wayne decided to drive over to see Marcus just to check on how he was faring. Marcus had booked the day off to recover from the bout. Wayne rang the bell and was greeted by Marcus at the impressive period Victorian front door. Marcus's flat was on the top floor which required going up two flights of stairs. He wasn't expecting any visitors so was only half dressed.

"Marcus, me old mate," was Wayne's enthusiastic opening line, "I just came round to see how you are, is that okay. I couldn't just forget about you, could I?"

"Why man, of course …," said Marcus, a little confused, "follow me up." The two climbed the creaking wooden stairs to the top of the building. Marcus felt slightly ashamed that his landlord had left the communal parts in a poor state. Wayne was oblivious to the fact that paint was peeling off the walls, the ceilings were dark and grubby and the stair carpets looked at least fifty years old. Sometimes the communal lights did not work.

The sound of Pink Floyd's 'One More Brick in the Wall' was booming from a cassette player somewhere in the flat.

"Got any bruises," said Wayne, as the door closed behind the two.

"Well, just a few coming," replied Marcus, "it's not too bad." Marcus went over to a small table beside his bed and switched off the cassette. He moved across in front of Wayne pulling his faded white vest up on one side to reveal the worst of the damage.

"You expect this if you've been in the ring," explained Marcus, "or if you've had a brawl in the city centre."

"Have you," enquired Wayne, looking shocked and surprised. Marcus chuckled and then sat himself down in one of the threadbare chairs in the main room. He took a few moments to reassure his concerned visitor that he had never brawled in the street, nor had he any plan to do so.

"If you come across any more tournaments, can you let me know," enquired Wayne, becoming ever more animated, "it's just that I'm keen to see another fight." Wayne was looking at Marcus expecting him to reel off a list of bouts to come.

"I didn't realise that you were *that* interested," said Marcus. On reflection, that seemed a silly remark for him to make.

Wayne went on to explain that he got really interested in the recent bout. Marcus acknowledged that Wayne had played a key part on the day, thanking him again for his support. Wayne had done some judo at an after-school club but always harboured a strong desire to box. Although he spent seven years in the Royal Navy the chance did not come his way.

"Marcus, mate," said Wayne, "do you consider I'd be any good?" Wayne was keen to get Marcus's approval. Marcus explained that there was a lot of training involved in boxing, not just learning techniques and moves but developing stamina and resilience.

"So, I wouldn't be any good at it, then," Wayne continued.

"Not sure," replied Marcus, "I can't say, although you seem keen enough, which is a plus point." Marcus suggested Wayne take up running and weight training and then, perhaps, investigate joining a gym. Wayne's eyes lit up as he heard this, taking it as positive approval from his new friend.

Marcus was subtly willing Wayne to stand up so he could edge him to the door. It was getting late and it seemed Wayne was unaware of the time.

"Oh, and another question, mate," said Wayne, his eagerness still on the rise, "do you … have you … do you know anything about barn boxing?" Marcus was stunned and almost fell straight out of his chair. Now standing, he wondered why Wayne would ask such a strange question.

"Barn boxing," said Marcus, "Well, yes, I do know what that is." Marcus explained that the term referred to unlicensed bouts put on in out of the way places, like empty warehouses or barns on remote farms. These bouts were illegal but well attended by selected people making the organisers good money. Bouts were usually kept very secret until the last minute so that the authorities could not be tipped off. It was akin to cock fighting, explained Marcus.

"Why did you ask that question," Marcus enquired of Wayne, who had been listening with silent interest.

"It was just that this geezer at the Optimus bout gave me his card. He organises barn boxing, I think," said Wayne.

"And man, you're interested …," Marcus enquired.

"Marcus, me old mate, how about us going to one together. I could telephone him and get more details," continued Wayne, looking straight at Marcus. Within an instant Marcus gave the idea his blessing, although he did not know why.

--o—

Two days after Wayne's visit, Marcus decided to 'phone Malcolm to elicit his 'considered opinion' on the bout.

"My nephew, Oliver, would have loved it," he said.

"I didn't know you had a nephew. Is he a fight fan," Marcus enquired; he was genuinely curious.

"Oh, no, not really …" Malcolm sounded embarrassed and hesitant. After a pause he began to speak.

"I enjoyed it more than I thought I would," he revealed. Malcolm said that there was a well-dressed, middle-aged man sitting next to him who kept asking what he thought about the participants and boxing in general.

"Not knowing much about boxing I tried to avoid eye contact," he explained, "He did seem to know a lot about the subject. He was some sort of promoter," he continued.

Malcolm said that at the end he must have been distracted, as he was a bit slow in realising that the bout would end in a draw.

"I was slightly annoyed with myself that I did not understand the scoring," he remarked, "but in my opinion as an observer you and Luke looked well matched in size and height; even stamina. I did notice that Luke was a bit more tanned than you." Marcus thought this was a strange thing to pick up on, but said nothing.

Marcus was hearing more about the man who had tried to engage his 'chaperone' in conversation, asking Malcolm what he thought about Marcus as a fighter.

"Well, I hope you said I was good," laughed Marcus playfully.

"Sort of …," replied Malcolm, "This guy thought you showed talent and had some good moves but realised you lacked recent experience. He judged that both you and Luke were good entertainment value and would like to see you fight again."

Going by all the chatter, Marcus guessed that Malcolm had enjoyed the bout. If he had not, he would have just walked out and gone home; although part of him wondered if Malcolm was simply trying to be polite. After all, he drove to the bout but declined to offer him a lift back home. Although Malcolm did not understand the scoring, he did say that there was a lot of action by the boxers; punches, jabs, quick foot movements and ducking and diving around. A colleague had told Malcolm earlier that the lighter the boxer weighed the quicker he moved, and that seemed to make sense to him.

"My thoughts about you seeming to be built a bit like a gymnast made more sense now," remarked Malcolm, "The same could be said about Luke Mills. The crowd were egging on both of you." It seemed to Marcus that Malcolm acknowledged that some parts of the audience were really involved, even though they did not leave their seats. Marcus pondered that they probably knew a lot about moves and scoring than Malcolm would ever know.

On a deeper level Marcus realised that Malcolm was glad that he witnessed the bout. He thought that Malcolm felt privileged to be given the opportunity to get right up close, where the action was. However, the whole experience obviously left Malcolm feeling confused inside. Some questions had been answered and Marcus knew Malcolm was no longer opposed to boxing on principle, but he had so many more questions that needed answering.

As Marcus ended with, "I'm off to get a tan," he knew that Malcolm was desperate for more information.

--o--

Marcus agreed to see Malcolm again and ended up in the 'Wild Boar;' the same pub where both had first met. Marcus guessed, correctly, that during the days before him 'phoning and the second pub meeting, Malcolm had tried to get his disjointed thoughts on paper. He tried formulating questions, but they just did not come easily so he decided to make rough notes to guide him on what more he wanted to know. Just before the meeting Malcolm had a terrible thought that he might be prying too much into Marcus's private life. What more did Malcolm need to know, Marcus wondered, and why?

Just like the time before, Marcus was the first to arrive at the pub, and sat near the main bar. He had begun sipping half a pint of cider when Malcolm walked over. He was wearing a smart brown three-piece suit with a dark red shirt, but no tie. Marcus wondered if Malcolm was trying to look less formal as he offered to buy him a drink.

"Pint of Guinness, thanks," Malcolm said. Marcus could sense he was searching for something to say.

"Why don't we sit in that corner," said Malcolm pointing to the only quiet area of the pub. Marcus remarked that it reminded him of 'The Rover's Return' snug in Coronation Street. Malcolm admitted to sometimes watching it, but got on with asking his first set question. He wanted to know who allocated the colours of the boxers' shorts. Marcus, replying, thought it was a strange opening.

"Well, the union told us what colour to wear but as mine was black, it was easy." Malcolm glanced at Marcus. "I had a black pair, so didn't need to buy anything... plus I still had my old boxing gloves."

Malcolm drank some of his pint. His mouth felt dry. There was an uneasy silence which was broken when Malcolm asked about what the final part of the pre-fight medical involved; the bit that he was not allowed to witness. Marcus was taken aback but started to explain but immediately felt that Malcolm wanted to withdraw his question. He looked slightly embarrassed.

"Before a fight they have to check, let's say, between your legs, if you get me." Marcus hesitated and wondered if he was using confusing language. "It's done in case of any abnormalities that could be made worse during the fight. Like it's an important safety thing, really," Marcus explained in a distant, matter of fact way.

"I guessed it must be something like that," Malcolm quickly responded, "The phrase below the belt comes to mind." Marcus wondered if Malcolm was naïve, but concluded that he probably did know about things like that.

"You're learning," he said, "and fitting the pieces together." Malcolm nodded. Marcus's willingness to open up gave Malcolm confidence to talk about the fight more.

"I decided not to sit near the front in the end, but did see everything from a distance," Malcolm explained, half apologising.

"That's okay, I didn't expect you to be right at the front despite people thinking you were my trainer," Marcus joked.

"Yes, being in the room behind the scenes was an extra experience, one I hadn't anticipated," replied Malcolm. "When

35

you changed down for the doctor, I expected you to look different," he continued.

"In what way different... I mean how different," Marcus asked.

"Well, you know, physically different ... slimmer or something," Malcolm said, trying to explain himself, "you both looked physically well matched." Marcus felt some anger building up inside him. Marcus pondered on the possibility that Malcolm was saying that he expected him to look 'weedy' out of his clothes. He let the remark evaporate; trying not to dwell on it, but it had been akin to a punch to the stomach.

"Maybe I should have got an all over tan before the bout," said Marcus sarcastically. Malcolm pointed out that there was a new tanning salon opening up a few streets away. Marcus wondered how he knew that. Malcolm now felt he had the confidence to come out with what he was really thinking.

"I have changed my mind about being opposed to boxing but I am still very curious as to why someone would willingly allow himself to get knocked about, perhaps risking serious injury ... or death. Actually, this seems worse for the boxers with a crowd looking on and baying for blood. It also seems odder in the lower weight categories because the boxers look more ordinary... if you understand what I mean."

Malcolm was sounding as if he was giving a speech to an assembled crowd at a union meeting. Marcus remarked that real life was full of knocks, but not only physical. Lost in thought, and looking slightly vacant, Malcolm was wondering if there was some sense of weird masochism involved in boxing.

"By me being involved was I contributing to something brutal ... something Roman," was his next brief statement. Marcus's annoyance had abated.

"The Romans weren't all bad," laughed Marcus.

"I know, replied Malcolm, "I studied history at Cambridge." Marcus sensed that the space between them had changed. The relationship between himself and Malcolm had moved on, and he was eager to put his fight in context. He now knew that what he was to disclose to Malcolm during that evening was to both shock him and help set the record straight – in several ways.

Marcus reminded Malcolm that he had started boxing after being sent to an approval school. Looking back, he thought he came from quite a rough area and his lifestyle had meant that it was inevitable that he ended up there. His school was mainly geared towards sports, including boxing, in an attempt to bring some order into the lives of its 'wayward' pupils. The boys who were sent there had difficult, often violent, pasts. Some had been involved in crime at a young age.

Most of these lads had assaulted teachers, routinely set off the fire alarms and vandalised cars. Lots of them formed gangs to promote fights between rival schools in the same area. The pupils at the single sex approved school were well known to the local police. Marcus thought that he was not as bad as most of the boys he came into contact with at the school. He often dreamed of escaping, but even as a teenager realised that would be pointless.

In an effort to set an example the school ran a strict regime of corporal punishments ranging from the cane and belt to extra P.E. and cold showers. Marcus tried to convey that although corporal punishments were being phased out during the final years he was at school, the boxers were expected to continue to have them.

"I think this was to toughen us up and make us win more bouts for the school," Marcus explained. "Why, it wasn't just a case of bad boys box," he continued, "although you probably think this by the way I'm trying to explain it."

Marcus began reminiscing. He said that he enjoyed some of the exercises linked to boxing, like cross-country running. However, he thought he had lacked aggression and the desire to always be 'centre stage.' Marcus told Malcolm of one inter-school tournament that he was entered in around the age of sixteen.

"Before the bouts each pair of boxers had to go on a small stage, lit by bright lights above our heads, we were wearing only our shorts. When both were standing side by side, and the names read out, we had to flex in front of the audience," Marcus explained, trying to convey his anxiety and lack of self-esteem. Marcus said that he looked out into the crowd, which was in semi darkness.

37

"Despite appearing just as human shapes I sensed people were looking at me – and I guess the other guy – and I immediately felt self-conscious …," he continued, his voice fading away. Marcus was now gazing at the carpet. He found himself talking about this a lot and as the conversation continued, Malcolm started to feel a little more empathy towards him.

Malcolm said that he thought Marcus was obviously very shy deep down. He asked him if he felt that way during the recent bout.

"I did feel self-conscious at the beginning, as I had to box bare-chested, just like at school. It reminded me of that place again," Marcus said. He detected some residual anger in his own voice as he spoke. There did not seem to be any logic to Marcus's statement and he knew, by Malcolm's expression, that he was a little perplexed.

"How could someone who looked so right in the ring be so self-conscious," Malcolm asked.

"I know... I know...I thought you'd say that," said Marcus, "Well, I always felt too slim and I was embarrassed to be totally smooth-chested. I was shorter than a lot of the boys in my class too," Marcus's mouth was drying up, and he took a sip of his drink to recover.

Malcolm laughed saying, "we can't do much about things like that. I guess it would have been more of an issue for you after the age of, say, sixteen or seventeen." Marcus nodded in agreement. Malcolm went on to apologise if he, earlier, had implied that he thought Marcus looked too 'skinny' or too pale to box. Malcolm now seemed very perceptive and in tune with Marcus's emotions and feelings, so took the opportunity to probe more deeply and look for answers.

"Why were you sent to the school in the first place," he asked.

"Why, I can't give you an easy answer, man," Marcus replied. He thought he would only be there for a year at most, but then his mother died, and so he ended up remaining for longer in the confusion. As a result of staying on he was obliged, at the age of sixteen, to sign a boxing contract. In it there were many controlling, clauses including some about physical appearance.

After the contract was signed Marcus had to have a chest shave before a bout, even though he did not have any chest hair at all.

Malcolm could see how this would be embarrassing and could become a humiliating ritual for Marcus, if repeated over time.

"It's because they sometimes set up bouts between smooth versus hairy fighters," Marcus pointed out, trying to add some retrospective logic to the situation.

Once, Marcus explained, he lost three fights in a row. If that was not bad enough, one of the boxing trainers decided to humiliate him some more by ordering him to lie on a bench, bare-chested, and spending the next ten minutes using a dry razor on his skin. He only stopped when it was raw and pink. As Marcus told the story Malcolm's face contorted at the torturous thought.

"Boxing training is like martial arts; you have to put up with everything thrown at you by your trainers. They know best how to treat their trainees," he said.

"I'm not sure I could stand that," said Malcolm, taking another sip of his pint, "It doesn't sound right, approved school or not." Malcolm had tapped into Marcus's inner place allowing him to talk openly about his past. Marcus was now in full flow; it felt strangely therapeutic. Malcolm was listening intently as his companion mentioned getting the cane and the belt at his approved school.

This was common in schools in the 1960s, but it seemed to have continued at Marcus's school for longer, at least for the boxers in training. "At our school boys could be caned over a stool or wooden horse, and after the age of fifteen could get the belt, or Scottish taws, on the backside," Marcus explained.

"That seemed a bit harsh for the seventies in Britain," Malcolm responded, "I'm more than a bit shocked by what you are telling me."

"Sorry, man, I'm probably speaking too much," said Marcus wondering if he should bring the conversation to an end.

"No, no, you're alright," Malcolm responded half choking on his drink. Marcus wondered why he had a perverse need to shock but told himself he was merely stating the truth.

"Well, some of the older boys claimed that they had the taws on the back. I'm not sure if it was true," said Marcus, looking directly at Malcolm. Caning, at least, seemed fairly common practise right up until Marcus left, but he thought he detected Malcolm wondering about the use of the taws.

As he was recalling his teenage years, Marcus was becoming aware that the theme of humiliation as a punishment ran through his earlier life in the boxing classes. Marcus paused and took another mouthful of cool cider. He did not want to deliberately shock Malcolm but it was as if his drinking companion had opened a door that was difficult to close.

Marcus decided to risk telling Malcolm about how even football matches could be utilised by his school for punishments. He said he did not particularly like team sports such as football or rugby.

"I agree," said Malcolm, "I was more of a tennis person." Malcolm sat attentively, awaiting the next shocking revelation from Marcus.

"As a punishment I had to go in goal," the younger drinker said, "It was winter, and I was only allowed to wear a pair of shorts... nothing else."

Malcolm shook his head on hearing this. He did not really understand why the approved school needed to punish and humiliate but was beginning to understand the importance of regular boxing medicals.

"We all had regular medicals and check-ups, especially before bouts," Marcus explained, "Our school preferred boxers to be 'cut,' as well, he continued, lowering his voice slightly and looking around the pub to see if anyone was listening in.

When Malcolm heard this expression, he looked at Marcus blankly, asking, "What do you mean by cut?"

"Circumcised," Marcus pointed out. This Malcolm understood, although he thought this was only usually carried out for religious reasons on babies and very young boys.

"My reaction is ouch," said Malcolm, "and it sounds very military.

"Don't worry, it never happened to me," Marcus explained.

The silence that followed said more than words could express. Marcus felt uneasy inside, as if someone had walked over his grave. He knew Malcolm did not blame him on his stance and pondered on what it would have felt to be 'cut' at the age of sixteen, or even thirteen.

After leaving school Marcus pointed out that his boxing contract was passed on, or sold, to a local family business in the area.

"I never did find out if the school actually sold the contract, and for what amount," Marcus said, "and I used to think about that for a long time afterwards." He did not receive any significant money at the time.

Marcus thought that the family who acquired the contract had several interests from amusement arcades and gyms to organising wrestling and boxing tournaments. He explained that the father ran the businesses.

"We didn't see much of him," laughed Marcus, "but he was known as Fat Fred." His two adult sons oversaw the boxing training and the enforcement of any punishments they thought were necessary to get better results. Malcolm found it strange that appearing smooth-chested in the ring was part of Marcus's initial contract.

"I had to undergo those chest shaves all the way to my twenty-first birthday," Marcus said smiling, "and I never did grow any chest hair; so, what was the point of all that?"

Bouts were usually scheduled for weekend dates and Marcus had to train hard in the family gym at least one month prior to the fight. "The training mainly consisted of jogging round a large green, which was at the front of the gym, and exercising with weights and a Bullworker machine," he said, "At any time leading up to a fight the two sons could ask for a physical check-up, virtually on demand when I was on their premises," he continued.

"That also sounds pretty controlling," Malcolm replied, awaiting a response. The remark hung in the air like smoke from a pub cigarette.

"Well, they looked at the boxers under their contracts as their assets and considered they were entitled to examine us," Marcus responded. Malcolm could see that this could be quite intimidating, as well as controlling. Marcus was in full flow once more.

The family gym had a steam room, which doubled as a punishment room if the brothers thought any of the boxers were not training hard enough, or were likely to lose a fight.

"We could be left in the heat for up to twenty minutes at a time, standing up, in a locked room like a small shed," Marcus said. "To make sure you were standing all the time there was a small glass window in the front door that could be opened by anyone, at any time. I remember that one boxer was found squatting down. He had extra minutes added to on the time he was in the steam room," continued Marcus.

Bit by bit Malcolm had been drawn into Marcus's former world, and whilst still on the subject he decided to ask what he thought the worst punishment had been.

"There were a lot over the years…really difficult to say," Marcus pondered, "You sort of get used to them and a lot become a blur." Malcolm pushed for a more definite answer but then thought he had overstepped the mark by him prying into a sensitive area. Malcolm politely apologised.

"No," Marcus said, "I'm still trying to think. I guess something with water." Marcus confessed to not liking water too much. He explained that he never did learn to swim despite going with the school for several years. He just did not gain the trust of the water.

"Did you get many injuries whilst boxing," Malcolm enquired, slightly changing the subject.

"Not as many as you'd think," Marcus said pondering, "I did injure a hand and a foot on different occasions, but they weren't breaks in the end. I had to have them X-rayed." Marcus was deep in thought. "Plus, I've had a hell of a lot of bruising over the years." Marcus also explained to Malcolm how the rigorous training helped to cut down serious injuries.

"Wow, you went through all of that stuff in the past," said Malcolm, "and you still decided to allow your name to go forward for the bout at Lowgate Hall." Malcolm sat back in his chair awaiting a response. Marcus bowed his head before speaking.

"Yeah, I guess it does seem strange," he replied, looking pensive. It was the best answer he could think of.

Marcus suddenly felt himself in the limelight; the centre of attention again. He instinctively tried to leave that place by asking Malcolm a question.

"You must be so bored with me prattling on like this," he said, "What about you?" Malcolm apologised for putting his younger colleague under pressure, and then emphasised that he was not finding the conversation boring.

"Far from being bored I'm learning a lot, and if I'm honest, finding myself somewhat shocked too," he said as he got up to go to the bar for another round of drinks.

When he returned to the table the conversation had moved back to Marcus. "Do you think you'll ever box again," Malcolm said enthusiastically. Marcus wondered if, like Wayne, he was hoping that something more had been planned.

"No, not at present. The last fight was a one off really … a bit of a favour to the boss," said Marcus, slightly perplexed. Marcus explained that he enjoyed most of his boxing training. He really only enjoyed sports that he could do on his own, like running and gym-based exercises. Marcus also liked the weight training and exercises to develop stamina.

"I guess I was always I bit of a loner," he disclosed, "As I said before, what I did not like was the feeling of being put 'centre stage,' especially at the beginning of public bouts."

Malcolm was right in thinking that Marcus was shy. Marcus knew that Malcolm had absorbed a lot about the world of boxing just by listening to his experiences. Malcolm considered, too, that he had learned a lot about Marcus as a person. He respected his frankness.

It was approaching closing time and Marcus had to get back to his flat. He quickly gulped the last of his cider and made his way to the door, pausing only to look back through the tobacco smoke of the public bar. In a split second he was gone, like a black cat slipping into the night. Malcolm, deep in thought, was left staring into a half-finished pint of Guinness.

Chapter 4

ONWARD AND UPWARD

Malcolm decided to pop into his local newsagents. He was interested in looking through any boxing magazines. Three different ones were on display on the shelves. Malcolm picked them up, one by one, and slowly flicked through the glossy pages. This did not give him any further insight into the way boxing was regulated or scored.

It seemed to him that you had to know more than a bit about the sport beforehand to appreciate the articles in the magazines. There did not seem a lot about boxers fighting at the lighter weights, such as Flyweight or Featherweight, or any articles on school boxing.

Yet, as Malcolm absorbed more of the spirit of the magazines, the more his confusion about boxing started to clear. He had to admit to himself that he had substantially changed his mind. So long as boxing was legal and carried out by two consenting participants, he now did not see what was wrong with it. Malcolm *did* continue to wonder whether boys at school were given 'hard times' learning to box but then he conceded in his mind that it was a legitimate sport of contact and aggression.

Malcolm also conceded that school boxing was going out of fashion. He thought that most of his questions had been answered, at least in part, but he knew he was left with the image of Marcus in front of the doctor before the fight – he had introduced this into the conversation on more than one occasion.

It was then that he realised Marcus was a different type of character to his once imaginary stereotype. He had expected Marcus to be of a different physical build as well. Malcolm also had the very real image of Marcus immediately after the fight drinking from a bottle of water. The word 'determination' came into his mind. 'Yes, you had to be determined to be a boxer,' he admitted to himself.

There did not seem anything in print to explain to Malcolm the different styles of boxing and why some boxers were in the ring bare-chested or bare-footed, whilst others wore vests and boots. Malcolm did remember that Marcus said something about the style he trained in originating from southern Germany. Perhaps he was looking in the wrong place for his information.

"Are you after for anything in particular," asked the helpful shop-keeper. Malcolm shook his head and said he was just browsing. He felt under pressure to explain himself, and decided to leave the shop.

Perhaps *not* coming back from the newsagents with something on boxing made Malcolm think he still had a few things to learn. He had been reflecting on his religious like conversion from 'anti' to 'pro.' He now had the urge to convey this to Marcus, but waited a few more days before making contact. Malcolm wondered if he was doubting himself, or was just trying to get his head around things.

--o--

"I wonder if we could meet up again," Malcolm said to Marcus down the phone. Marcus let him know that he was about to go on holiday for a few weeks but was more than happy to talk to him about anything now.

Malcolm admitted that he had started off very 'anti' boxing and was on the brink of trying to stop the Optimus tournament. He also said that he had appreciated Marcus's openness about his past and his willingness to show him things he was unaware of. He admitted that he had a complete change of mind within a relatively short space of time.

"I'm glad to hear it," said Marcus. Malcolm wondered if Marcus was feeling smug, but he said later that he did not detect that in Marcus's tone of voice.

The two chatted about boxing, politics, the troubles in Northern Ireland and life in general for well over an hour. They did not arrange another meet up, but as Marcus put the receiver back on the 'phone he realised that he had left an impression on Malcolm that was difficult to define. Malcolm would no longer be the self-righteous 'stick in the mud' who opposed boxing. However, something else had happened. Marcus detected that something deep inside Malcolm had changed, and it felt both fascinating and confusing for him.

Marcus's mind wandered to Oliver, a nephew of Malcolm, who had started Japanese martial arts training as a teenager. Malcolm said that he was pleased when he had to give it all up because he got glandular fever. Malcolm had realised what a mistake he had made in not supporting Oliver's sporting ambitions. He was twenty now, fully recovered from his illness, and Malcolm knew he was still keen on judo and boxing. Marcus had become convinced that Malcolm wanted him to meet Oliver.

--o--

Malcolm was mowing the grass in his back garden when his 'phone rang. He rushed indoors.

"Malcolm Bauer," he said down the receiver. His mind was still in office mode.

"Hello, Malcolm, it's Marcus, how are you," came back. Malcolm was surprised, but pleased, that Marcus had contacted him again. He started to thaw.

"How did your holiday go," Malcolm enquired. Marcus told him how he had taken two weeks off work and had driven up to Liverpool to take the ferry to the Isle of Man.

"The scenery was fantastic," he said, "and some of the roads go all the way up a mountain. You go so high that you can put your hand out of the car window and feel the clouds."

Malcolm had wondered if Marcus had gone for the motorcycle racing. Marcus explained that he just needed a break from work and had always wanted to visit the Isle of Man.

"It's got its own parliament, you know," Marcus continued.

"And very sensible rates of taxation," said Malcolm, chuckling to himself.

Marcus was coming across quite excited as he spoke about his trip.

"Marcus, I've got this idea, just hear me out," Malcolm interrupted. The next five minutes was spent by Malcolm expanding on the story of his nephew and how he had not supported him in his passion for martial arts. He told Marcus that he wanted to put things right by showing him that he was wrong.

46

"You've made me realise that," Malcolm tried to explain to Marcus.

"I see," Marcus said, "well I think I do." It was Malcolm's desire that Oliver and Marcus meet each other as both seemingly had a lot in common. Marcus's gut instincts were correct. According to Malcolm his nephew was three years younger, and slightly taller, than Marcus. Seemingly, both had similar builds. Although Oliver had not trained in boxing, both of their characters, apparently, were complementary. As Malcolm spoke, Marcus was trying to picture Oliver in his mind. Malcolm was outlining a plan. It would be great if Marcus could teach Oliver a bit about boxing. He had an idea that maybe Oliver would agree to meet Marcus at his house and they could all take it from there.

"If I could get Oliver to meet you, do you think you could teach him a few boxing tricks," enquired Malcolm.

"I had a feeling you would ask that," Marcus replied, "Are you thinking of inviting us both to your place?" Malcolm confirmed Marcus's thoughts that he wanted both to go a few rounds together, if he could get Oliver to agree.

--o--

That night saw Malcolm, at home, running through some images in his mind. Some of them saw Oliver and Marcus boxing in a bout. Malcolm was acting as referee. Other fantasies saw Marcus sparring with Malcolm at his home in the back garden. The thought of him boxing sent a shiver down Malcolm's spine and brought him back to reality.

How could he, at 38 years old, have any chance of scoring anything against Marcus? His imagined opponent was fifteen years his junior and had trained over several long, tough years. Malcolm had only boxed a few times whilst enlisted in National Service. He hated it; his peers thought of him as a skinny geek.

As if to draw a line under Malcolm's thoughts his black cat, Toby, jumped onto his bed with a thud.

"Toby, am I losing the plot," whispered Malcolm, as he stroked his pet. There was no reply, only purring from the cat.

--o--

47

Marcus strolled over to Malcolm's house on the day they had arranged. It had taken him over half an hour, but he enjoyed walking and being out of doors. The plan was for both of them to discuss a possible fight between Marcus and Oliver. Marcus had a lot of questions in his mind as he rounded the corner into Grosvenor Crescent. It was an affluent area to the north of the city, with wide, tree-lined avenues.

The neighbourhood was full of individually designed houses and bungalows occupying large plots on both sides of the road. Most had perfectly manicured front gardens. Suburbia meets heaven, Marcus thought. He glanced across the road to see the number 27 on a neatly painted door. The property sat well on its plot, which looked more generous compared to some of the nearby houses. The Prussian Blue door was where Marcus was ending his walk.

Malcolm's place was a large detached house with a side garage and gravel drive. There was an impressive 3 litre Capri parked just in front of a triple garage. Toby was looking out of one of the downstairs windows. A neatly mown lawn and a perfectly clipped privet hedge completed the picture. You can tell a lot about a person by the state of their front garden, thought Marcus with a grin on his face.

Malcolm had been expecting his guest and opened the newly painted door as he stepped up to the porch. The door still retained an original art deco window. Malcolm looked strangely tense as he appeared at the threshold.

"Hello," Marcus said, pausing briefly under the canopy.

"Well come on in," said Malcolm moving back. Marcus stepped up and was in Malcolm's hallway.

"Quite a big place you've got here," Marcus said glancing into Malcolm's back room. Malcolm agreed that it was a large house, especially for someone living on their own. He had been left the property by a distant relative, who also had a business in Bonn.

Marcus wondered why Malcolm had not considered taking in lodgers to make a bit of money. He could tell that the house was solidly built, fairly typical of the workmanship of quality homes fifty years ago. Malcolm's house had an enchanting atmosphere all of its own. Some of the original features had been kept, but it was more than that. Malcolm's house was warm and inviting; somehow a bit special.

The house décor was a tad old fashioned with dark wallpaper and dado rails but it did benefit from a large, solid lean-to on the back. There was plenty of room to build outwards, as Malcolm's garden was a lot larger than typical for the area.

"Do you want to have a quick look outside," asked Malcolm.

"Yes," Marcus said, "I've already noticed you're quite a gardener."

Both were soon out on the back lawn. The sun was shining; it was a lovely afternoon. Malcolm explained that he needed to replace some conifers that had died off in the hot summer of 1975, but there was still enough shrubbery to create ample screening.

"The good thing is," explained Malcolm, "the lawns are quite large and I am not overlooked by anyone else here." Marcus could see the advantages.

"I guess it makes it easy for nude sunbathing," he said turning to Malcolm, who looked embarrassed.

"Oh, no, I don't do that."

"Only kidding, man," responded Marcus. He turned back to look at the back of the house. Everything seemed neat and well cared for.

Malcolm wandered back inside the house, just in front of his guest. There was a lot to sort out. Marcus still could not imagine why Malcolm was condoning a fight between himself and his nephew.

"So, are you really saying that Oliver has an interest in boxing," Marcus enquired.

"Yes," responded Malcolm.

Marcus needed to know more. The two were sitting in Malcolm's back room. Marcus looked round and noticed some family photographs in frames on the sideboard. Malcolm saw where Marcus's gaze had travelled.

"Yes, this is a picture of Oliver," said Malcolm, picking up a coloured photograph in a silver frame, "It was taken just over a year ago."

Marcus held the photograph and glanced up at Malcolm. He could see the family resemblance.

"What are you thinking," enquired Malcolm. Marcus told Malcolm that he thought Oliver looked very much like him. It seemed the eyes and the nose and mouth were quite similar.

"Yes," chuckled Malcolm, "some make the mistake of thinking we are brothers, although there is a bit of an age difference."

Marcus handed the photo back, and it took its rightful place on the sideboard. He was just about to speak when Malcolm suddenly started stringing his thoughts together.

"You would never guess …," said Malcolm, looking slightly dejected, "but Oliver wants to join the armed forces." He sank back in his chair, pausing and looking over to Marcus for a reaction.

"What's wrong with that," Marcus asked, not really following Malcolm's point.

The atmosphere in the room suddenly changed. Malcolm was now looking tense as he squeezed the arms of his favourite armchair.

"Well, surely there's better places for him than in the British Army," he said. Malcolm's voice was getting louder. "Don't you remember the Warrenpoint Massacre, not that long ago… 18 soldiers died there," Malcolm continued. He was now quite agitated.

"Man, I do," replied Marcus, "And maybe there's worse places than the Army for a young bloke like Oliver." Malcolm was quieter now. He looked frustrated; and felt that Marcus was not taking his fears seriously enough.

Malcolm told Marcus how he though his nephew would be bullied if he joined the Army. He admitted to lying awake at night worrying about it, especially as the troubles in Northern Ireland appeared to be getting worse. Malcolm then recalled his own sorry days in the National Service where he seemed to be out of his depth. It was Marcus who was now quiet. He began to understand more where Malcolm's dark fears were coming from.

"You see," said Malcolm looking over, "Oliver takes a bit after me … well you can see it in his photograph, can't you …"

Marcus tried to reassure Malcolm that things had changed since National Service; the Army was more of a career nowadays, more professional, despite the risks. Malcolm did not say anything, but judging by his pained expression Marcus would need to do more to convince him. The subject quickly changed.

"I think 'It's a Knockout' might be on," said Malcolm looking for the 'Radio Times' to check the listings.

Marcus said he was not that fussed about watching the television. It was now getting dark and he could just about see a large, orange moon appearing through some distant trees marking the end of Malcolm's garden.

"I've got a German Hock wine, if you want any."

"Okay," responded Marcus, thinking that white wine would be a change from the usual cider or beer. Malcolm thought he had a bottle in the fridge and walked off to look for it.

After a few minutes he returned and apologised for not finding the wine.

"Maybe you drank that one already," said Marcus, grinning. Malcolm was heading for the door again. He looked flustered.

"I've got more in the cellar," he called out as he disappeared along the hallway. Marcus thought that it was unusual that a house built after the First World War would have a cellar. He tried to envisage its size and depth, and wondered if it might be full of old, unused furniture.

The room was silent apart from the regular tick from an old looking wooden clock sitting proudly on the mantel piece. His host seemed to be taking his time finding the wine. Marcus decided to take another look at the framed picture of Oliver. Yes, he did look a lot like Malcolm, he concluded. Marcus also noticed that Malcolm still had a record player.

He walked over to take a closer look. Nearby lay a sizeable collection of records, in no particular order. Marcus pulled one out at random. 'Goodbye to Love.' The soft, airbrushed faces of Karen and Richard Carpenter were staring out at him. Marcus felt a ripple of emotion pass over him; he felt lonely. He wondered if that feeling had been released from deep within him, or had more to do with Malcolm and his choice of music. At that moment his host returned clutching a dusty bottle.

"If I stick it in the freezer part for a while," said Malcolm, "it should taste better."

"Okay," responded Marcus. He still had Oliver's picture in his hand but put it back before Malcolm noticed.

Over a glass or three of partially chilled wine, Malcolm and Marcus thrashed out a plan whereby Oliver would be asked if he wanted a bout in the back garden. If Oliver consented, it would be three rounds of three minutes. Malcolm agreed to keep time.

"It seems you have spent some time working this out," said Marcus.

"Shall we say next Saturday week?" enquired Malcolm, not rising to Marcus's point. "Yes, that sounds fine," Marcus replied. The details having been agreed, Marcus got up to leave.

"Time to go, I think," said Marcus rising from his chair, "I need to get the last bus back ... or walk."

"Stay longer, if you want. I can always arrange for a taxi," replied Malcolm, who was indicating that Marcus could still have any remaining wine.

After further discussion Malcolm said that Marcus was welcome to stay in one of the spare bedrooms. That would give Malcolm the excuse to drink more Hock, his favourite. Marcus agreed as it was already ten past ten at night and buses rarely ran after that.

"What you never explained from school," said Malcolm, taking a drink from his glass, "was your worst punishment. It was something to do with water, wasn't it?"

As soon as he said these words, he wanted to withdraw them, but it was too late. If he had offended Marcus he had just have to apologise.

"Good recall, Malcolm," said Marcus seemingly unphased by his host's direct question. Marcus reminded Malcolm that he went to a gym after leaving his school and the punishments happened there too.

"You couldn't seem to escape the abuse," Malcolm pondered.

Marcus told Malcolm that he always detested taking a shower at school. He hated the feeling of water coming down over his head. To him it felt akin to drowning.

Marcus looked across towards Malcolm wondering if he was going to laugh but Malcolm was listening intently. Marcus explained that during the first few months of his contract with the Tyneside family he was subjected to a water punishment.

This entailed Marcus doing sit ups on the hard edge of an indoor pool. One of the brothers – either Ali or Jas – held his ankles as he went backwards parallel to the surface of the water and then up to the sitting position again.

A set number of sit ups had been stipulated by his trainer but this eventually exhausted Marcus and he at first hit the back of his head on the surface of the water but then went down under it. The person holding his ankles then pulled them up not allowing Marcus up for air. Marcus paused his story before saying he was terrified, although to a swimmer this would not be such a frightening punishment.

"I'm not so sure about that," pondered Malcolm.

Marcus told Ali and Jas that he would do any punishment but not that one again. They took him at his word and that is how he ended up getting all sorts of creative physical punishments during his time at the gym.

"I guess they set the number of sit ups high so you would eventually dip into the water," said Malcolm.

"Got it," responded Marcus, "I could nearly do forty in the end but that wasn't good enough for them." Malcolm could understand how cruel this was for anyone, swimmer or not.

Marcus said that lots of the punishments were carried out with him wearing light blue jeans. Malcolm wondered if this was to emphasise the working-class background to most boxers under contract. Marcus considered that insight might contain more than a grain of truth. Malcolm was now glancing at the clock above the open fireplace. He yawned. It was well past eleven.

"Boring you, am I," asked Marcus.

Malcolm looked embarrassed but suggested the two get some sleep. Marcus felt drained and went upstairs, choosing what he assumed was the second bedroom, which was almost as spacious as the main bedroom. He switched on the light and shut the door behind him.

Marcus sat on the corner of the bed, bending down to untie his shoelaces. The mattress was quite bouncy, he thought, but that was fine. He noticed that there was an old tea making machine in the room. By the time Marcus was ready to get into bed he had also noticed another object.

His gaze had caught a carved head, complete with a slight beard, on a stand by the bed. He took a closer look and read the name on the base. 'Hadrian.' Amazing, thought Marcus as he switched off the light. He was in the dark with the head and shoulders of the Roman Emperor Hadrian!

It was cold outside but the central heating made the bedroom very warm. Marcus had forgotten to open a window, as he normally did at home. As the night progressed, he begun to have strange dreams and his disjointed thoughts formed a vivid nightmare. There were scenes of Roman Centurions marching four abreast down a lonely country road. Marcus was in the dream, sheltering behind a low stone wall, hoping not to be noticed.

Someone was looking for Hadrian but only found a creature with a human body and a raven bird head. The six-foot creature's body was dark and muscular and its eyes frightening and piercing. Marcus found himself floating in the air, looking down at the ground. There were ravens flying around him, trying to knock him down. The dreaming Marcus found himself tumbling towards a tree standing on a tiny island surrounded by water.

--o--

Marcus woke up at six thirty. He decided he would slip away before Malcolm got up. Marcus never got a good night's sleep in a bed that was not his own. He did not understand how the tea machine functioned. What he really needed was a 'caffeine hit,' and then he would go. Marcus thought it best to leave a note to explain his secret departure.

As Marcus was searching for a clean mug the sound of the kitchen door opening broke his concentration. Malcolm was coming through the eggshell painted door.

"I did not want to wake you," said Marcus, "I thought I'd make myself a cup of coffee and leave. Thanks for putting me up." Marcus looked as if he had slept outside and was wearing some of the same clothes from the night before.

"No problem," said Malcolm.

54

Malcolm was sporting a yellow knitted jumper and blue and white striped pyjama bottoms, tied at the waist with a white cord. Brown leather slippers completed the early morning picture.

"Ah, found one," said Marcus picking up a dark blue mug from one of the kitchen cupboards.

The kettle was already boiling and Malcolm was pointing to where the coffee could be located. Marcus glanced at Malcolm and wondered if he should comment on his attire.

"Nice jumper," said Marcus, sarcastically. Malcolm realised that his guest was not saying what he really thought.

"Oh, the jumper ...," said Malcolm in a sheepish voice.

Marcus turned to put some sugar in his coffee. At the same time Malcolm slipped off the offending yellow jumper and sat down on one of six identical wooden kitchen chairs beside the solid table. He was now showing a brilliant white Marks and Spencer vest.

"Before you go," said Malcolm, "there's something I want to say." He looked deep in thought, almost entirely lost for words.

"When you boxed in the tournament," continued Malcolm, "it was a kind of therapy for me.

Marcus put his mug on the table. Malcolm looked as if he was going to say something profound. After a pause he disclosed that during his National Service days he was teased and called 'Lilywhite' for being pale and uncoordinated. One of the corporals picked on him and called him a wimp for not being able to win boxing bouts. He was adding more detail to the story he had started to verbalised the night before.

"I've got a confession," revealed Malcolm, "When you were in the ring with Luke Mills, I was secretly willing you to knock him out."

Feelings of shock and then anger rippled through Marcus like a tide of emotion rising up from the ground. He was now sitting opposite Malcolm with his mug a few inches from his hand. It would have been easy for Marcus to throw his coffee in Malcolm's face, but he took a deep breath and resisted the urge. An uncomfortable silence hung in the air like toxic gas.

"Aah," grunted Malcolm, banging the table in frustration. The noise was too much for his cat to stand, and he could be seen rushing out of the kitchen.

Malcolm was trying desperately to summon the words to explain his feelings.

"When I did my National Service, I hated the times we had to box. I was never any good at it," he continued.

"That's okay," said Marcus breathing deeply and trying to force away any remaining anger like a Buddhist monk, "We can't all be good at boxing, now, can we?" Marcus noticed that Malcolm looked full of emotion.

"Here, take this coffee," Marcus said, sliding the half-drunk mug across the table. Malcolm gripped the warm object avoiding the handle, just letting the mug move backwards and forwards from one hand to the other.

"I just wish I could have been as courageous as you were," Malcolm said, his voice chocking with the emotion that had built up. At that moment Malcolm looked like a crumpled man.

"I think I'll go back to bed," he sighed.

"Maybe you've got 'flu coming on," Marcus said, putting his hand on Malcolm's shoulder.

On Marcus's suggestion Malcolm finished his coffee and started off towards his bedroom. Marcus decided to accompany his host up the stairs in case he felt dizzy or fell. Malcolm went straight to his bed and sat on it before slipping off his vest. He asked Marcus to hand him his pyjama top. He seemed more composed so Marcus bade his host 'goodbye' as he pulled the sheets up. Marcus hurried downstairs; he was now on his way down the hall aiming for the front door. Toby was scurrying the opposite way.

--o--

Wayne drove to Albert Road and parked his precious Blaze red Morris Marina opposite the detached Victorian house where Marcus lived. The building looked impressive from a distance being on its own, and standing back from the road in wooded grounds, with several yew trees at the front. As Wayne walked up the drive, he wondered what type of family had been its original occupants. People of importance and wealth, he concluded.

Wayne had once lived in a Victorian house in the city centre but this residence was a far cry from his parent's overcrowded two-bedroom terrace facing the railway. Although happy-go-lucky by nature, Wayne hated sharing a bedroom with his younger brother, Grant. He only managed to fully escape Belmont Terrace when he married Sandra.

This time Marcus had been informed of the visit, so he answered the front door soon after Wayne had rung the bell. The two climbed the creaking stairs to the top floor. Expecting Wayne, Marcus had tidied up. The bed was made, and all the old newspapers and magazines had been thrown out.

"Got some good news for you, me old mate," said Wayne pulling out a piece of crumpled, green coloured paper from the back pocket of his jeans. Wayne had a glint in his eye.

Marcus glanced at the paper and wondered where Wayne got all his energy. He was like a young child at a birthday party. Marcus thought that if he were ever feeling in a low mood, he would only need to invite Wayne over for a few minutes. That would be long enough to cheer him up for a whole week.

With paper in hand Wayne started to read out details of the barn-boxing event both were planning to go to.

"Saturday the thirteenth of September … Drive out to Church Green and stay in sight of war memorial …," explained Wayne.

"Okay," replied Marcus, waiting impatiently to hear the next bit.

"You will be met by someone there at seven and will be given further directions," Wayne continued, scanning the paper.

"I've heard about this before. I think we'll also need an Ordnance Survey map," said Marcus, "just in case."

Wayne knew where the village was and he was happy to drive there. A time was agreed for Marcus to be picked up to go to the fight.

"Keep quiet about it," said Marcus in a serious tone of voice, "I mean it, otherwise you won't be Mr. Popular." Wayne was still acting as if he was going to a party. After the warning he took the hint.

"Another thing," said Wayne, looking uncharacteristically sheepish, "take a look at these ..."

Wayne was holding some poor quality, slightly faded, holiday snaps of him and Sandra on a beach near Bournemouth. He was wearing his trunks; she a summer dress. Both looked as if they were gazing out to sea.

"Forget the misses," he said, "what do you think … physically, mate, could I be a boxer? Be honest."

Marcus was looking at the pictures of Wayne and his wife on a holiday.

"Can't really say from these," said Marcus, who then gave Wayne a lecture on what it would be like to train as a boxer. Marcus pointed out that he started at thirteen; most lads started a little earlier. In addition to physical fitness Wayne would need stamina and resilience, and would also need to learn boxing techniques. Marcus looked at Wayne. He looked slightly dejected but quickly bounced back saying he could do it, if someone had had some faith in him.

--o--

It was a sunny afternoon with not a cloud in the sky. Marcus was already at Malcolm's house waiting to see what Oliver was like 'in the flesh.' Malcolm had apologised for being so grumpy the last time both were in the house together. He said that he was suffering from a virus. Marcus gave him the benefit of the doubt and started some small talk bringing in Toby and the weather.

"Not a bad afternoon for this time of year," he said.

The front door bell rang and interrupted any further conversation. Malcolm went ahead of Marcus to greet his visitor. He and his nephew, Oliver, were coming along the hall as Marcus went into the back room. He could hear voices in discussion and then Oliver, followed by Malcolm, entered the room. Oliver was carrying his sports bag.

"This is Oliver," said Malcolm. Marcus politely greeted Oliver before everyone sat down.

"Would anyone like a drink?" asked Malcolm breaking the silence. Oliver and Marcus agreed on water, Marcus pointing out that anything else would not be appropriate before a fight.

Marcus sat back, sipping the clear liquid from a bright blue plastic tumbler. He would have preferred soda water.

"Now you don't have to do this ... either of you," blurted Malcolm. He still had not handed over Oliver's tumbler, and looked as if he was about to spill the water contained in it.

"Well, I'm up for it, if you're agreeable, Oliver." Marcus said. His prospective opponent nodded, but looked sheepish. Eventually Malcolm placed a bright green tumbler of water in front of his nephew.

Marcus pointed out that the contest would be short, with three rounds of three minutes each Malcolm would keep time. There would be no referee as such, as agreed at Malcolm's house nearly a fortnight before. Malcolm would mark out a square on the lawn with chairs, which would represent the ring.

"If anyone goes down, we stop the fight," Marcus said firmly, "and remember that what we are doing is barely legal, so we'll call it training."

"That's right ..," added Malcolm," and Oliver, don't breath a word of this to your mother, I mean it."

Marcus said that as there was not a doctor or referee, he would have to satisfy himself that Oliver was capable of the bout, and that he was a willing participant.

"Now, you don't have to do this, Oliver," repeated Malcolm.

Malcolm had designated his second bedroom for Marcus to change down and the smaller third bedroom for Oliver. Marcus followed Oliver up the stairs, as he needed a pre-fight chat with the brave novice.

"Just a quick word, Oliver," Marcus said standing at the door. He moved inside the bedroom and sat on a chair opposite the bed.

"I know you've had some martial arts training when you were younger," Marcus remarked, "Malcolm told me about it, but are you willing to fight today?"

Oliver nodded and looked over to his sports bag that had been dropped beside the bed. Marcus instinctively felt unhappy with this and wondered if Oliver was agreeing just to please either his uncle or someone else.

"Why do you want to fight," Marcus insisted, "You might get hurt."

Oliver revealed that he was thinking of joining the Army and knew life would be tough. He realised that a boxing bout could be part of the assessment procedure and he really wanted to pass.

Marcus still felt that Oliver was trying to prove himself, perhaps to his uncle. Marcus looked at Oliver and thought that he looked more suited to being a catalogue fashion model than becoming a solder.

However, Marcus was satisfied with what he was hearing and instructed Oliver to change down to his shorts. As Marcus had not met Oliver before he said that he would leave the room and return again after a few minutes. He went back into the second bedroom and quickly changed down into his black shorts. Malcolm was to supply his nephew's gloves. Marcus waited just outside the door for a few minutes and then re-entered.

Oliver was standing at the side of the bed in a new pair of red shorts and a white T-shirt. Marcus beckoned him, indicating that he wanted the T-shirt removed.

"Do I have to," whispered Oliver, looking down. "You can wear it for the fight but I need to check you out to satisfy myself that you're capable of the bout," insisted Marcus.

Oliver seemed very reluctant to comply and was becoming slightly flushed in the face. He looked embarrassed. Marcus offered to go out and come back in again but this seemed not to make any difference.

"You don't have to go ahead with this, Marcus said, "no one would think you a sissy, or anything."

Marcus could not understand what the problem was. "I do want to fight," retorted Oliver, "I really do ... please."

Marcus felt frustration building up inside him but tried not to show it. There was a long silence. Oliver looked at Marcus, and then looked down towards the floor again.

"Stand up straight," barked Marcus, still feeling the frustration simmering inside.

Marcus was thinking of removing Oliver's T-shirt himself and took a step towards Malcolm's nephew. Oliver knew what was about to happen and stood in front of Marcus passively. Oliver had to make a decision, but Marcus knew that he had already won the bout.

"Arms up," said Marcus trying not to be too harsh on the nervous younger man standing a few inches away from him, "I've seen your uncle shirtless, now I'll see you the same."

Oliver did not fully comprehend what Marcus was saying but complied, and he was soon facing Marcus bare-chested.

"Nice tattoo," Marcus said, looking at a red England flag contained in a shield on Oliver's upper left arm.

The colours were sharp; it looked new. Oliver remained silent, looking down to the floor once more and trying to hide the tattoo with his right hand. Marcus could still imagine Oliver modelling sportswear.

"Oh, I've guessed it," Marcus said gleefully speaking in a loud voice, "Malcolm doesn't know you've had a tattoo done, does he?" Oliver shook his head.

"No one else does ... right," continued Marcus. He was now on a roll.

The two came down the stairs wearing shorts and T-shirts. Fortunately for Oliver he brought a longer sleeved T-shirt with him for the bout. Malcolm was waiting for them in the back room, boxing gloves ready.

"A bit cold for you, boys," he quipped with a hint of sarcasm. Neither rose to the bait. Marcus told Malcolm that they had agreed that if he lost he would do a forfeit, but if Oliver lost that forfeit would be down to Malcolm.

Looking across to Oliver, Marcus gave him a concealed wink of his left eye. Oliver smiled; some of his earlier apprehension was disappearing. Without further talk all walked out into the back garden. A chilly breeze blew across the lawns.

"Oh, okay, I can see why you wanted the T-shirts," said Malcolm.

Marcus glanced around. Malcolm had done a good job of creating a flat space on the grass with chairs marking the boundaries.

Malcolm stood in the middle, as previously agreed, with Oliver and Marcus facing each other. He glanced at his watch and waved the two together, moving himself quickly out of the improvised ring. Marcus dodged around Oliver willing him to make the first contact. A flurry of punches into the air was meant to draw Oliver into the bout.

Oliver looked, and acted, if he hardly knew what to do. Marcus was aware that Oliver was younger and less experienced than him and that both fighters were not wearing head or mouth guards. He did not want to act like a bully. He would not go in hard, he thought, as that would be unfair. Marcus vowed to keep the blows away from Oliver's clean, baby face, just in case the soldiering career did not work out. A bent nose would not look good in a photo-shoot, thought Marcus.

Oliver leaned forward and assumed a crouching, defensive stance. His fists were in a good position to protect his face but he looked as if he was fixed to the spot like an expensive cherub garden statue. Marcus weaved in and out of Oliver with some fast footwork. He was still holding back. Oliver started to move more, and loosen up. Both boxers were now engaged in the fight and making contact.

Some mild grunts pierced the fresh autumn air. Marcus looked focused and moved in to strike Oliver twice in quick succession on his right arm. Oliver dropped his guard and Marcus moved in again punching him in the chest. The older fighter was determined to pace the rounds so that Oliver would not be defeated in the first. Both boxers were moving around on the grass as if they were ritual dancers. A flurry of blows rained down on Oliver pushing him backwards.

"Time," shouted Malcolm, holding his watch up.

Marcus returned to a chair in one of the corners. He looked across at his opponent who was standing around looking lost.

"Go to that chair," beckoned Malcolm, pointing to the chair diagonally opposite Marcus.

A grin came over Marcus's face and he moved his head down, his glove up, to hide it. Marcus quickly glanced up again. A group of swans were flying in a V formation high in the sky. Marcus's thoughts started to drift. He wondered what it would be like to be as free as a bird, flying with his companions to some lonely, secret place. His thoughts soon returned to the fight. Should he use round two to lay into his opponent and thus end the fight, he wondered.

Malcolm called time again and both boxers swiftly moved into the middle of the improvised grass ring. Oliver sprang forward to meet Marcus. He now looked more confident. Marcus held back and Oliver managed to land some good punches. Marcus responded with lightening reactions with a left hook.

More sporting grunts broke the silence. Oliver was stunned into inaction. Malcolm looked on, worried for his nephew's safety. The second round was now over. Marcus and Oliver went back to sit on a chair in their respective corners. Oliver was breathing deeply. Concerned, Malcolm walked over to get a better view.

"Want to continue," asked Malcolm, hoping his nephew would say 'no.'

Oliver, more determined, simply nodded. Malcolm asked again.

"Yes," retorted Oliver, standing up.

Malcolm, still looking concerned, waved the two fighters into the middle again. 'If anything went wrong, I'll get the blame for it,' he anxiously thought. As the two boxed on it was clear that Marcus was in control. He was dodging around his younger opponent and landed some light punches. Oliver fought back but this provoked Marcus into landing one heaving punch on Oliver's right shoulder.

Oliver moved backwards but was distracted by a stone under his bare foot. Looking down he lost all concentration, which gave Marcus his final chance before the bell. Marcus landed another heavy punch on Oliver's torso, the blow tripping him backwards. Oliver landed ungracefully on his backside.

That marked the end of the bout. At first Oliver just sat on the grass, his head down. He looked as if he was waiting for someone to say something. Marcus held out his right hand and both boxers symbolically tapped each other's glove. Oliver stood up. Both embraced warmly. Marcus could feel the heat from Oliver's body. It felt comradely and somehow 'safe.' The two were now members of the same club. Malcolm had become the outsider in his own environment.

Marcus held out his hands for Malcolm to remove his gloves. Oliver copied the victor. Everyone was now walking back into the house.

"Okay," said Marcus wiping the sweat off his forehead, "that was good, but next time remember to hold your gloves high." Oliver absorbed this advice in silence.

"Let's go back upstairs and get changed," Marcus suggested.

The two went inside and back to their changing rooms. After five minutes both were fully dressed. They stood at the top of the stairs talking in whispered voices.

"Malcolm is the one that has to do a forfeit," Marcus pointed out, "What do you think it should be."

Oliver was in deep thought. He felt uneasy and did not want to fall out with his uncle. They had been emotionally distant for years but the bout on the lawn had mended a few bridges on all sides.

"Maybe he ought to jog around the back garden for twenty minutes," said Oliver.

"Yeah, followed by twenty press ups in front of us," Marcus added, looking over towards Oliver.

He felt his boxing opponent's uneasiness with this suggestion. Oliver looked concerned, still thinking that he ought to protect his uncle's position. Marcus, detecting Oliver's loyalty, pondered that blood was thicker than water. He had learned a lot by just observing Oliver.

Marcus and Oliver returned downstairs to join Malcolm.

"Ah, there you both are," he said, "For a minute I was wondering what you were up to."

Marcus and Oliver looked at each other knowingly. Oliver pointed out that it was Malcolm who was supposed to undertake a forfeit now that Marcus had won.

"Anyone for a beer," enquired Malcolm, moving into the kitchen.

Both guests told him that he could not get out of the agreement by simply offering alcohol. Malcolm returned with a couple of cans and put them on the coffee table in front of his white leather sofa. Marcus grabbed a Stellar, pulling the ring then carefully pouring the foaming contents into a glass.

"Can I exchange my forfeit for a treat," asked Malcolm.

Marcus glanced over saying, "I guess it depends what it is."

Oliver and Marcus tried to guess what the treat could be. Suggestions ranged from ice cream to money.

"I know you are into aircraft," said Malcolm, looking towards Marcus.

"Yes, I am," came the reply, "but what are you saying?"

Malcolm spelled out his idea saying that he knew someone, a friend from school, who had restored an old bi-plane to full flying condition. The aircraft was based at the main airport and was designed for passengers.

"What sort of plane is it?" asked Marcus enthusiastically.

Malcolm explained that it was an aircraft from the 1940s – a wood and fabric Dragon Rapide.

"Ah, a very famous old English design," said Marcus knowingly.

Marcus turned towards Oliver, but Oliver remained silent. Malcolm explained that his forfeit could be traded in for a flight on the Dragon Rapide. It did not take long for Marcus to agree. Oliver also said he would like to experience a 'flight from the past.'

With the deal struck Marcus finished his drink and got up to leave. He was chuffed that he was to get a freebie flight on such an iconic aircraft. Marcus paused at the front door.

"Bye, Oliver," he shouted down the hall. "Before I go," he said turning to Malcolm, "I want to know something that's been bugging me." Malcolm enquired what it was that needed an urgent explanation.

"Why did you allow the union fight?" asked Marcus.

"Well in the end, it wasn't the message, it was the messenger," was Malcolm's cryptic reply. Marcus did not wait for a translation, and was soon heading for home.

Chapter 5

SHOCKS AND SURPRISES

Wayne called round to pick up Marcus. He was a full twenty minutes early. No sooner had Marcus answered the front door, Wayne was rushing up the stairs to the top floor flat.

"You're a bit keen," said Marcus, trying to tune in to Wayne's energy.

"I didn't want to be late for the important event, did I, me old mate," came the reply, "That would never do." Wayne hurried in to the flat like an excited, young terrier after a rat.

He sat down, he stood up, he moved about, finally settling on looking out of the window on the overgrown gardens below. He was oblivious to the sounds of the Sex Pistols coming from on Marcus's cassette player. The track over, Marcus only needed to check his keys and grab his denim jacket from the back of a chair before both were leaving. Wayne was racing ahead and almost tripped down the creaking staircase before ending up in the fresh autumn air.

"You need to pull the door again," said Wayne, noticing that the car's passenger side was only closed on the first lock. Marcus secured the door and pulled down his seat belt, clicking it into place.

"Nice jacket," commented Wayne as he started the engine. Marcus explained that he bought it cheaply from a work colleague, who no longer had use for it.

The car was soon on the ring road looking for the route that would take them south and away from the city. Wayne had settled into driving the car and had little to say. Marcus looked out of the window, noting that the distance between the suburban streets was getting wider. They were soon out into the countryside with farms and scattered buildings on each side. Marcus thought he had noticed a bird of prey overhead but when he looked again it had gone.

Suddenly Wayne came into life, a big smile on his face, reaching for the radio and turning up the volume. Gary Numan's

'Cars' was now blaring out. Marcus guessed that his driver liked the song.

They were soon arriving at Church Green. Wayne parked the car near the stark white war memorial. Marcus and his faithful driver each looked out of the car windows, scanning anything that moved. They dared not to be too conspicuous in case someone noticed them. A Wagtail was strutting on the grass near the car, its tail moving up and down at every step. It was deadly quiet; no one else was around. There was little point in the two getting out of the car as the air seemed bitter, although there was no breeze to speak of.

"See that pub over there, beyond the pond," said Wayne pointing to a building across the green, "It's a funny thing but that's now run by Ian, a former Chief Petty Officer."

"From your Royal Navy days," added Marcus.

Wayne nodded. He said that they both served on '*HMS Andromeda,*' a Leander Class frigate.

"She was a special ship," he said with deep conviction and a trace of emotion in his voice. They had seen action in the Icelandic 'cod wars.' Wayne explained that on one occasion the ship was damaged when a Nordic tugboat rammed them.

Marcus listened intently and tried to imagine Wayne as part of a frigate's all male crew. Ian had taken over the running of the pub with his wife and teenage sons, after he left the Royal Navy. Wayne had visited twice and had spoken to Ian on the 'phone several times recently.

"I bet you've got some stories to tell," said Marcus. Wayne looked momentarily vacant.

"They were good days," he mumbled.

Wayne looked as if he had drifted into another world. His eyes were glazed, his face frozen and expressionless. Marcus pondered on Wayne's meditation. He suddenly realised, that as well as sometimes acting the drama queen, Wayne could be quite reflective. The two had only met a few months beforehand but Marcus was beginning to respect Wayne on a deeper level. Perhaps they had known each other in a previous existence, he pondered.

Marcus and Wayne were looking for signs of human activity. They were scanning the horizons for other people. After a few

67

minutes of tense waiting some people came within sight of the car. Wayne and Marcus looked at each other, and without saying a word both got out.

"Waiting for something," asked a distinguished man dressed in a tweed jacket.

"Yes," replied Marcus, "We are looking for a venue for an event." Wayne looked full at Marcus wondering why he was talking in coded terms.

"Can I trust you," asked the gentleman.

"You can trust us both," Wayne said winking, "I didn't get to where I am today without knowing nothing." The stranger in the tweed jacket was trying to sum Wayne up.

"That's a silly phrase to use," whispered Marcus, showing his disapproval.

"Robert," said the man thrusting his hand forward. Robert's grip was as firm as you would ever come across.

Within a few minutes Wayne had been given a basic, hand sketched map of how to get to the venue. Robert had also verbally explained the route, adding that it was nearby. Marcus and Wayne were quickly back, inside the car.

"We need to turn around and go towards the end of the green," explained Wayne, "I think I can get to it without the map." Marcus was impressed.

Moving cautiously, they turned off the main road and towards a school. The road was much narrower now and had a few bends in it. Tall hedges appeared on both sides giving a claustrophobic feeling. As they continued a bit further, they caught sight of the rear lights of what looked like an old Land Rover. As Wayne caught it up it turned left into a long, rutted dirt track.

"They must be going where we're going," said Marcus. It was soon apparent that they were on the edge of a large, bleak farm complex.

Wayne parked the car alongside the Land Rover they had spotted earlier. Marcus approved of the dirty, green 'series one' vehicle. The two got out of the car and followed a group of three men in through the opening of the nearest wooden barn.

"This looks ancient," commented Marcus as they moved into a large space. They could hear the hum of several voices ahead of them.

"Here for the entertainment, boys," came a female voice. Wayne looked around to see two young women approaching. "Yes," he responded. "That'll be eight pounds each." Marcus started to sort out his change but Wayne insisted that the bout would be his treat, saying that it was the least he could do. Cash paid, the two walked deeper into the barn. The atmosphere was eerie, but at the same time electric. Most of the space was in darkness but the area of the ring was lit up with dozens of bulbs. A generator hummed in the background out of sight.

"Let's sit here," said Wayne choosing two seats at the edge of the third row. Marcus edged in followed by Wayne. The wooden benches were quite hard but served a purpose. Marcus could see that Wayne was looking round. A man was approaching the seating area from the right. He seemed to be heading their way.

"I recognise you," said the middle-aged man in a confident way.

Marcus was thinking that their guest would be a successful double-glazing salesman. He looked bold and engaging.

"How are you both doing," he asked. Wayne explained to a confused Marcus that this was the man at the Optimus bout. He was the one who had given Wayne the business card.

"Max, in case you've forgotten," the man continued.

"Oh, of course," said Wayne stretching his right hand out towards the grinning Max.

It was not long before Max had Wayne away from his seat and was talking to him out of Marcus's earshot. Marcus, suspicious of the conversation, speculated what was going on. Did Wayne really want replacement windows for his house, he wondered, or maybe a cut price conservatory was on offer.

As more people were arriving and taking their seats facing the ring Marcus began wondering what the two could be discussing. He did not have long to wait for an answer as they were walking back again. Max was just about to say something when Wayne spoke.

"Marcus, me old mate… how about you helping out today?"

"Helping out," Marcus replied, wanting to know more. Max explained what had happened. A local lad of nineteen had put himself forward for a bout and although an opponent had been allocated, he had not shown. Max was looking for someone to fill the space.

"The thing is," said Max looking at Marcus, "this is his first fight so it would be an easy forty pounds if you agreed... No one need get hurt ... just do three rounds of convincing sparring."

Marcus turned to Wayne angrily wanting to know if he had been set up.

"No, absolutely not," said Max, "it's just that I've seen you box, and we are short of an opponent for Dominic ... that's the lad's name."

Wayne was now urging Marcus to agree to the bout, emphasising Dominic's local connection. Marcus added nothing to the conversation. Sensing a deadlock Max suggested Marcus first meet Dominic in the fighters' area before ruling out a bout.

"Okay", sighed Marcus, giving in, "let me see him." Max led the way.

"This is Dominic," said Max, introducing the shy novice before moving into the background.

Marcus put out his hand in a friendship gesture. He was pleased that Max had moved away and he now felt he was not being put under further pressure. Marcus tried to sum Dominic up. He was taller than his more experienced fighter, with dark hair and soft green eyes. Physically, Dominic would not be much of a challenge, Marcus calculated, despite looking as if he participated in sports.

Some of his initial anger had gone, but he was still a little suspicious as he quizzed Dominic. Marcus wanted to know how he had got involved in barn boxing, and what motivated him to fight. Dominic was very local to the bout venue but seemed quite naïve. He said he had overheard details of the event in a pub and wanted to participate himself.

"This is a rough sport," explained Marcus, "Are you really sure you want to get directly involved?"

Marcus was subtly trying to persuade the person in front of him to just be part of the anonymous fee-paying audience. He did not want to see Dominic hurt.

"Why put yourself through it," he asked. Dominic looked slightly dejected but soon perked up saying he still wanted to fight.

"What have you decided," enquired Max, coming over, "If it's a no, it's a no." Dominic turned to Marcus who then agreed to the contest, speaking for the both of them.

The two boxers had soon changed down. Marcus had been handed a donated pair of shorts, and Max helped him with the gloves. As instructed, Dominic stood wearing his black trousers. They looked as if they could have been his last school pair. Dominic soon had his gloves on. Marcus could now gauge him better. He had a reasonable physique, some chest hair and seemed fit enough to fight. Max said that medicals would be waivered. He had agreed to make them the first bout.

Earlier Max had indicated to Marcus that what was really required of him was a mentoring role, both in the ring and immediately afterwards. The older fighter led the way to the contest area, followed closely behind by Dominic. The combat zone was an illuminated square, packed with sawdust, and held in place by wooden edging.

As they came out the piped music faded and some extra lights were turned on. The referee for the evening had stepped forward urging both a clean fight for each three-minute round. Dominic and Marcus nodded before slapping gloves to cement their sporting agreement.

Marcus could see what looked like the compare come into the space clutching a microphone. He was sporting a distinctive red jacket that would not have looked out of place in a circus ring.

"We are just about to start," he said, looking towards the crowd.

There were some cheers and whistles from the restless audience. As Marcus looked forward, he could see Wayne, his eyes fixed to the ring, sitting impassively in the same spot. The rows of benches appeared quite full. More people must have come in whilst we were 'back stage,' thought Marcus as he tried to scan the faces. A few looked like they had military connections, but the majority looked like young farmers out to be entertained.

"Our first bout is between two fighters from Norfolk," said the compare, "On my left I have well-established, well-respected boxer Marcus Ingram." More whistles could be heard from the crowd.

"On my right, first time in the ring, I give you Dominic Giles."

Marcus detected even more cheering and whistling. He knew the crowd were behind the underdog so he had two choices – go in hard and mean and wind them up or be more moderate in his attack. He decided on the latter course, as this was what Max had said he wanted.

The referee appeared again as if by magic and urged the two boxers on. The bell rang and Marcus came straight in for an encounter. He quickly moved forward to meet Dominic near the centre of the improvised ring. A few seconds later he was testing his opponent with some light blows to the chin. Most were getting through as Dominic was poorly guarded against the onslaught.

Marcus eased off to allow Dominic to throw some punches. Most were wide of the mark. Both boxers weaved in and out of each other until Marcus decided to attack again landing two quick blows to Dominic's upper body.

It was clear to Marcus that although Dominic was up for the fight, he had had little training. The first round was soon over and both boxers went back to their corners. Marcus drank some water but was looking over towards Dominic trying to work out his next moves. He sensed that the crowd were expecting more, yet he did not want to bruise Dominic too much.

"Seconds out, round two," barked the compare.

This was Marcus's moment to move quickly into the middle of the ring. Dominic followed. Marcus stepped up the pace. It was almost as if it was a school boxing lesson. Marcus weaved effortlessly around Dominic, scoring some direct hits at will.

'Come on Dominic' could be heard from the crowd and 'Get in there.' As Marcus returned to his stool at the end of the second round, he briefly looked through the faces towards Wayne. His friend appeared to be obscured by the people around him. Marcus was perplexed by Wayne's apparent lack of interest in the bout. Why was not Wayne cheering him on, he wondered, and why was he sitting so low in his seat? The bell rang again to announce the start of the third round.

Marcus had planned to finish Dominic off almost at the end of this round. He would have to quicken the pace and move in convincingly before the bell. Now is not the time to hold back, he told himself, as the audience had paid to see a fight, not a ballet dance. Marcus took a deep breath and moved in to lay multiple punches on Dominic. Most hit his upper body and face. He could see that Dominic was struggling and the sweat started to form on his tanned torso. Despite the younger fighter's bigger build, his lack of experience was being shown to an enlivened audience.

'Dominic' and 'Fight back, Dominic' were intermittent cries from the spectators. With one clean upper cut Dominic was sent reeling backwards, thus ending the bout.

After the promoter formally declaring Marcus the winner, the two fighters quickly left the ring and headed back to where they had left their clothes. Max was already waiting for them.

"Spot on," he said as he handed both their brown envelopes before disappearing again into the vastness of the barn.

"Good job our clothes weren't left over there," said Marcus looking towards a flood of water coming down one of the main supporting beams of the barn.

"It must be pouring outside," remarked Dominic.

Both Marcus and Dominic were seated whilst other boxers were preparing for their bouts. Marcus could hear the compare introducing the next two fighters. He wondered if Wayne was enjoying being a spectator, but could not understand why he had appeared so 'distant' during his bout. After all, he pondered, it was Wayne's grand idea to come to the venue in the first place.

"So, what do you think," said Marcus, smiling, as he tried to find out how Dominic viewed their bout.

Marcus's anger at being 'dropped in it' by Wayne had now changed to elation and he was feeling pleased with himself that he had easily won the fight. Dominic was still clarifying his thoughts but he was pleased that he had entered. The end of an adrenaline rush was still carrying him along. It felt to him similar to scoring a goal for his football team.

Dominic loved football and was hoping that one day he would be spotted and play in the big league for a famous team like the Canaries. For now, he had to accept that he was a reserve at the Tangerines. Marcus was almost fully dressed. He looked at Dominic, who was still seated, and had a vision of his opponent working on a fishing trawler. Marcus wondered where this image had come from.

"Hey," said Dominic, looking up, "I knew you'd win but I'm glad you helped me out and allowed me my dream." Marcus detected a tear in his eye.

He held out his right hand; words were unspoken. Turning, he nodded at Dominic in recognition of what he had achieved and walked towards the spot where he had left Wayne. Fortunately, Marcus arrived at the seating area during a natural break. There were no boxers in the ring area and most people were just sitting quietly or chatting and laughing with friends. As he made eye contact with Wayne, he detected something was not quite right.

"What's up," enquired Marcus, "You look as if you've seen a ghost."

"No, mate … no, not a ghost," came the response.

Marcus looked round, aware that some of the people in the audience were looking at him. For a moment he wondered what it would be like to be a famous person; someone who is recognised by everyone in the street. He refocused on Wayne.

"What's the problem, then," asked Marcus. Wayne was usually very good at communicating his thoughts but he looked 'punch drunk.'

"That bloke you were boxing …," said Wayne, his voice trailing off, "well, I know him. I know his father." Marcus sat down beside Wayne waiting to hear more of the story.

At that point another bout was about to start. Marcus beckoned Wayne away from the audience and they walked over to the back of the barn. The illuminated ring was just visible in the distance. It was easy to have a private conversation in this dimly lit part of the barn, but still keep one eye on the contest. Wayne explained that Dominic was the elder of his friend Ian's two sons.

He had no idea that Dominic was interested in martial arts, let alone connected to the secret world of barn boxing. He doubted if Ian knew anything about it. Marcus suggested Wayne keep their knowledge to themselves.

"I could hardly believe what I was seeing," Wayne said. He still looked shocked.

The two decided to view the remaining bouts from their distant position near the back of the barn. Wayne was half hoping that he would spot Dominic somewhere, which would give him the excuse to say hello.

"Well, it's a small world," remarked Marcus, leaning back on one of the wooden supports that held the barn roof up. Wayne agreed.

"Oh, sorry, me old mate, I'm being selfish... do you want to sit down again," said Wayne looking over to his friend.

Marcus admitted that his left ankle was hurting but said he was fine just 'winding down' in the dimmer light.

"You missed a good bout," Wayne said enthusiastically, "Two heavyweights slugging it out, one a Russian bloke. Sergey, they called him ... don't know where he came from."

"Probably the Soviet Union," responded Marcus. He was feeling a little tired. "Maybe he's a defector from the Afghanistan war," Marcus added, knowing Wayne still had an interest in most things military.

Wayne and Marcus half watched another bout from the back of the barn before deciding to leave. Marcus was beginning to ache in several places. They slipped out without being seen. It was evident by the number of cars parked around the entrance to the barn that quite a few people had turned up to witness the fights. Wayne even managed to spot another Morris Marina amongst the assorted vehicles. Marcus's eye was on a smart white Range Rover with tinted windows.

Wayne turned the key in the ignition of his cherished car.

"That's it, Lisa," he mumbled under his breath, "come on, start."

"Lisa," remarked Marcus, "Who is she, and old girlfriend of yours?"

Wayne chuckled, explaining that the person he had bought the car off called her 'Lisa,' and the name had stuck. Fortunately, Lisa fired up first time. Unfortunately, the black plastic seats were very cold to sit on. Everything seemed damp. The rain was torrential and putting on the headlights only served to create a wall of dazzling white light in front of them. As the car moved off it seemed they were driving through a long car wash.

"This is going to be bad getting back," said Marcus, winding down his side window.

He was leaning right out to try to get a better view of the way out. He only served to get his head wet from the downpour. The car slowly moved forward picking its way long the dirt track a few yards from the car park.

"I know we have to go straight for quite a while before we get to the road," said Marcus, "and then it's a right turn towards the village."

Wayne felt 15 m.p.h. was all that he could offer until he hit the main road. The car was slipping and pulling to one side. Wayne was aware that there was a ditch on both sides of the track and to veer off course too far could be disastrous. After a few minutes the usually reliable Marina was turning onto the country road that had brought them to the secret venue.

"We may be able to go a bit faster, if I could clear the windscreen," announced Wayne as he wiped his fist along the inside of the glass.

"This is getting silly," said Marcus as the car drove alongside a hedge. The passenger window was half open and sharp twigs were hitting the wing mirror on this side.

"Don't fuss, me old mate, I know what I'm doing ... I've got a plan, you'll see," replied Wayne. Marcus saw that he had a cheeky grin on his face.

"Okay, okay," he said, as he started to wind up the window. "Oh, I don't believe it," exclaimed Marcus just as he had got the window closed, "Some idiots only dumped an old bike in the hedge ... some people."

Wayne glanced over and noticed how annoyed Marcus had become on seeing the apparent fly-tipping. As the two reached Church Green again Wayne decided to pull in. Marcus looked at Wayne, who had a strangely knowing look about him.

"Don't say the car is breaking down," Marcus complained, "It's too wet to be marooned here. I'm not in the mood. I just want to get home and to bed."

Wayne was now urging Marcus out of the car. Fortunately, the downpour was easing up. After checking the car doors, Wayne was beckoning Marcus to follow him to the pub.

"We're staying here for the night," announced Wayne, opening a side gate and hurrying into the grounds of the pub.

Marcus wondered why they were in the pub's garden late at night. Wayne pointed to a caravan a few yards in front of them.

"This is it," said Wayne pulling open the door, "It's a little Sprite."

The caravan was small but was hooked up for electricity. Wayne soon found a light switch and the cramped space was illuminated. Marcus observed that the inside was tiny. It looked as if it could only sleep two or three people at a push.

"It must have a heater somewhere," Wayne said. He was looking around for anything that resembled an electric fire. "Ah, I think this must be it," he said flicking a switch.

Marcus looked around. He could see that two small beds had been made at the rear end of the caravan. Marcus was equally quick to see that some Jameson whiskey had been left in a small cupboard.

"I guess this is for us," he said, "unscrewing the cap on the bottle.

Wayne agreed to have some of the whiskey and the two sat opposite each other on the front seating drinking from plastic tumblers. Marcus still wanted to know if Wayne had set him up concerning the bout, but Wayne insisted that events had not been planned.

"It just happened, mate, it just happened," he insisted. Marcus was not convinced and decided to press him further.

"Oh, come off it man," said Marcus, "you knew the bloke … the fight organiser."

Wayne's face was now flushed with fury. Without speaking he got up and stormed straight out of the caravan, pushing the door closed behind him. Marcus, fearing he had insulted his companion, stayed inside. He guessed, correctly, that Wayne would soon return. After all, he thought, it was very cold outside. The caravan door soon clicked open. Wayne was now coming through the door, bringing a wave of damp air with him.

"Sorry, Wayne," Marcus said, "I should have believed you the first time. You're a sound bloke. I don't distrust your motives."

77

Wayne returned to the bed area, but was icy silent. Marcus tried to explain that when it came to certain things, including boxing, he lacked trust.

"It's no excuse," continued Marcus, "but when I was a teenager I had to go to an approved school."

Wayne had calmed down and was glancing sideways at Marcus. The approved school was news to him. Marcus looked at Wayne, who had a strange expression on his face; a look that was half way between surprise and shock. Marcus let Wayne know a little about his earlier life, pointing out the many times he felt forced to box.

A claustrophobic silence followed broken only by Wayne holding out his right hand in gesture.

"I didn't know any of that," he said in a soft voice.

Marcus noticed that Wayne had gulped down his whiskey and was pouring out a refill.

"You see, Marcus, me old mate," explained Wayne, "I've reached thirty and it should have been me in the ring today … that's what *I* wanted." Marcus, in a rare show of emotion, put his arm around the person sitting next to him.

The two friends moved to the front of the caravan, which had the illusion of being more spacious. More whiskey was consumed as Wayne spoke about his thinly suppressed boxing ambitions. Marcus suggested that Wayne find some weights and a punch bag to get started, but pointed out that the world of boxing could be quite sinister.

"That's what I was trying to convey to Dominic before the bout," explained Marcus.

Wayne was still listening as he stepped back to the rear of the caravan. He rested on the bed, leaning forward to take off his shoes and socks. He continued undressing in silence, ending up in just a pair of dark red Y-fronts and a string vest.

"Anyway," asked a perplexed Marcus, "why did you arrange to stay in this caravan. Obviously, that was planned."

Wayne agreed that they could have driven back to the city but he wanted the event to be a mini holiday. Marcus looked around the tiny space they were staying in and wondered to himself if it could be described in any way as a holiday.

"I'd like a better holiday," said Marcus, looking at his friend on the bed. "Besides, no one shares a room with me wearing a string vest," he joked, "Come on, take it off."

Wayne briefly glanced at Marcus, and then obliged, throwing the vest onto the floor.

"Anyway," mumbled Wayne, "it's a Sprite ... a Sprite," as he got into bed, "HMS Sprite."

Having got his friend to remove his vest without a word of protest Marcus went on to mischievously suggest that Wayne should slip off his underpants. This he did, tossing them onto the floor, before pulling his cover up towards his chin. With his eyes closed, and a broad grin on his face, Marcus also drifted into sleep. The light was off; tomorrow would be another day.

--o--

Marcus was the first one up, out of bed and dressed. He hated wasting half the morning lounging around, unless there was good reason. Wayne was also awake, but resting. Marcus noticed a plaque on the caravan wall saying 'The Wanderer.' He thought it might have been put up for his friend.

"Hey, mate, pass me my underpants," he suddenly instructed. Marcus picked up the pants but changed the subject.

"On the wall there is a plaque called the wanderer, he said." Wayne looked around but then noticed it.

"Ah," he exclaimed, "That was me in a previous life... but, mate, hand over my pants."

"What did your last servant die of," Marcus asked, as he walked to the caravan door, resting his hand on the handle.

Marcus decided to get Wayne out of bed by pretending that he was going to throw the pants outside. The ruse worked and Wayne leapt out bed, coming up behind Marcus and trying to grab his underwear back without revealing his nakedness.

There was an unexpected knock on the caravan door followed by a rattling sound. Fresh air gushed in the part open doorway. Marcus used himself to shield his friend's embarrassment as Wayne quickly put his underpants back on. He could see someone trying to enter the space; it was Ian's younger son Jason. Marcus moved aside.

"Do you like my friend," asked Marcus, "don't you think he's got a cute body?"

Wayne's face flushed red but Jason was un-phased by the schoolboy banter and simply announced his mission.

"Dad thought you'd like some toast... I've got some coffee outside too," he said, placing a plate on the side.

"No cooked breakfast then," remarked Wayne in jest, trying to gain some control.

Jason shook his head explaining that his parents had gone out in the car to look for Dominic. All they could work out was that he went out for a bike ride the evening before but he had not returned. They were quite worried. Ian had 'phoned some of Dominic's friends thinking that he might have gone to a party and stayed over, but no useful information had come through.

Suddenly a small dog rushed in through the part open doorway. It was soon on the bedding and had taken a slice of toast from Wayne's plate as he tried out sort out his clothes.

"Get down, Hayden," said Jason, trying to control the dog. He looked embarrassed.

Wayne recognised the breed straight away asking Jason when they had got the Jack Russell.

"It's a rescue dog," replied Jason cheerfully, "We've not long had it. We're not sure of its age, but it's lively enough."

"Ah, a Jack Russell," said Marcus grinning at Wayne, "Typical."

Jason hesitated, looked round at Wayne, and then left the caravan alongside Hayden, closing the door behind him.

"Why, Jason's a fat bastard," said Marcus, picking up one of the mugs. After taking a sip of coffee he decided that he needed more sugar.

"That's unfair, Marcus," said Wayne, indignantly.

He had finished his toast and the plate was sitting on the blankets. Marcus walked over and removed it, returning with a mug of coffee for Wayne.

"Ian knows Jason's a bit overweight," explained Wayne, "That's why they got him the dog – for exercise."

"It's just as well he never went to my school," said Marcus, "Then again, maybe he could train as a rugby player, rather than a footballer ... or a boxer."

Wayne just stared silently out of the caravan window, focussing on the form of an ash tree. Marcus detected he had annoyed Wayne, which was not his intention. The subject was not mentioned again.

"Okay," said Wayne, "I'm getting properly dressed."

Marcus took the few steps to the other end of the caravan and sat down. He turned his head just as Wayne was zipping up his black jeans. Wayne was bare-chested and had his string vest in his hand, trying to straighten it.

"Man ... stop a minute," said Marcus, looking at Wayne.

Marcus remarked that Wayne had once shown him a picture of himself on the beach and had wanted to know if his physique was good enough for boxing. Wayne listened with his full attention.

"Your build's not that bad, but you have a bit of a beer belly," observed Marcus, "It's because you sit all day in that Transit van."

Wayne insisted that it was a disabled access minibus but this only served to irritate Marcus.

"Now look, Wayne," he said, "if you're not going to take this seriously ..."

Wayne interrupted insisting that he was listening and taking on board his friend's observations. He had a mischievous glint in his eye. "Not that bad, hey," said Wayne grinning. He was now bold enough to flex his muscles.

Marcus found himself repeating earlier advice, suggesting that Wayne invest in a skipping rope and a punch-bag and start some fitness training.

"You could go jogging each morning, or evening, around the streets," said Marcus.

"Like pounding the beat," replied Wayne, "I could do it after work." Marcus advised Wayne to look in at his local sports shop to see what was on offer, reiterating that he ought to invest in a good punch bag.

"Okay me old mate, I'll do that, you'll see", said Wayne, "I'll soon be the next Dave Green."

Both empty mugs and the plate had been left on the bench in the caravan. Marcus and Wayne were both fully dressed and about to leave their small overnight room.

"Oh god," Marcus shouted. Wayne was taken aback and did not have a clue what had come over his friend. Marcus was staring at Wayne.

"What's wrong, mate," he said.

"That bike in the hedge ... don't you get it," Marcus shouted.

At first perplexed, the colour suddenly drained from Wayne's face and he collapsed down in a squatting position, holding his head before springing up again like a tiger. Marcus and Wayne were now in tune with each other's thoughts, but hoping that what they were thinking could not be possible. They hurried to the car. The two front doors of the Marina slammed closed as Wayne flicked the ignition. The engine turned over but failed to start.

"Come on, come on, Lisa, start ... start," demanded Wayne.

On the third attempt the engine sprang into life, now in harmony with the occupants. After a frantic three point turn the car was soon on the main road.

"Turn off here," barked Marcus, pointing to where the school was.

"I know, I know," replied Wayne, his face hardened to the mission.

Wayne remembered the spot along the lane where Marcus mentioned the bike. He was driving slowly, window fully down, so that he could get a good view of the hedgerow. The road was still damp but the sun was out. A rusting, white painted metal railing interrupted his view. Wayne pointed out a gap in the hedge and pressed the brake pedal. The speedometer dial dropped away. Marcus was first to leave the car and rushed over to the gap.

"That's the bike," he said.

"See it ... see it," responded Wayne, who was only a few feet behind.

Marcus gingerly moved forward pushing some springy branches aside with each step.

"Careful," responded Wayne.

He could see Marcus was approaching a dip in the ground. They had ventured a few feet into the thick undergrowth. Wayne was now beside Marcus. He pushed past and took a few steps towards the dip. An arm, then a whole body, came into his view. It was Dominic.

"Dominic, Dominic," said Wayne sharply, "Wake up."

Dominic looked awful. He was lying in a damp, mossy ditch at an uncomfortable angle. One leg was twisted awkwardly to one side. It looked broken. He had several cuts and lacerations, but worst still he looked pale and was barely conscious. Dominic was mumbling something. Wayne moved closer to try to catch what he was saying.

"Hang on in there. It'll be alright soon," said Wayne.

Marcus was making his way out of the undergrowth.

"I'll go and get help," he said as he made his way back to the road.

He had only been running a few minutes when he spied a police car heading up the lane. He stopped and put up his hand. The police were soon at the scene and radioing for an ambulance to be sent. Dominic was carefully moved onto a board and carried out of the undergrowth. He still looked ghostly white but was able to speak. He asked that his parents be informed but then kept saying that the accident was not his fault. One of the police officers surmised that a larger vehicle, perhaps a lorry, had run him off the road. The ambulance doors were now firmly closed and Dominic was being transported to the main hospital in the city centre.

"Let's go and inform Ian," said Wayne.

He looked drained of all his energy. They were soon back at the pub. Marcus went back to the caravan to check for anything that might have been left behind in their rush to look for Dominic.

"Okay," said Wayne, as he came in through the caravan door, "It's time we were off. I've explained to Dominic's parents what we saw." Marcus asked how they had taken the news.

"They were shocked," replied Wayne, "really shocked."

--o--

It seemed a long, sad drive back. Wayne said little. His gaze looked fixed, which concerned Marcus. It was as if the car was travelling on autopilot and Wayne was a passenger in the driving

83

seat. Outside fields, farms and villages flashed by as the Marina sped on.

"I hope Dominic's accident has not disillusioned you regarding boxing," said Marcus, interrupting the silence. Wayne refocused.

"No, mate," he said, "I know the accident had nothing to do with boxing."

Wayne started to get some of his familiar expressions back.

"I just hope he's okay," he continued.

"Yes," agreed Marcus, "He seemed like a nice lad." There was little else he could say. His thoughts started to drift back to the bout he had had with Dominic the day before. Marcus was thinking about how a person's life could change in the course of a few hours.

"Life can be weird," he said. Wayne was silent again.

"Looks like we're here," Wayne announced as he drew up outside Marcus's flat.

"I know it's Sunday," said Marcus, "but you can't just drive off."

Wayne agreed to come inside for a coffee. Marcus put his key in the large Victorian front door and went inside. There was a hand written envelope addressed to him on the windowsill where the residents left the post. Marcus picked it up and walked upstairs to his flat. The two were soon inside and discussing the weekend and how events had turned out.

"Strange how life turns out," pondered Wayne.

"I guess it is," mumbled Marcus, whose attention was focussed on reading the letter.

Wayne was agitated and kept getting up from his chair. He asked Marcus if he could use the communal telephone in the hallway to check on Dominic's progress.

"Sure," responded Marcus, "You know where it is ... It'll take 50p coins."

Marcus pointed to a tray at the side of where Wayne had been sitting where he kept some spare coins for the 'phone. Wayne left the flat to make the call whilst Marcus looked over the letter. It was from one of his friends, Paul, who had, apparently, got his dream job as a P.E. teacher in New Zealand. He would be

84

emigrating in a few weeks' time. Paul had some items of furniture to sell, plus his gym equipment.

With a bang on the door Wayne was back in the flat. He had been able to speak to Ian who said that Dominic had a broken leg and was suffering from concussion. He also had several bruises on different parts of his body, including his face. Ian thought Dominic would be kept in hospital for at least a week but that he should make a full recovery.

"It's a good job we discovered him when we did," commented Marcus. Wayne agreed.

"This is from a friend of mine," said Marcus, changing the subject and holding up his letter. Marcus explained Paul's circumstances and asked if Wayne would be interested in buying the gym equipment. Marcus knew that Paul had two good punch bags.

"Yeah, mate, yeah that's good," commented Wayne on the suggestion.

He looked a bit vague. Marcus wondered if he was still concerned about Dominic.

"Well, you don't have to make a decision now," said Marcus, "Just think about it."

Wayne still looked as if he was only half listening, but did acknowledge his friend. Marcus decided to follow Wayne back to the car. 'Keys,' thought Marcus as he shut the door behind them. They were soon out in the fresh autumn air again. The leaves on the trees had turned wonderful hues of yellow, orange and red. Autumn was Marcus's favourite time of year.

"Aye, you," shouted Wayne at a youth standing near his car, "What do you think you're doing?"

Marcus could see that the unidentified lad had one of the Marina's hub caps in his hand. Another was resting oddly by the kerb. Wayne's shout had startled the thief, and he momentarily froze. Wayne moved in and grabbed the youth by the throat, pushing him back into a yew hedge. A hub cap dropped with a loud clatter. Marcus stood back, perplexed.

"What's your name, mate?" asked Wayne. "Please sir, be gentle … have mercy on me," said the youth. Wayne repeated his question.

"Sean," he said. "Second name," demanded Wayne. "Smith," came a frightened reply.

"Yeah, right," responded Wayne, "You're all called Smith."

Marcus could see that Sean had not expected to be confronted; his face was frozen as white as a sheet. Sean was surely one of the travellers from the site on the edge of the city, Marcus thought. He looked seventeen or eighteen and was wearing faded blue jeans and a dirty green and cream jumper. Wayne punched Sean in the face, sending him down to the floor. Blood appeared on his upper lip.

"Leave him, he's had enough," Marcus said.

"Had enough has he, Marcus," replied Wayne angrily, "I've only just started." Marcus could see that it was 'no contest' and moved himself in between Sean and Wayne.

After a few minutes Wayne had calmed down, the redness leaving his face. It was agreed that Sean would put the hub caps back on the Marina and then leave the area, agreeing not to come back.

"Thanks, Mister whatever you name is," said Sean as he left, "You've saved me life, truly you have, now."

Marcus smiled inwardly. Sean's broad Irish accent and exaggerated way of speaking had amused him. He had to admit to himself, too, that he had felt a bit sorry for Sean, despite not agreeing with his thieving.

"See," said Marcus, looking at Wayne, "No harm done."

Wayne gave Marcus a look of bewilderment and got into his car, uncharacteristically slamming the door. He was soon accelerating away.

Chapter 6

There was a fresh feel to the chilly November air as Marcus stood around waiting for his lift. The sky was a clear light blue with only a few white, wispy vapour trails to spoil the canvas. A bird was signing somewhere not too far away, although Marcus could neither see nor identify it.

He did notice a black cat across the road, which seemed to be walking up every path of a row of houses and listening at each of the front doors, before moving out of sight into some dense shrubbery.

Marcus was at the top of Half Mile Road as previously arranged with Malcolm and was feeling quite the part in his brown leather flying-jacket. He had managed to scrape together enough money and was pleased to get it at a bargain price, last spring, when the shop ran a closing down sale. It did not matter to Marcus how cold the morning was; he was wrapped in sheer 1930s retro luxury.

Marcus glanced at his watch it was five past nine. He wondered if Malcolm had been delayed somewhere, but in the end, he had not long to wait. The piercing sound of a car horn disrupted Marcus's anxious thoughts.

A cream-coloured estate car had driven passed and stopped a few yards from the junction. Marcus looked down the road but did not recognise the car that had so suddenly pulled in. He was just about to walk towards the vehicle when he saw someone at the open passenger side window.

"Marcus, come on, get in the back," shouted Oliver, who was now leaning fully out of the open window. Oliver was wearing sunglasses, something which had added to the confusion.

Marcus sprinted to the car, opened the rear door and jumped inside.

"Nice set of wheels, Malcolm," he said, "I didn't realise you owned a Triumph 2500S, and the estate version at that."

Malcolm pointed out that when Marcus called round to his house the smart Triumph was in his garage, out of sight. Marcus thought that the Triumph suited Malcolm's personality, more so than the familiar Capri, which he saw as a bit of a 'boy racer' motor from 'The Professionals.' He never saw Malcolm as a Bodie or Doyle type. As it happened, Malcolm had built up quite a collection of interesting cars over the years, but was thinking of selling a few on.

The sound of Val Doonican was playing soothingly on the car radio as Malcolm continued the short drive to the airport. They were already to the north of the city, beyond the ring road. Traffic signs for the airport soon started to appear.

"Great, nearly there," exclaimed Oliver in an overly excited voice.

Oliver kept pointing the way ahead, to the annoyance of Malcolm, who knew precisely where he was going. They were soon driving through the airport gates and following signs to the back of an industrial estate.

Marcus decided to wind down the car window so that he could get a better look at the aircraft. He noticed a row of colourful tails behind a large modern building.

"We're not going to the terminal," announced Malcolm, suddenly.

He explained that his friend's aircraft was hangered in a different part of the airport, between a maintenance area and the apron where executive jets parked up. The car was now approaching its destination near some old, military looking hangers. Marcus was eagled eyed looking for anything that resembled a bi-plane.

"Can't see the Rapide anywhere," he finally said, voicing his disappointment.

The car came to a halt and Malcolm's friend was soon bounding out of his little office at the side of one of the hangers. He stepped out to greet the visitors as if he had never seen another human being all year.

"Hi, Keith," said Malcolm grasping his friend's hand, "Is it alright to park here?" Keith assured him the car was fine where it was.

"This is my friend Keith," Malcolm continued.

Both Marcus and Oliver politely shook his hand. Marcus was keen to know where the Dragon Rapide was hiding. Keith apologised saying that the 'old timer' had 'gone down with a cold' and was in the hanger being worked on.

"An unexpected engine problem," he explained, "It sometimes happens with these old girls".

The visitors looked slightly confused on hearing the news but Keith explained that they could fly in another aircraft called a de Havilland Dove. As if on cue the Dove was being towed out of the hanger behind them.

"Just a *different* sort of plane for your thirty-ninth birthday, Malcolm," said Keith glancing over, "This one's made of metal."

Malcolm looked embarrassed and nervously glanced around, making little eye contact. Marcus turned towards Oliver. Their thoughts were in unison but neither exchanged words.

"Who owns this one," asked Marcus looking at the graceful lines of the Dove. Keith confirmed that he was the proud owner of both de Havilland types.

Marcus broke away from the group to take a closer look at the plane. He knew the Dove was around thirty years old but beautifully turned out in a 'retro' blue and grey colour scheme. 'Waveney Air Services' was painted on the upper fuselage in dark blue paint. The plane even had its own name; *'Siggson'* was in a bold handwriting style of script on either side of the curvaceous nose. Marcus ran his hand over the smooth paintwork. It was almost as if the aircraft had a personality of its own.

He let his mind wander. 'This aircraft has seen a lot,' thought Marcus before noticing the others staring at him. Oliver and Malcolm approached the plane from the rear, led by Keith, now sporting a luminous yellow jacket. He opened the small door to the cabin, putting a step in place. It was fairly easy to get into the Dove, even though the cabin space was tiny by modern standards. As Marcus went through the oval shaped door, he noticed the four rows of light blue seats. Every seat had a window view.

Marcus sat down on the right-hand side. He was three rows back and had a good view into the cockpit. The inside of the Dove reminded Marcus of a 1950s coach. It smelled slightly musty. It even had metal framed luggage racks above each seat, complete with webbing that reminded him of Cornish fishing nets. Malcolm sat opposite Marcus, with Oliver nearer the front.

"This is great," remarked Marcus, turning towards Malcolm. "I might buy one myself," he joked.

"It's not too small for you then," said Malcolm, smiling.

"No," replied Marcus, "if it's good enough for Maggie Thatcher to fly in, it's good enough for me."

Activity was increasing around the aircraft. Someone outside closed the door and there was more movement on the tarmac. A younger man walked around, pausing every so often, to check the Dove's wings moving parts. Another man dressed in a thick, padded fireman's uniform was near the right-hand engine. He had the propeller in his gloved hand and was rocking it from side to side. Marcus was fascinated by this, not really understanding the reason behind it, and by the careful actions of Nigel, the pilot for the pleasure flight.

Nigel now had his fingers on switches near the cockpit ceiling. With a rough popping sound, one after another, the Dove's two engines burst into life. Marcus was looking out of the window again. Each time an engine started a small cloud of smoke appeared from the exhaust and then drifted away in the late autumn breeze.

'That was the start-up genie leaving,' thought Marcus. The veteran piston engines were now in harmony, like identical twins, no longer arguing. With a slight jerk *'Siggson'* began taxiing forward.

Marcus was looking at the ever-changing views of the parked aircraft and hangers as the Dove taxied closer to the end of the runway. He beckoned Oliver to move to the seat in front of him.

"That's a Handley-Page Herald," said Marcus after tapping Oliver hard on the shoulder. He then pointed out a blue and white Shorts SD3-30 and a larger Viscount.

"You seem to know all these planes," commented Malcolm, seeking more of an explanation. After pausing, Malcolm said that he had flown Pan Am 747 to New York and Swissair Caravelle to Geneva a few times several years ago. He knew Keith's heritage flight would be totally different.

There was more activity in the cockpit, with switches being moved. Marcus looked forward. He was diagonally opposite Nigel, who was now glancing back into the passenger cabin. The aircraft had lined up with the runway and was ready for take-off. Marcus made eye contact with the pilot and nodded to indicate everyone was ready for the experience. With a distinctive hum the engines became more powerful and the Dove started skipping along the runway, shedding some of its years. It was soon in the air making a slow, steady climb away from the airport.

Marcus felt pleased about giving the nod for take-off. It was the nearest he had been to his schoolboy ambition of being an air traffic controller. He turned his gaze through the window onto the ground below. The widely spaced houses and trees were getting smaller by the second. He tapped Malcolm on the shoulder, pointing out a bright blue swimming pool in the garden of a grand house below. It seemed to be set in very large grounds. This view soon gave way to farms, hedges, hamlets and connecting roads.

Malcolm was pointing out something on his side. Oliver was also looking in that direction. Marcus unbuckled his seat belt and half stood up to understand what they were fixated by. It was a little river, glinting and turning as it travelled towards the freedom of the sea.

Marcus settled back down into his seat, just before some air turbulence caused a sensation akin to going over a hump-backed bridge. Oliver looked back towards Marcus, who just laughed. He was in his element; a natural flyer, unconcerned about a few bumps during the flight. He secretly hoped there would be more. Marcus preferred the take-offs and landings and anything that put an aircraft under a bit of pressure.

The 'bump' passed, and the aircraft settled into level flying at 1,000 feet above the ground. Marcus thought the Dove was a very refined aircraft, considering its age, and the fact that its engines originated in the 30s.

Everyone experienced a sharp turn to the left. Marcus could see only fields, and then beyond them more open stretches of water. As the Dove levelled off again it became obvious that these were the Broads. Save for having a drink at a waterside pub, Marcus had not really discovered this stretch of England. He tapped Oliver on the shoulder.

"That's one of the Broads," he said. Oliver nodded. "I've never been on them, have you," Marcus continued. Oliver shook his head. All the white coloured boats moored up fascinated him. His eye caught some geese flying below.

"Uncle's been on the Broads," commented Oliver without taking his gaze off the mirror like water below.

"Oliver, are you a water baby," asked Marcus, playfully. Oliver did not answer. "Why don't we hire a boat sometime," Marcus, a confirmed non-swimmer wondered where his illogical idea had come from, but Oliver acknowledged it by nodding approval.

More air turbulence pushed the Dove over another imaginary 'hump' in the sky.

"It's going to crash," Marcus whispered into Oliver's ear. The air turbulence had given Marcus the opportunity to try to scare his younger friend. It was working. Oliver now looked worried and put on his sunglasses again. Teasing, Marcus pulled them off, suggesting that Oliver see the fullness of his imaginary death in a fireball of mangled aluminium and electrical cables.

Just as Oliver was wondering when the Dove would be landing Marcus launched another verbal attack.

"In the air you're a big jessie, Oliver," he said, "Get a grip, man." Marcus sat back into his seat. He was concerned about where all the aggression had come from. After all, he knew Oliver was a pleasant lad with no obvious bad traits. Predictably, the Dove's Gypsy Queen piston engines were performing brilliantly and continued to pull the travellers through the chilly Norfolk air.

It was not long before the Dove started to lose height. It was a carefully controlled descent with Nigel speaking frequently to the control tower. The tone of the two trusty engines changed; there was no longer the sound of pistons straining. The aircraft was losing height, but so gradually it was hardly felt by the passengers. Looking out of the window, Marcus started to notice the ground getting nearer. Houses, fields and trees were becoming larger and moving cars could be observed driving along busy roads.

Finally, the engines made a sort of strange popping sound and then the skid of tyres as the Dove was back on firm tarmac again.

Malcolm found it easier to exit the aircraft by going backwards down the few steps to the concrete. Everyone was now out and standing around waiting for the pilot to appear.

"So, did everyone enjoy that," Nigel asked. Malcolm appreciated the experience. He had flown many times before from Heathrow and Gatwick, but normally on modern Boeings. He realised how flying had moved on enormously since the austere 50's. Marcus looked across to Oliver, but said nothing.

"Would you like a tour of the hanger," enquired Nigel, knowing the answer would be positive.

"That would be lovely," replied Malcolm glancing over to the large corrugated metal door ahead. Nigel led the way, followed by Malcolm and the others. As soon as they were all inside the hanger Nigel left them to look around, saying he was in the little office, next-door, if anyone needed anything. They were under strict instructions not to touch anything that looked dangerous.

The inside of the hanger was dim, smelled strongly of grease, and felt cluttered. It was like grotto of complete aircraft and others in various states of rebuild. Marcus could identify a blue and white Piper Aztec pointing towards them, plus a thirty-year old Auster. On the other side of the hanger the unserviceable Dragon Rapide could be seen with its nose pointing up at an angle. The party walked over to it to get a better look.

"It's made of wood," explained Marcus, "and covered in fabric." Malcolm took a closer look, running his hand over the wing.

"Strange," he remarked, "And a lot different to a Jumbo Jet."

"Just a bit," quipped Marcus, laughing.

As Malcolm wondered how something made of wood could carry eight passengers one of the mechanics suddenly appeared from the back of the aircraft.

"Hi," she said, "were you the group that went up in the Dove?"

Malcolm acknowledged her and explained that he was expecting a flight on the Dragon Rapide but could now understand why it had to be the Dove. Marcus focussed on the embroidered name on her grubby, grey overalls – 'Lynn

Marshall.' She wiped the grease from her small hand on to her overalls and offered it to Malcolm, who shook it firmly.

"I didn't realise ...," said Malcolm stopping himself abruptly in mid-sentence. Keith's voice sounded through the aircraft.

"She's our best mechanic." Malcolm took note of this.

"We've just got the engine back in," said Lynn, confidently, "but there's still a bit of work to go, plus the testing and the paperwork."

Malcolm was at the front of the Rapide whilst Marcus had taken Oliver to the aircraft's door, near the back.

"Yes, you can take a look inside," spoke a male voice from behind them.

It was not Keith, who had slipped out of the hanger, but another mechanic. Marcus read his name – 'Bradley Thomas.' This was truly Marcus's world; a world where he felt safe and appreciated. He could never get too much of it.

The interior of the Dragon Rapide was even smaller than the Dove's. Once inside, Marcus had to squeeze himself along the tiny aisle between the faded fabric covered seats. Oliver followed him inside the plane.

"Look at the front," said Marcus, perplexed at how simple the cockpit controls looked, Oliver sat down in one of the few passenger seats, commenting how claustrophobic he felt. The feeling was made worse for being in the darker light of the hanger.

"I was only teasing earlier," said Marcus, as he touched Oliver on the arm. Oliver smiled.

"I'll have to fly on one of these one day," Marcus quipped, enthusiastically, as he left the plane through its small, flimsy looking door.

--o--

As the Triumph exited the airport gates the three flyers started comparing experiences. Predictably, Marcus enjoyed his Dove day; he knew he would. He was the sort that was always scanning the skies for anything unusual, and the Dove fitted that description. Flying in the Dove was a dream come true. Marcus

94

felt sure that, one-day, he would also fly in the older Dragon Rapide.

Malcolm too had got a lot out of the visit. Although he normally flew in larger aircraft, it was a chance for him to catch up with Keith and see the little aviation business he had created for himself. Malcolm hoped that Keith could fulfil his boyhood dream and see the venture expand.

There was a silence surrounding Oliver, who seemed fixed on gazing out of the car window. Marcus asked him what he thought of the Dove.

"It was alright," he replied in a noncommittal tone.

"Just *alright* ...," repeated Marcus. He was irritated by Oliver's lack of enthusiasm.

"Someone spoilt your day, did they," quipped Marcus sarcastically, pulling on the back of the seat in front of him.

"Well, I wouldn't mind flying in one of those executive jets I saw," came the unexpected answer.

Marcus was not prepared for this view on the day and curtly told Oliver that he did not appreciate anything historical. Marcus did not want to start an argument in the car; Malcolm had his full concentration on the driving. Something inside Marcus could not let things rest.

"There's always one ...," he said as he slipped back in his seat. "Mind, Oliver, you won't be flying in any fancy executive jets if you join the British Army," he continued.

The cutting remark just slipped out and Marcus instantly knew it was one jibe too many. He also knew that Oliver had not said anything about joining the Army; that had come from his uncle.

"Let's just stop this *now*," said Malcolm.

Neither Oliver nor Marcus had seen him that annoyed before. As Marcus glanced forward, he got sight of Malcolm's flushed face in the driving mirror. Oliver was busy looking for something in the glove compartment and soon found his sunglasses.

They were now nearing the familiarity of the city centre and Marcus suggested he could get out of the car and get the bus back home from where they were. He was feeling a little guilty about his earlier outbursts.

"Actually, I thought we could find a pub to get something to eat," was Malcolm's calm response.

His annoyance had left him just as quickly as it had been triggered and he was now back to his old, measured self. Marcus decided to stay in the car. All knew that the 'Green Man' was only a few minutes' drive away. It served good food all day and, for Malcolm, had a large car park.

Malcolm suggested stopping at the pub. There were no objections.

"Here it is," said Oliver pointing to the faded sign a few yards ahead.

Malcolm drove into the pub car park, bordered on three sides by a thick, untidy hawthorn hedge. It could accommodate over fifty vehicles but was less than half full.

"Where's best to park," asked Malcolm.

Oliver pointed to an area near the rear door. He did not really like walking far if it could be avoided. The three got out of the car and headed straight for the back entrance of the spacious building.

They were soon inside and making their way to the bar. The pub was relatively empty, save for a group near the jute-box and another playing pool. Malcolm picked up a menu.

"My treat," he said, "Choose what you want."

Marcus wondered if Malcolm had been embarrassed earlier on when it was revealed it was his birthday; he also knew Malcolm was a generous person. Cheeseburger and fries were on special offer. Malcolm had already decided he wanted a curry. The special offer found favour with both Oliver and Marcus.

Malcolm carried three half pints of a local ale across to a sturdy round table with a numbered flag in the middle. 'Message in a Bottle' was playing in the background. Oliver and Marcus soon joined him. They started talking about music, and comparing tastes. Malcolm was fond of any type of jazz and had been thinking about booking a concert later in the year. By contrast Oliver was into a new band from the Midlands called 'Duran Duran.'

"Never heard of that group," said Marcus, turning to Malcolm, "Have you?" Malcolm shook his head.

"Where did you hear about them," enquired Marcus.

Oliver explained that he had a pen pal in Birmingham and this friend had seen them somewhere locally. Oliver's pen pal friend thought they would break into the charts one day. The conversation moved on.

Malcolm was the first to bring up the subject of the boating holiday. He said he had been on the Broads with family over fifteen years ago and had enjoyed it greatly.

"Someone always falls in," he said, grinning, "Often it was a family friend called Sidney."

Oliver said he remembered Sidney, a large, overweight man, who was always telling crude jokes.

"You shouldn't have been listening to that sort of humour," said Malcolm. He genuinely looked shocked.

Malcolm paused, then took another sip of his drink before recalling the story of Sidney standing on the back of the boat and taking a Polaroid photograph of another boat passing the opposite way. As he pulled out the developing picture the wake of the other boat made a wave, which then caused Sidney to fall in. Oliver thought this image highly amusing.

Marcus looked at them both and, in an instant, knew that they had a blood-bond that cemented them together despite the strained past. He felt a wave of darkness overtake him, and then it had passed. In that fleeting moment Marcus realised he was the outsider. He was not laughing, only seeing how stupid Sidney had been to put himself in danger for the sake of a photograph. This grey thought was broken by the meals being placed on the table.

"Did you order a side salad," asked a young waitress bearing a false smile. She looked a little confused, just like her frizzy light brown hair, which was sticking out in all directions. Everyone looked at each other for guidance before Malcolm said 'no.' Too late; it was left on their table.

The conversation drifted on to television and 'Dad's Army.' Marcus had always liked the comedy series, based on the wartime Home Guard. It was something he was allowed to watch at his school.

"Did you see the one where they made crude radios from coco tins and string," he asked. Marcus recalled the scene in his mind.

"Captain Mannering then demonstrated how to use it," he continued.

"Oh yeah," said Oliver, "very funny, and they got caught up in the string."

"I saw that one too," interrupted Malcolm, "I think the verger ended up cutting the string to let the vicar through."

Malcolm admitted to remembering the first episode when it was screened in black and white.

"I bet you like Hi-de-Hi, don't you, Oliver," said Marcus out of the blue. Oliver looked away, but Marcus could see him blushing.

"Why, you've got a crush on Gladys, I bet," continued Marcus.

Oliver revealed nothing, despite Marcus goading him with a couple of 'Hello *camp*-ers.' After reminiscing about 'It's a Knockout' and 'The Likely Lads,' the group ended their meal by comparing episodes of 'On the Buses.' Marcus particularly liked the comedy and the way the bus drivers always ended up teasing Blakey, the uncompromising inspector.

"Well," said Malcolm, sitting back in his seat, "did we decide anything about the Broads trip."

The water-based holiday was back on the agenda, which left Marcus with a dilemma. On the one hand he wanted to be a part of what looked to be a fun break away from work. However, he wondered how he would cope with several days on board a boat, not being able to swim. He knew he had no liking for water but had no problem about holidaying with Oliver or Malcolm. His two companions were in deep conversation whilst Marcus was churning the 'pros' and 'cons' in his mind. It would be silly not to be involved, he thought, but doubts still lingered.

Suddenly a different image appeared in his mind's eye. His thoughts now turned to Wayne; involving Wayne seemed to be the logical answer. Marcus remembered what he had said about his days in the Royal Navy, and how it enjoyed it so much. Marcus considered that if Wayne were to be part of the trip, he would enjoy it more. Wayne made Marcus laugh without him trying. He brought his thoughts back to the group.

"I have an idea," said Marcus, suddenly thrusting himself fully into the conversation. Malcolm and Oliver stopped talking and looked at Marcus for clarification.

"Malcolm, you remember a bloke called Wayne, don't you," said Marcus, looking at his friend for an answer.

Malcolm said he was not too sure who this Wayne was. After Marcus reminding him of the union boxing bout Malcolm was clear about the other person in the room after the fight.

"What you probably don't know is that Wayne was in the Royal Navy," explained Marcus enthusiastically, "so, he's great with boats."

Oliver wanted to know what Wayne was like, which irritated Marcus. He had just explained that his friend was good on the water. Trying not to feel further annoyed, Marcus set out his argument for inviting Wayne on the holiday. He explained how Wayne would be able to steer, and park, the boat and would find it easy to judge distances and read charts of the waters.

Marcus spoke without interruption, holding his audience for a full five minutes. A moment of silence followed, broken only by the waitress clearing the tables. Marcus looked over to Malcolm.

"Yes, I'm impressed, aren't you Oliver," he said, "Why don't you see if Wayne's interested." Marcus was quick to respond.

"I'll do better than that. I'll give him a call right now."

With that he shot up from the table to look for the public 'phone. Whilst Marcus was away from the table, out of earshot, Oliver began to quiz his uncle about Wayne. He wanted to know more about the boxing bout that Marcus had talked about.

"I might have been interested in going to it, if I'd have known," said Oliver.

Somewhat flustered, Malcolm tried to make an excuse saying that he only decided to go at the last minute. Oliver probed him for more details.

"Who, won, uncle," he asked. "Well, I'm not sure … a draw, I think … I … I … was sitting at the back, not taking it all in," came the reply. Oliver wanted to ask more questions but could see a grinning Marcus returning to their table.

"He was in and he's coming over here now," blurted Marcus, "I've given him a few details, and he seems keen on it." Marcus paused.

"Oh, I'm sorry," he continued, "I'm getting ahead of myself. I'm assuming everyone is okay with Wayne joining in."

Oliver answered for both of them, in the affirmative. Marcus realised it was a good time to offer to buy the next round. He went over to the bar and was served almost at once by a middle-aged man wearing a bow tie. Marcus took his change and was immediately aware of someone standing beside him. He turned to see Oliver.

"I'll help you with the drinks," he said. Marcus realised Oliver had something else to say.

"I'd like to go to a proper fight," said Oliver. "I see," replied Marcus smiling, but why not ask your uncle." Marcus had formulated a deliberately sarcastic question; he already knew the answer.

"Alright, Oliver, if I hear of anything, I'll let you know," continued Marcus, speaking in whispered tones, "Put your phone number of this piece of paper."

Marcus quickly took the paper and spirited it away in an inside pocket. They agreed not to mention the conversation to Malcolm, lest he disapproved.

"I see you've all got yourself drinks," said Wayne suddenly appearing beside the table the group were sitting at, "I'll get myself a pint ... anyone want anything?"

No one answered and Wayne went to the bar. Marcus looked at Oliver in silence. Oliver said nothing but looked across at his uncle. It seemed that everyone wanted to say something but were afraid of being labelled 'stupid.' The uneasy atmosphere was shattered by Wayne appearing with his drink. He sat down next to Marcus and launched straight into his dialogue.

"Good job you rang me," said Wayne, looking at his friend, "because I was going to ring you."

Marcus looked perplexed. Oliver and Malcolm looked at each other and smiled. Wayne, ignoring the other two said that he had been in contact with Paul and, as Marcus had suggested, bought his gym equipment. Paul had helped him transport the items back to Wayne's garage where they were stored.

The original idea was for Wayne to create a mini gym in the garage and get Paul to give him a few sparring sessions. Neither plan had worked out. Paul had been asked to fly to New Zealand earlier than planned and now Wayne's wife was complaining that she could not get her precious Riley Elf in the garage. Wayne had been given orders to move the gym.

Marcus asked Wayne where he was going to re-home all of the gym items.

"That's just it, me old mate, haven't got a clue," Wayne explained. Grinning, Wayne glanced at Marcus.

"Oh, no," responded Marcus. He knew what Wayne was thinking. "I've only got a tiny flat – no chance."

Wayne looked forlorn and took a mouthful of lager. Marcus beckoned Wayne to get up and follow him to the bar area.

"I've got an idea," said Marcus. He looked thoughtful and serious, as if he was going to negotiate an important business deal.

The two were out of earshot. Marcus told Wayne he had been to Malcolm's house that that there appeared to be plenty of storage space. Wayne listened with interest as Marcus described the layout of the house and its basement.

"If you agree," remarked Marcus, "we'll have to persuade Malcolm. He can be a bit of a stick in the mud, but I reckon that Paul's gear can be stored in the basement." The two wandered back to the table.

"Can I have a quick word, Malcolm," said Marcus, who was now standing up again. He did not want to lose any momentum. Malcolm instinctively got up and the two wandered over to the bar area.

"Wayne's got this problem with where to house his gym equipment," Marcus started to explain. Malcolm acknowledged that he had been following the conversation.

"Well, why don't we house Wayne's stuff in your basement," Marcus continued, it would be out of the way, and it would be good for Oliver's training if he really wants to join the Army." Malcolm looked at Marcus with a knowing expression.

"You don't have to bring Oliver into this," Malcolm grunted.

Marcus was about to speak, to justify himself but before he could utter a sound Malcolm had said he would go along with the idea. Marcus wondered why Malcolm had seemingly given in so easily. He certainly was not about to put that thought to Malcolm, in case the magic disappeared.

Everyone was in agreement that Wayne's gym equipment had to be moved. Malcolm was persuaded that there was no time like the present.

"Thanks for that," said Wayne extending his right hand towards Malcolm. "And yeah, if you'd have me on the Broads holiday I'd love to come."

Wayne gave a good account of his life in the Royal Navy before explaining that he would be good at manoeuvring the boat into tight spaces for parking.

"It's not that easy, you know," he explained, "unless you've had experience." No one raised any objections, so Malcolm suggested doing the trip around the May Bank Holiday and said he would order some brochures from the local companies that hired out boats.

"Last one … drink up," said Marcus, staring at Wayne. He got the message and gave a mock salute before gulping down the dregs of his pint.

The glass was placed on the table with a thud as Wayne scrambled to his feet. The plan was for all four to drive to Wayne's address in Malcolm's car. It would be easy to take all of the gym equipment in the back. Four people would make light work of the move. Everyone in place, and the car engine running, Malcolm started driving out of the pub car park. They were quickly on the main road heading for the other side of the city. The sun had almost disappeared from the gloomy horizon; it was getting dark.

Wayne seemed in his element giving directions. He saw a small part of his life moving on.

"Next right, mate," he signalled, "Follow that white Jaguar."

After driving for over twenty minutes, they entered a narrow road comprised of red bricked Victorian houses. Most were terraced but every so often a solitary grander property appeared like a sentinel.

"Keeping driving," said Wayne, "Almost there, but we need to go down the back alley."

The passengers were bumped in all directions as Malcolm tried, unsuccessfully, to avoid the numerous potholes along the track. The car slowed down, finally stopping opposite a row of sad old garages. The majority looked neglected; as if they had not been used in years. Marcus noticed that the first one had ivy growing over its asbestos roof. Half had drably painted rotting wooden doors. They looked worse in the near darkness.

The front passenger door was flung open. Wayne sprung himself out of the car, rapidly moving towards a garage with a white painted metal up and over door. Marcus and Oliver followed Wayne as the door was lifted revealing an Aladdin's cave of items ranging from ladders and paint to an old cycle propped against the wall. Marcus could see some of the gym equipment. Malcolm had the Triumph's tailgate open and was assessing what needed to be moved to accommodate all of Wayne's new collection.

Oliver and Malcolm soon left the garage struggling with a set of weights. Wayne was not far behind with a Bullworker exercise machine and some boxing gloves. The rear of the Triumph was fast filling up but two punch bags had still to be brought out, plus several rubberised mats. It took the entire team to manipulate the remaining bits into the vehicle. The tailgate now firmly closed; everyone was back in the car.

"We should have got a van," Wayne suddenly remarked. No one dared comment.

Malcolm started the engine and gingerly pulled away. He hoped that the extra weight would not push the car too low and damage the exhaust. That would be expensive. This time Malcolm knew where he was going. Marcus sat diagonally opposite Wayne in the car and he caught Wayne's look of satisfaction. 'A dog that got the bone,' he thought to himself. The traffic was light on the main road. Marcus glanced out of the side window. The neon lights of the shuttered shops looked weird and reminded him of the sinister side of any city. His thought chain was broken by Oliver's voice.

"I can get out here, if you want." Marcus regained his focus and wondered if he had misheard his companion. "I can walk back from here," continued Oliver as the car slowed to a halt.

The seatbelt flicked back, the door opened and Marcus caught a 'thank-you' as Oliver slipped into the night like an owl. A wave of anger came over him but Marcus hoped it had not shown. He was disappointed that Oliver did not see fit to complete the day.

The car moved off again and it did not seem long afterwards that they were turning into Malcolm's drive. The powerful headlights cast eerie, dark patterns against a garage door and the house wall. Marcus was deep in thought, but not knowing what he was particularly thinking about. For a brief moment he was convinced that he had seen a ghost in the shadows. He dismissed it as a trick of the mind. Malcolm was already at his front door, fumbling for the right key to open the lock.

"If we all take a bit each…" he shouted back.

Bits of gym equipment were now being taken through Malcolm's hallway and into the centre of the property. He opened the small door that led into the basement, feeling for the light switch that illuminated the stairs that descended into the bowels of the house. At least it seemed clean, thought Marcus, as he started down with one of the weights in both hands.

"There's another light switch in front of you," came Malcolm's voice from above, "Have you got it?"

Marcus looked for the next switch and on clicking it was confronted by a cavernous space that opened up in from of him. He had not expected such a room but it felt inviting, akin to discovering a secret den. With three people moving the equipment it was soon safely in the basement.

"Okay then," said Malcolm, "who wants a lift back?" As if acting like schoolchildren volunteering for milk monitor, both Wayne and Marcus waved their arms in the air to get attention.

"Fine," said Malcolm turning to Wayne, "I'll drop you, navy boy, off first." Wayne and Marcus were soon sitting in the back of the Triumph, and as Malcolm had arranged, Wayne was dropped off near the top of his road.

The roads were clear and it did not take long for Malcolm to be turning into Albert Avenue. The Triumph came to a gradual halt opposite the old house where Marcus rented his small flat.

"Thanks for the lift," said Marcus opening the rear passenger door, "and thanks also for accommodating Wayne's equipment. I know that means a lot to him." Malcolm said that he was glad to have been able to help and that the basement was not getting much use anyhow.

Marcus was just about to leave the car when Malcolm enquired why Oliver's actions had irritated him. "Did it show... Sorry," Marcus replied thrusting himself onto the pavement. Malcolm wanted to say more and Marcus found himself speaking to his chauffeur through the front passenger window, which Malcolm had wound down.

"Why don't you try to work with Oliver in some way," enquired Malcolm.

"Work with him, I'd sooner ..." Marcus's words faded into a mumble as he stepped back. He hoped he had not upset Malcolm by his heart-felt reply.

The Triumph moved forward. Marcus waved, turning back towards the long drive that led to the Victorian house. There was no gate to close, just a gap in the weather-warn, red brick wall. The sound of gravel crunched underfoot as Marcus headed for the front door. A dark, humanoid shadow appeared from near the front of the property. Marcus could barely make out the shape as he moved forward in the half-light. Just as Marcus was thinking once more about ghosts the shadow took on a more solid form as it turned towards him. Marcus recognised the voice.

"Mister Marcus, now don't be cross. I guess you never thought it would be me showing up again," said Sean.

Surprised, Marcus made it known that he was, indeed, taken aback to see the cheeky traveller on his doorstep. He formed his lips to say something more but Sean spoke again.

"Now, don't turn me away, sir. Hear me out, you're my only chance," said Sean. Marcus looked bewildered. He thought he had seen the last of Sean.

"I was wondering if you could help me out," Sean continued.

"Help you out," replied Marcus, amazed at his bluntness. He had now imagined that the police were looking for the cheeky thief, and he wanted nothing to do with a plot to assist him. Yet a part of Marcus allowed Sean to explain himself.

"Me pa's thrown me out, so he has," said Sean.

Sean looked cold and dejected. Marcus listened as the traveller explained that his father had disowned him and had thrown him out of the caravan the family lived in on the edge of the by-pass. Apparently, his father also did not want anything to do with him and now Sean was homeless.

Marcus thought that there must be more to the story but could get little else from Sean. Besides it was late, and it had been a long day. Marcus drew a slow, deep breath. He now realised he had a dilemma. In a split second he realised that he felt sorry for Sean, although he did not fully understand why.

"You can use the garage for this one night," said Marcus abruptly. "It's full of old furniture, but no one uses it," he continued. Marcus led Sean to the back of the property and to the old communal double garage that most people had forgotten still existed. It was covered in ivy but the handle-less side door could easily be pulled open.

"Stay here for a minute," said Marcus, "I'll be back with a torch." Sean had already gone into the garage. There was a loud clatter as something inside fell down.

A few moments later Marcus had returned with a torch and an old blanket. He realised it would be cold sleeping in a garage overnight, not long before winter. The dim light of the torch caught Sean's slim outline. Marcus could see that his short, sandy-brown hair was dishevelled and he still wore his old, dirty jumper and jeans. His face looked innocent and showed a glimpse of fear and desperation. Marcus could also feel deep sadness as he stood near the traveller. Perhaps it was this that prevented Marcus from turning him away.

Marcus instructed Sean to be gone by the morning, pointing out that he should not be seen by any of his neighbours. He said nothing about the blanket and the torch. In his mind Marcus had already written these off with the thought that they were only material objects. Maybe he was also feeling generous towards someone in a difficult situation.

"And don't be telling your friend, Mister Marcus, that'll never do," said Sean. Marcus thought for a moment and then recalled the last time they had met and the way in which Wayne had lashed out.

"He won't know," remarked Marcus. "Another thing … just call me Marcus, not *Mister* Marcus … it's annoying," Marcus quipped as he left the garage.

The next morning was cold and frosty. Marcus decided to check the garage before leaving for work. He closed the large front door behind him and went around to the back of the house. His mind was already buzzing with 'what ifs' and he needed to reassure himself that Sean had gone. The garage door seemed a bit stiff but he managed to pull it open, quickly stepping inside. He knew the garage area was not overlooked by and of the other flats so would not be seen by curious eyes. Marcus made his way through the jumble of discarded chairs and tables that helped fill the inside space.

There was very little light but Marcus was sure Sean had left. He took a deep breath and began to relax. Glancing around the dim space, something caught his eye. It was his torch, neatly placed on top of the blanket, and left on a brown leather chair. Any doubts Marcus had regarding allowing Sean to stay immediately lifted. He was now convinced that it had been the correct thing to do. Pleased with his findings, Marcus carried on to work and the rest of his predictable day.

As usual, he was the first to arrive at the office. He decided to use the office 'phone, before his boss got in, to make a quick call to Malcolm. He wanted to arrange to see the gym equipment again but after speaking with Malcolm they both agreed to wait until after Christmas and the New Year festivities.

Malcolm had been summonsed for jury service and he had a feeling that it would be a long, complicated case. Marcus agreed that as it was approaching winter there was little point in trying to get a gym organised when people had other things to occupy their time.

Chapter 7

A NEW CONSENSUS

The dying, damp days of late autumn 1980 merged into a full, fresh winter and then the western world seemed suddenly to be a very different place. It was spring and bright yellow daffodils were flowering in gardens and on roadside verges.

Ronald Reagan, the 40th President of the United States of America, was installed in the White House leaving political pundits to speculate how this would affect Britain's special relationship with America. Prime Minister Margaret Thatcher had already visited the White House and it appeared the two leaders shared more than a common hatred of Communism and high taxation. A month after the visit, Reagan had been shot in the lung by an assassin.

Marcus was keen to follow the fresh political landscape with renewed interest. He had always thought of himself as a politician in waiting. However, nearer home, Marcus had decided to leave his small space in the Victorian house – but only to relocate to a different flat in the same tired building.

The new flat was twice as large, and had been redecorated by the landlord before it was offered for rent. Marcus was now the proud tenant of No.5. It had two decent sized bedrooms, which Marcus saw as more civilised when putting people up. He thought the bedrooms had been made from one original room, and briefly wondered what it would be like living in such a large property when it was a Victorian family home. His new sitting room had a view of the untamed back garden. He was in a buoyant mood; the winter had passed.

There was no reason to put off plans any longer. Marcus had agreed to finalise a date for the Broads holiday and he needed to 'phone Malcolm to sort out the details. Marcus hurried down to the dreary hundred-year-old staircase to the communal phone placed strategically on a small table in the hallway.

As he started to dial Malcolm's number he wondered if it would be worth getting his own line installed, especially as he now had a better property. As he had been promoted at work, line cost would not be a problem but Marcus wondered if the number of calls he made would justify having his own 'phone. The ringing tone suddenly stopped with a click.

"Malcolm, hello, this is Marcus."

"Good to hear from you," Malcolm replied. Marcus was aware that Malcolm was coughing down the 'phone.

"Are you alright," enquired Marcus.

"Yes... yes, just a bit of a frog in the throat," he responded,

"I guess you've called about the boat trip." Marcus confirmed he was not much of a sailor, or a cook, but was keen to be involved.

"Well, why don't we all get together sometime soon," said Malcolm coughing again, "and see if we can agree details."

"Great idea," responded Marcus enthusiastically. Before ending the call, the two decided to meet at Malcolm's place, Saturday week, to look at what everyone wanted from a boating holiday.

Marcus placed the mustard-coloured receiver back in the cradle and then picked up some of his post from the hall floor before returning back upstairs to his flat. Marcus had seen nothing of Oliver for months, but had been in contact with Wayne. He was aware that Malcolm was fearful that his nephew was slipping out of regular contact. They had not seen each other since a family get together just before Yule.

--o--

The front door of Malcolm's house swung open just as Marcus was about to press his finger on the bell.

"Good to see you again," said Malcolm, "Come on in..." Marcus burst into the hallway and was heading for the kitchen. Although Malcolm was quick to offer, Marcus declined a cup of coffee. He was determined to get to the basement without wasting time on pleasantries.

"I haven't touched the stuff since we all brought Wayne's gym gear here," explained Malcolm. Both agreed that it seemed too long ago.

"And your friend hasn't been here either," Malcolm continued.

"Not sure what he's up to," Marcus responded, "but I did hear there's some sort of domestic problem."

"Married, is he," asked Malcolm in a tone that suggested he had already guessed the answer.

Malcolm unlocked the robust door that revealed the stairs, putting the equally impressive key in his back pocket. The stairs to the basement were now eerily illuminated as the two descended into the little used part of the property without saying a word; the silence only broken by the creak of the wood underfoot. It felt colder the more they got closer to the cavernous space that lay under the house. Malcolm entered the basement first, and switched on more of the lights.

"I know you don't want me to say this," said Marcus on emerging through a heavy steel door, "but hear me out. If Oliver is determined to go into the Army he needs to toughen up and get fit, otherwise he'll struggle." Malcolm, head lowered, looked towards the grubby floor.

"He'll be bullied, mind...," blurted Marcus. Malcolm seemed in a trance. "This space could be turned into a sort of gym," continued Marcus. Malcolm listened dispassionately, his face giving nothing away.

"If you don't agree with that," continued Marcus, "well, maybe Wayne and I could use it. What do you think?"

Marcus was expecting to be pushed back and he geared himself up for disappointment, but Malcolm had already worked out what Marcus was after.

"It's not such a bad idea," replied Malcolm, "but I can't guarantee that Oliver would get involved. You know what he's like." This statement was music to Marcus's ears, and he had not expected what was total approval by any other name.

There was certainly enough space for an underground gym, but Marcus knew the rooms under the house had the atmosphere of a castle dungeon. The space lacked proper heating and would be cold for, maybe, half the year.

"At least it's got lighting," Malcolm suddenly chipped in, as if reading his friend's thoughts, "and I could donate you two paraffin heaters." Marcus thought that sounded reasonable.

"I think we could make it work," he concluded.

His mission over, Marcus accepted Malcolm's earlier offer of a coffee. Both sat in the lounge in deep thought until a voice broke the uneasy silence.

"I guess I want Oliver to be the person I wasn't at his age," said Malcolm. Marcus looked over. He felt he knew what Malcolm was going to say before the words were verbalised.

"I was proud of him, in the back garden last year, accepting that bout..."

Marcus was trying to find a suitable response but Malcolm continued.

"He wasn't that good, but at least he tried."

"He did that," said Marcus, "I know you fear losing him after just getting to know him..." Malcolm was deep in thought again and did not answer. Marcus took the opportunity to leave.

--o--

It was not long before Wayne had been called to Malcolm's house so that he could sort out his stored gym equipment. Marcus got a 'tip off' so cheekily invited himself over on the same evening. He could hardly wait to see Wayne again and tease him on any subject that would guarantee a 'wind up.' Marcus was walking towards Malcolm's front door when he heard a car pulling into the drive. He glanced round to see Wayne's Marina slowing to a halt; headlights flashing on and off. Malcolm was at the door, checking that it was Wayne who had arrived.

"Oh," said Malcolm, noticing Marcus, "I didn't realise you were coming too ... but that's fine."

The two visitors soon found their way into the basement. It was difficult finding a light switch in the dark. Wayne commented how cold it was under the house, although it did not seem damp. Marcus declined to follow Wayne's mood so, changing the subject, he asked him if he liked the Bond films.

"Yeah, mate, yeah, I do ... great stuff," he replied enthusiastically, his energy returning. Wayne went on to say that his favourite was 'The Spy who Loved me.'

"That's the one where James Bond is a naval officer," Wayne explained.

Marcus had seen the film, although it wasn't *his* favourite and was not particularly keen on Roger Moore playing Bond.

"The one where Bond's Lotus car drives under water and comes up on the beach," Wayne continued, making a dipping motion with his hand, "I liked the bit where he dropped a fish from the car window and surprised the children on the sand."

Marcus confessed that he preferred the earlier Bond films starring Sean Connery.

"I thought Bond would be the tough guy with the beautiful woman in the opening sequence," said Marcus, "but he was that Soviet agent who got killed by Bond early on."

Wayne agreed. Marcus went on to say that he always thought of the 'real' Bond as being hirsute, adding that the strong guy had to be hairy.

"Well then," quipped Wayne, "you could never be the next Bond, then, could you!" Marcus grinned; he did not see himself as a Bond archetype.

Wayne, oblivious to his friend's lack of further dialogue went on to say that, like Commander Bond, he once had some shore leave in Cairo.

"Got a bit of a tan, too," he said, rubbing his arm. Marcus found it difficult to imagine Wayne sun-bathing and said as much to his animated friend.

"So, you came out with a torso looking like a trawler boat net then," said Marcus in jest.

"Ha, ha, very funny ... I've given up on the string vests," Wayne responded, "Anyway, you didn't say which Bond film was *your* favourite." Marcus thought for a bit and then said his was 'Goldfinger.'

"That's the one where Bond gets his new Aston Martin DB5," said Wayne, his voice rising, "with all those gadgets ... great stuff."

"It's also the one with the 1930's Rolls-Royce ...," Marcus responded, "and those aircraft."

Wayne looked on with a vague expression until Marcus pointed out the Lockheed JetStar business jet and the piston Carvair.

"The one where Goldfinger's Rolls-Royce is loaded on for his flight to Geneva," Marcus explained. He had just started to describe the Piper training aircraft from Pussy Galore's Flying Circus when Wayne cut him short saying, "Rabbit, rabbit... Have you forgotten why we are meant to be here? We are like a pair of old biddies prattling on – wasting time ..."

There was silence, and then footsteps followed by strong cigar smoke. Marcus turned around to see Malcolm had joined them.

"Aah, Condor," said Wayne sniffing the air. Malcolm just smiled politely in response before asking Wayne his plans.

"We could use this as a gym," Marcus said, butting in before his friend could speak. Wayne agreed. He paced around the basement switching lights on and off and pulling some of his equipment out.

"It's a bit dingy, but it'll do," he concluded.

"Okay, it's over to you," said Malcolm with a look of smug satisfaction. With that he was gone, leaving only the slightest smell of cigar smoke behind as a reminder that it was his house.

Wayne found a broom and started sweeping the floor, moving a small bag aside.

"Shall I get you an apron?" asked Marcus laughing. Wayne swiped out with the broom but Marcus skilfully ducked and jumped aside.

"Why, you'll have to do better than that if you want to make a boxer," quipped Marcus.

The two, play fighting, pushed each other around before Wayne continued sweeping. After a full ten minutes of effort there was a small pile of dusty rubbish to one corner of the basement room. Marcus located a dustpan and brush and swept the pile into the plastic pan. They both agreed the place looked better for their efforts.

"Did I tell you, me old mate, that I've got a new job," enquired Wayne.

Marcus replied that he was surprised, and had not heard that Wayne was not working for social services any longer. To him, being in social services was Wayne's ideal job.

"You see," said Wayne, "I got this offer as a housing caretaker. It is just a change ... I got a bit bored with the other job."

Wayne went on to describe his duties as a caretaker, pulling out the bins on a large council estate before the dustmen came, and then putting them back; sweeping and mopping floors in a block of flats, and providing a handyman service.

"You've certainly proved yourself with a broom," said Marcus teasing his friend again.

Marcus and Wayne were now grouping the gym equipment around various areas in the basement room. There was more than enough space for everything.

"Let's celebrate a new beginning," said Wayne.

He moved over to where he had left a small bag and began rummaging around in it. Marcus looked on from a distance whilst Wayne pulled out a pewter tankard and a small bottle of what looked like stale urine.

"What's that," asked Marcus. He was genuinely perplexed.

"It's mead," replied his friend, "mead me old mate... mead of the Vikings."

Marcus watched on, moving closer to get a better view of the drink being poured into the grey metal tankard.

"This means a lot to me," said Wayne. Marcus could detect some emotion in his voice.

He wondered if he had spotted Wayne's eyes watering up. Now was not the time to make sarcastic remarks, but a time for stillness and respect. As Wayne lifted the filled mug to head height Marcus momentarily thought he was attending a solemn military ceremony.

"To our future," said Wayne looking at Marcus for a response.

"To our future," Marcus replied. Wayne smiled, bringing the mead slowly to his lips and taking some before handing the tankard to his friend to finish.

"Why, that's strange stuff," said Marcus. Wayne smiled.

"At least it's warmed us both up," Marcus laughed.

Wayne agreed and took back the empty tankard being thrust at him. The two were soon climbing the austere stairs that led back into the main house, Wayne talking all the way to the door. He said that he thought his new caretaking job, involving more manual work, would assist him in getting into shape. Marcus agreed; he was aware that Wayne had proven he had the commitment to train hard enough for the ring.

"Ah, there you both are," said Malcolm as the two emerged, closing the door to the other world behind them.

"It's a bit like a medieval dungeon down there," suggested Wayne. Malcolm was keen to confirm that the gym equipment had been kept in good working order over the winter months. Marcus pointed out that everything was fine.

"Apart from the cold," added Wayne.

"You big Jessie," said Marcus pushing Wayne towards the front door, "You'd never guess he was once in the armed services."

Malcolm though the two were 'as thick as thieves' but wanted to get everyone back soon to finalise the Broads holiday.

--o--

A few weeks had passed and Marcus was keen to be the first to get to Malcolm's house again, ahead of the others. The door opened before he had a chance to place his finger on the round button that started the bell.

"Come in, Marcus," said Malcolm, "You're the only one so far."

Marcus wanted to know whether Oliver was attending, but Malcolm was unable to give a definite answer. Marcus pressed him for more, but he remained only a 'maybe' at this stage. Marcus knew that having said 'yes' Wayne would not let him down. After all, he thought, Wayne had served in the Royal Navy for several years, so was probably keen to grasp any opportunity to be on the water.

"Wayne's a good character," said Malcolm, "I can feel his sincerity." Before Marcus could process the remark Malcolm handed him a cup of coffee, whereupon they sat down to look through some boat hire brochures. It was useful to see the pictures of the boats, but the technical specifications meant nothing to either of them. Picking a boat would probably be down to the size and number of cabins, they thought. Just as Marcus was wondering about Wayne, the door bell rung with its familiar jarring tone.

It sounded to Marcus like a half-hearted fire alarm, especially if the visitor kept their finger on the button for more than a few seconds. Wayne had arrived.

"Of course, you remember Wayne," said Marcus sarcastically. It was not really a serious question. Malcolm got himself a bit tongue tied.

"Yes, yes, I do ... ," he eventually replied. He looked a bit embarrassed. Wayne soon had a cup of coffee in his hand and was sitting next to Marcus on the brown leather settee.

"You know about boats," said Marcus, handing Wayne the brochures, "have a look through these."

Marcus glanced at the clock on the sideboard. He was thinking about Oliver, now twenty-one. His non-appearance had only served to confuse the situation. Marcus was wondering what Oliver was doing, and his commitment to the holiday.

"This is the sort of size of craft we need," said Wayne pointing at one of the medium sized boats on offer.

Marcus noticed that Wayne had slopped some coffee over his hand. Malcolm looked on, awaiting more information.

"Three reasonably roomy cabins, one with a double bed," he continued, "and, I'd say, reasonably priced too for what it would give us."

There was a thud coming from the hallway and then the door of the lounge swung open. It was Oliver. He was dressed in a pair of smart dark brown corduroy trousers, a green and red check shirt and expensive looking pointed, tan coloured shoes.

Marcus looked towards Malcolm for an explanation. After all, no one had answered the front door.

"Oh," said Malcolm, "Oliver's now got his own key to my place." Wayne caught Marcus's gaze.

"We were just looking at boat hire," Marcus said firmly. He enquired of Oliver if he intended to join the Broads party.

"Yes," snapped Oliver in a tone that said 'do not ask.' Wayne went further and queried if his shoes were made in Italy.

"They were," Oliver replied grinning, "and how did you know."

"Us sailors know everything," Wayne jovially responded. Marcus looked irritated by the dialogue.

No sooner had Oliver arrived he was making plans to leave.

"Uncle, can you give me a lift out to that pub next to the station," he asked.

Marcus felt angry inside but tried not to show it. He wondered why Oliver had been given a key to the house and considered that he was taking advantage of Malcolm's easy-going nature. Malcolm said that he had an appointment in the city centre so would give Oliver his lift in. Wayne and Marcus could stay on and sort out the gym if they wanted to.

"Thanks, we'll do just that," replied Wayne, glancing at Marcus for support.

"Can we agree on a boat," said Marcus, feeling impatient and not wanting the meeting to break up before something definite had been decided.

After a discussion the choice was between *'Odalstone'* and a more classic cabin cruiser called *'Encounter Group.'* In the end *'Encounter Group'* won. Its layout was along the lines of Wayne's earlier suggestion, with three cabins. The finer details were given over to Malcolm before he and Oliver were out of their seats and finding their jackets.

The two friends were soon the only people in the house. Wayne went to his car and brought out a new sports bag, carrying it back inside. He intended to get stuck into some intensive gym work for the first time in the basement. Marcus found two old paraffin heaters and once they were alight carefully carried them through the basement door. By the time Marcus descended the stairs Wayne was kitted out in a new T-shirt, black shorts and modern training shoes. He was already doing some chin ups on a bar. Marcus was displeased by his friend's new sports clothing.

"Stop a minute," said Marcus sternly, "what do you think you are wearing?"

Wayne was sure his friend would be impressed by his new sports gear. After a brief exchange of words Marcus pointed out that Wayne better get used to dressing in what he would be wearing at a real bout.

"Shorts only," insisted Marcus looking on.

"You're a hard taskmaster," said Wayne as he changed down. "The next Bond," he announced, wearing only his shorts.

Marcus instructed Wayne to stand on the mat and flex. Wayne obliged, moving his arms up. His mind had regressed back to his basic naval training, and he would willingly do anything his mentor asked of him. It was the only way to progress, he thought to himself, and it would be tough.

"Leading Seaman Bradshaw – W, reporting for duty. Sir!" said Wayne standing to mock attention.

"Why, you'd be a laughing stock if you entered the ring today, Leading Seaman," said Marcus. Wayne relaxed.

"I know you can train me to get into better shape, that's why I'm here," his friend replied, "and also get me into the ring safely."

"Man, I sure can," Marcus responded," because I know you are going to do everything that I ask of you."

Wayne continued his workout as Marcus looked on, giving instructions on what to do next. The orders came thick and fast.

"Thirty press-ups ... twenty-five sit ups ..." There seemed no let up to Marcus's orders.

"This is worse than basic training in the navy," Wayne eventually remarked.

Marcus looked on and then allowed his friend to rest, handing him some water he had brought down. Wayne gulped it back and sunk on to a mat.

"No resting," barked Marcus, "Get a move on, man... twenty press-ups or a forfeit."

Wayne was, by now, genuinely tired and sat on the mat. Half of him wanted to start the press-ups but the other half said he needed a break. He wanted to know what the forfeit would be.

"Feel the lash, sailor," barked Marcus, waving a rolled towel.

Wayne momentarily froze, speechless. He was taken aback; Marcus's words sounded genuine enough. Marcus could now see that his friend was in need of a break. He threw him the towel.

"You're finished," announced Marcus, "Get dressed." Wayne was still confused. He needed time to rearrange his thoughts, and to catch his breath. He stood up, with his back to Marcus who shouted something.

"Why, don't tempt me," his trainer said. Marcus felt irritated that his friend was not getting dressed quickly enough.

Wayne moved over to his sports bag and grabbed his clothes from inside.

"It's a shame I couldn't use these," he said, pulling out his new blue and white sports shoes.

Marcus agreed that next time Wayne could wear the shoes on the basis that the basement floor was dusty. He reiterated that in a real bout it was likely that Wayne would have to box bare-footed.

"Fair point, mate," his friend replied.

Nevertheless, Marcus was interested to know where Wayne had bought the shoes. Wayne handed them to his friend urging him to try them on.

"They're a good size for me," replied Marcus, "and I know the shop where you got them."

"So how do you think I'm doing," enquired Wayne, eager for some encouragement.

Marcus conceded that Wayne had made a good start. He realised his friend was capable of boxing but did not want to give him blanket praise, nor false hope, at this early stage.

"Mind, it's a big space down here," said Marcus trying to change the subject.

The light bulbs that illuminated the area were barely adequate but created an atmosphere that begged exploration.

"I want to be the next bloke that strikes the gong on those Rank films," said Wayne catching his friend up.

Marcus was standing in a different part of the basement where the two quickly found another heavy steel door in one corner. Wayne commented that he had seen such doors on government buildings. Marcus told Wayne that Malcolm had said that he thought the military had taken over the house during the war, and reconfigured the lower part.

"That makes sense," replied Wayne.

With a ghostly groan the newly discovered door was opened. "Needs oiling," said Marcus sarcastically.

The two moved carefully into another space. It looked like a passageway of sorts. Wayne groped for a light switch, finally allowing the two to get a clearer view.

"Wow," said Wayne, "this place is full of surprises."

Marcus looked along the space but turned back to Wayne with, "We better leave it; it's not our property."

119

Wayne agreed and they dragged the old steel door back to its closed position. The two decided to move into the relative normality of the main house closing the protective door behind them. Wayne put his sports bag in the hall.

"Very strange place," he said, "A very strange place, indeed."

Marcus persuaded his friend to take a look at some more rooms in the house. He was confident Malcolm would not be back for a while longer. They quietly moved into the lounge like a pair of burglars. Marcus pointed to a photograph of Oliver, and then to the record collection. Wayne pulled out a few record sleeves at random – Tom Jones, the Beetles, Val Doonican, and then the Carpenters.

"I always think of this as sad music," whispered Marcus, pointing to the album in Wayne's hand.

"Yeah, sort of," he replied, "I know what you mean... why are we whispering." Wayne left everything as it had been and the two moved back into the hall.

"Let's take a look upstairs," said Marcus.

He stepped aside to let Wayne go up first. The stairs made a creaking sound as they turned the corner, half way up. Wayne took a single step onto the landing. Marcus, not realising his friend had stopped, bumped straight into him.

"Move, man, move," said Marcus, pushing Wayne towards a bedroom.

They both peered inside the first room without entering it. Marcus remembered the Hadrian statue in the bedroom he had occupied and was eager to show it to Wayne.

"Look," said Marcus, beckoning his friend into the room. "What is it," enquired Wayne as Marcus lifted the image of the Roman Emperor.

Marcus had now thrust the heavy bust into Wayne's hand.

"Don't be so ignorant," whispered Marcus, "it's the famous Roman Emperor Hadrian."

"As in Hadrian's Wall," mumbled Wayne.

"He did other things. Anyway, we had better put it back," said Marcus as he quickly snatched the statue from Wayne's grasp. Hadrian was returned to its rightful place.

Marcus beckoned his friend to leave and return to the ground floor. It suddenly felt wrong to be in one of Malcolm's bedrooms without permission. They both hurried down the stairs like a pair of naughty nine-year-olds about to be caught out by a teacher in the stockroom.

"Interesting," said Wayne, "very interesting."

Put your interest on hold," Marcus replied, "we better be off." As they reached the front door Wayne offered to give his friend a lift back.

The two were soon driving away from the leafy, middle-class area where Malcolm lived.

"You seemed keen to leave the house," said Wayne, "I was just getting into nosing around."

"That's you all over," commented Marcus.

Wayne slipped the Marina into fourth gear on the second attempt. The car was happily cruising along the main road back to Marcus's flat.

"Sure it wasn't something to do with that statue?" asked Wayne. Marcus gave a vague reply, hoping that Wayne would change the subject but it only made him more curious.

"It *was* that statue... I know you like the back of my hand," said Wayne.

During the short drive back, Marcus decided to tell his friend about the time he was taken to Hadrian's Wall to box another schoolboy. Wayne remained silent during the retelling. Just as Marcus was finishing the story the car was turning into Beaumont Drive, near the property.

"Why don't you come in," said Marcus, "I've got a new flat ... number five." Wayne got out of the car awkwardly, almost stumbling as he checked both doors were locked.

"Can't be too careful," he said, looking around.

Marcus put the untarnished silver key into the lock and newly painted door 5 swung open. Wayne stood near the threshold; he still seemed in a daze. A tug from his friend and he was ushered through the opening and into the lounge. He appeared strangely confused. The only word that came from his lips was 'magnolia.' Marcus explained that he was not permitted to change any of the colours on the walls but was happy enough with the neural look of the decor as it seemed fresh and clean.

"Sit, man," said Marcus pointing to a chair, "Do you want a cup of tea." Marcus had to repeat the question again before

Wayne said he would prefer a coffee. He gathered his thoughts and was soon on the subject of the Hadrian's Wall incident.

"Was that for real, what you said in the car," asked Wayne.

"Well, man, you don't think I was just making it up to entertain you, do you," Marcus snapped back. The two argued back and forth about the fight and what it meant until Wayne said he would have liked to have seen the posed 'corpse' photograph.

"What kind of 'sicko' are you," retorted Marcus, "You're saying that you don't believe me."

Wayne put his cup down and offered to leave but Marcus was determined not to let him run away from a disagreement.

"I'm sorry, said Marcus, "I know you were not there so how could you know..."

"No, it's me who needs to apologise," Wayne replied. He said he never meant to doubt his friend and that hearing about his earlier life at the approved school had stirred deep emotions within him: surprise, shock and some sadness.

"How could anyone do that to you," Wayne murmured, his head lowered. Marcus told him not to worry as it was in the past and he ought to take it on board as a lesson.

"Boxing is tough, bare-knuckle or not," said Marcus, "You better believe it." Wayne nodded his head in silence. He was still staring at the carpet. Wayne asked for another coffee but Marcus waved his hand towards the kitchen.

"Make it yourself ... the coffee is on the bench; sugar in the usual place," he said. As Wayne was boiling the water his friend cheekily came up beside him and asked for one for him too. Wayne looked pensive.

"I guess it's a case of what doesn't kill you makes you stronger," he uttered.

Marcus replied that he hoped Wayne's coffee would not kill him. Wayne saw him fetch a half empty whiskey bottle from another room.

"Here, man," said Marcus, "Put some of this in mine ... and pour a little for yourself, if you're brave." Wayne added a generous amount of alcohol in both.

"Ah, I can smell the whiskey from here," said Marcus as he picked up his favourite blue mug. Wayne sat down to finish his coffee but it took a whole thirty minutes before the mug was empty. He constantly spoke about his wanting to sign up for a boxing bout and told his friend he was fit enough, pausing only to get confirmation.

Wayne suddenly sprang from his seat, leaving his mug on the floor, and asked Marcus if he could have a shower. Marcus looked perplexed at this request, but Wayne explained that regular cold showers were now a bit part of his training regime. "Give us your mug first," said Marcus holding his hand out. Wayne apologised and offered to wash up.

"Good... and whilst you're doing that, I'll find some towels," explained Marcus as he disappeared into his bedroom.

A cupboard door banged closed. Marcus was soon in the room again with his friend, giving instructions.

"The bathroom is across the landing... you can have a bath or a shower, it's up to you... plenty of *hot* water, mind," Marcus continued, grinning. Wayne insisted he needed a cold shower to freshen up and walked across to the bathroom clutching two brand new white towels.

With Wayne under the shower Marcus decided to slip out to the local corner shop off-licence to stock up on another bottle of Jameson whiskey, plus some lemonade. He was gone and back before Wayne had even noticed. Marcus managed to open his front door just before his friend, sporting a white towel around his waist, was coming out of the bathroom. Marcus held the door open as Wayne wandered inside, water dripping from his wet body.

"I gave you two towels for a reason," said Marcus sternly.

"Okay me old mate, replied Wayne, "keep your hair on, you're as bad as the missus."

Marcus pulled the almost dry towel from Wayne's hand, quickly rolling it up tightly.

"Oow, that hurt," Wayne exclaimed as the impromptu whip flicked across his back.

"See, I told you I'd get you," laughed Marcus, "Come on then, get yourself dressed." As Wayne got his clothes together, he saw the new bottle of whiskey on the table.

"Any lemonade," he asked. Marcus went into the kitchen and took out two glass tumblers and came back with a large bottle of lemonade to go with the alcohol. Marcus poured two generous measures.

"This is also part of your training regime," he said, handing one to his friend.

Wayne had almost finished dressing when Marcus provocatively spoke about seeing Sean. He knew he would get a reaction from his friend and wondered why he had brought the subject up in the first place.

"Mate, you're joking," said Wayne with a look of surprise and disgust.

"I'm not joking... it's true," Marcus replied, "He stayed in the garage overnight last November." Marcus retold the full story, indicating that he had felt sorry for the young traveller. Wayne gulped his drink down with a look of anger.

"He'll be back, mark my words, and when he does, I'll be straight over," said Wayne.

"Reserve your anger for boxing, mister high and mighty," retorted Marcus, "it's more useful there." Marcus spent the next ten minutes reassuring Wayne that nothing had happened, beyond Sean staying in the garage.

"He even left the torch behind," said Marcus, "and the blanked I leant him." Wayne was still unconvinced.

"Come on then, come on ... what would you do if he came back," blurted Wayne. Marcus wanted to know what sort of a question was it that his friend was asking. Wayne looked agitated but Marcus decided to pour Wayne another drink.

"Drink up, and keep the noise down," said Marcus. He felt in control of the conversation. "If he turns up again, I'll invite him to Malcolm's for a bit of sparring with an ex-sailor turned drama queen." Wayne suddenly saw the funny side of the situation and quickly calmed down.

"Yeah, I'd be on for that," he replied, showing his innate sense of humour. Wayne was beginning to slur his words.

"Why, you'll have to stay here overnight," chuckled Marcus, "unless you want the wife to come over and pick you up." Marcus was waiting for a reaction.

"Good on you," Wayne said, "I think slaying here is the best option." Marcus chuckled.

"Well, man, you'd be slain if you went home now... that's for sure," he said looking at his friend. Wayne went on to say that he had not been getting on with Sandra lately. He was thinking that she was trying to control his movements and kept asking him where he was.

"I feel so hemmed in," explained Wayne as he sipped his drink, "It's not good..." He said he thought the most important thing in her life was her little Riley Elf, with its expensive looking interior.

"Real red leather seats," he muttered. Marcus listened patiently trying to work out what Wayne really wanted from life. After thirty more minutes he felt his friend was repeating himself so changed the subject.

"I was talking to Malcolm the other day," said Marcus, "and he was saying it was possible to change the rooms above his garage." Wayne pulled himself up in his chair and looked at Marcus who continued to detail a plan. He explained that there was a lot of space above the area where the cars were parked that was once an office. Access could be had through the basement and up some stairs at one end.

"Apparently, there's even a toilet and sink fitted," said Marcus enthusiastically.

"Are you thaying what I'm sinking," Wayne enquired, slurring some of his words.

"Go on, man," said Marcus, "what is it you are thinking?" Wayne wanted to know if there was enough space for a gym and if he thought Malcolm would allow this.

"Is the Pope a Catholic," asked Marcus.

"Is Ronnie Reagan the cowboy President," replied Wayne, ... yes! ... yes!" Wayne took some more whiskey and sat back with a gleeful look in his eye. With that he slumped to one side and was asleep. Marcus decided to leave him in the chair and carefully removed the almost empty tumbler from his hand before it dropped. 'No good wasting it,' thought Marcus as he took the last swig from Wayne's glass, before moving silently into his bedroom.

--o--

Wayne was back at work by seven the next morning despite a slight hang-over. He needed to pull the big, metal communal refuse bins out early as it was collection day on the Corinium Estate. If he did not get them out on time they would not be emptied and would soon overflow with household rubbish from the flats. Wayne tried to focus on the task in hand but his mind was not on the job of providing a good standard of caretaking to the council tenants living in four large sixties-built blocks.

He looked around at the grey environment and longed to be out at sea again. He pondered on the direction of his life. It seemed to be becoming as drab as the flats around him despite his new friends. Wayne felt as if something was sadly missing, but could not identify what that was.

With all the bins out and the lifts checked he decided to go to his den at the back of Octavia House. He pulled out his bunch of assorted keys and immediately found the one for the caretaker's office. Wayne entered the main room, switching on the light and moving over to the kitchen area where he checked the kettle had enough water in it to make a coffee. He was in a pensive mood. He knew he was feeling depressed but could hardly work out why. Thoughts of his marriage were pushed aside, but they kept intruding.

The empty coffee mug was placed in the sink. Wayne turned the tap and began washing the stains away. 'I need a shower,' he said to himself, 'a cold shower.' Luckily, he did not need to wait until he got home to have one as his caretaker's room had most things to hand. Wayne opened the wooden door to the shower cubicle and reached for the wheel that turned on the water. He put his right hand under the spray to make sure it was cold.

Undressed, he now stepped tentatively inside. The feeling was of stock as the water hit him but also exhilaration. He was finally awake, and felt alive. 'That's *exactly* what I needed to sort myself out,' he said to himself as he stepped out and found a towel to dry himself off.

By the time he returned to Bibury House the bins had all been emptied by the refuse collectors. It was time to start putting them back in the bin rooms again.

126

"Are you our caretaker," asked a slightly haggard looking woman pushing a forlorn buggy that had seen better days. Wayne acknowledged her whilst peering down at the young boy asleep.

"Only that I'm locked out, and can't get in." Wayne walked alongside her until they had reached the eighth-floor.

"Eighty-three," she said, pointing to a faded red door. Wayne was keen to help but knew that his locksmith skills were limited.

"At least you've only got a Yale lock," he said wondering what to do. "Isn't he cute," Wayne continued, looking at the buggy again. He was playing for time.

"I could smash the glass," Wayne continued. The look on his tenant's face was a mix of shock and disbelief.

"Then I'd have to get the emergency glazier out," he continued, trying to be helpful, "Or I could see if I could slip a piece of plastic between the frame and the lock, just like James Bond." Wayne's tenant gave him a sideways look and was just about to say something when a youth came running up to the flat. He looked more than angry.

"What's this, then ... what's going on," he shouted. He was a teenager changing into a raging demon.

"Reece, we are just trying to get in," his mother tried to explain but her son was in no mood to understand her words. Wayne told the lad to keep the noise down. The front door was now open and Reece rushed into flat 83 followed by his mother.

"Sorry," she said quietly, as the door closed behind her. Wayne walked away, turning the corner at the end of the block. He had plenty of tasks to catch up on; the stairwells needed mopping. Suddenly he could hear the vibrating sound of footsteps pounding the concrete floor behind him. Turning, Wayne could see Reece running towards him like a mad bull.

"You leave my mother alone ... right," he shouted. Wayne looked at a face contorted with rage; eyes vacant.

"Hey, hang on a minute," replied Wayne.

It was at that point he saw the knife. Wayne took a half step backwards but Reece kept coming forward, accusing him of all sorts of violations. It was as if he were possessed.

"Calm down... it's Reece, isn't it," said Wayne, trying to gain control of the situation. The lad did not respond other than wave his knife towards Wayne. Things looked bad. Reece was now accusing Wayne of all sorts; sleeping with his mother, trying to take advantage of her, trying to move into their flat. Wayne knew it made no sense but Reece, for now, believed it as if it *were* true.

Wayne took another step back and glanced at an object at his side. It was an old wooden chair that had been left outside one of the flats. He had often told the tenants to keep the communal areas free from rubbish but he was thinking the chair could come in useful in fending off an out-of-control teenager. As Reece waved the knife again Wayne picked up the chair and thrust it towards him, pinning him against the wall. He then pulled it back and used it to knock the knife away.

It was a swift, effective move and the knife fell to the ground. Wayne kicked it away and then grabbed Reece by the throat, pushing him against the wall. He detected that Reece had calmed down, but looked shocked. His facial expression even showed some remorse.

"Get away," instructed Wayne as he thrust Reece back towards his flat. The lad took a few steps of retreat, allowing Wayne to safely dispose of the knife down a rubbish chute. With a series of metallic clangs, the weapon ended up in one of the communal bins below.

"Sorry, mate," said the lad. The energy had drained out of him like a deflated balloon. Wayne could see a different person standing in front of him; a passive, sheepish boy who looked lost in the world.

"If you want your little knife back, see me in my caretaker's room in half an hour ... right," instructed Wayne. Reece nodded and walked away dejected; his head bowed in embarrassment.

Forty minutes later Wayne heard a faint knock on his den door. It was Reece.

"You're late," snapped Wayne as he beckoned Reece into his private space.

"Sorry, mate," replied Reece. Wayne noticed that his attacker was not sporting any footwear and he enquired what had happened to his Dr. Martens boots. Reece did not elaborate.

"Who do you think you are," said Wayne, gripping the lad and pinning him to the wall nearest the door.

"Please don't hurt me ...," he replied, "else I'll report you." Wayne pointed out that Reece's actions earlier in the day could get his mother evicted. He could see that his warning had hit home.

Reece was not unintelligent despite his outburst of anger.

"I've got your knife locked in my drawer," said Wayne, "but if you want it back, you'll have to work for it and earn my respect." Reece realised that his mother's caretaker had the upper hand and just awaited his fate. He felt helpless and consumed by a heavy feeling of guilt. He knew that it was wrong to rush at someone with a knife without thinking but also knew his flashes of rage controlled him like an underworld monster.

"Sorry," said Reece, his head once more bowed to the floor.

"I believe you," responded Wayne. He saw that Reece was far from a bad lad – lost, maybe. As Wayne looked towards Reece, he saw a little frightened boy. By now his eyes were welling up with emotion. Wayne took a step forward and gave Reece a hug. In that sacred moment Reece had a father; Wayne a son.

Chapter 8

CRUISING THE BROADS

Wayne leaned against a red pillar box at the end of his road, his mind deep in thought. Jack-in-the-Green's scent, emanating from an unruly hawthorn hedge, wafted through the morning air as a cheeky robin looked curiously on, all knowing, from a distance. He pondered that he felt a real connection with nature but felt a 'nothingness' when he pictured his wife who was still at home. Wayne's thoughts drifted, nostalgically, back to his years out at sea, and his beloved Leander Class frigates.

Suddenly the peace of the universe was broken by the distinctive low humming sound of a distant Volkswagen approaching. Wayne was expecting it. A pink and white minibus, sporting psychedelic 'hippy hearts' on each side, soon appeared and pulled in on the opposite side of the road.

Malcolm sounded the horn just as Marcus slid open the side door and looked out. With a broad grin on his face Wayne swung his kit bag onto his shoulder and dashed nimbly across Dunmere Drive to join the group. Marcus jumped out of the vehicle to greet his friend, almost stumbling on the kerb.

"Why, that looks very military," he commented, slowly running his hand down the canvas. Wayne explained that he had saved the bag from his naval days.

"It comes in handy for outings like this," he said, peering inside his ride. Oliver indicated a good place for the bag at the back and Wayne was quickly inside what he was already calling 'the love wagon.' Marcus opened the front passenger door.

"I'll sit here then," he announced as he climbed back in.

"This is a new one on me," chuckled Wayne.

"Oh, the van," replied Malcolm.

"Uncle loves his Volkswagens," explained Oliver, "but I'm not sure about the decals on the side. I think it used to be some sort of hippy pilgrim bus, going to Glastonbury, or something." Malcolm asked Oliver how he knew that, and his nephew had to admit he was just guessing.

"I've heard a lot about Glastonbury," said Wayne, turning to Marcus. The front passenger wondered if he was referring to the music festival, or the town. "It's supposed to be quite a mystical place," continued Wayne as Malcolm drove towards the Broads and their hire boat.

The hum of the minibus's engine sounded deeper as, some thirty minutes later, they pulled into the entrance of the marina. Malcolm held it in first gear, giving it a bit more power.

"Look out for a sign for Tideswell," said Malcolm as he drove slowly along a dirt track lined with tall, mauve weeds.

"Over there," said Wayne, "That way." He was pointing to another small track on the right. The minibus rocked from side to side as it continued along a narrow, rutted track but quickly emerged past a row of stately ash trees onto the marina car park.

As Marcus opened his door, he could see the sun-baked white tops of a row of moored cabin cruisers ahead. Malcolm switched off the engine and his passengers quickly disembarked like a group of excited schoolchildren on a field trip. Malcolm made his way to the boat hire office to confirm the booking and sign some paperwork. Minutes later Ivan was the first to step onto 'Encounter Group,' quickly followed by Wayne.

The hire boat owner was a portly, laid-back, but quietly confident man with a face that had been weathered by many seasons working on the Broads. He had seen life; he had been to places.

"This is your craft for your booked days," he said as Malcolm and Oliver joined him on the boat, "I hope it suits." Malcolm nodded but he was concentrating on Ivan's moth-eaten jumper that had seen better times.

"Come on, Marcus," shouted Oliver, turning around, "... *do* catch up." Marcus took a deep breath and quickly stepped on to the pretty floating holiday home with its unusual name, and lots of natural wood. It moved gently in the swell of the river. He was aware that it was not a stable platform and wondered if he had made the right decision in agreeing to a boating break. He knew he was outside his comfort zone and looked around for Wayne, who had gone to the front of the boat checking out the cabins.

Marcus joined him. He felt reassured on seeing his friend.

"Well, there are three cabins," said Wayne, "Two are the same size and one is a lot bigger." Marcus was craning his neck to look inside the larger cabin.

"This can be the one where we have two people sharing," suggested Marcus. They agreed that was the sensible, and only, thing to do.

"Up 'ere boy," called Ivan. He wanted everyone to witness his nautical demonstration. The holidaymakers were now all making their way to another part of the boat to see how it was fired up, stopped and steered. Ivan saw that Wayne was the one who wanted to get more involved, despite his focus on the sleeping arrangements. He explained how *'Encounter Group'* was started, and how power from the engine was applied.

"You don't need to go above five knots, okay," said Ivan sternly, expecting a reaction.

The ropes securing *'Encounter Group'* to the side were untied and Ivan gave Wayne a demonstration on how to position the boat. Marcus was already wearing one of the cruiser's bulky orange life jackets, which he had found below.

"Yeah, that's it," said Ivan, "You've already got the hang of it."

"He was in the Royal Navy," interjected Marcus in a flat tone.

Ivan was happy that Wayne could be left in charge of one of his favourite cruisers. Wayne put *'Encounter Group'* into reverse and manoeuvred her back to the bank. Ivan leaped off like an agile, young puma, only turning around to give a brief farewell salute.

"Before we properly get going," said Malcolm, "we ought to agree who is having the single cabins, and who is sharing. We should have done it earlier."

Marcus said that perhaps Malcolm and Oliver might like to share. Oliver looked unsettled and waited for the conversation to move on. Wayne picked up on Oliver's unease and suggested that he and Marcus take the larger cabin. Oliver and Malcolm quickly agreed with their new captain. That would leave uncle and nephew with an individual cabin to themselves.

"That sounds fine by me," said Marcus.

Wayne apologised for not consulting him. After a few minutes all the bags and cases were in the correct cabins and

Wayne had *'Encounter Group'* in mid water. It was an unusually warm May Saturday and the group had the boat until late Friday.

"A whole week on the water," said Wayne, "... great."

His eyes were fixed ahead avoiding a line of oncoming white and blue cruisers. Marcus stood next to Wayne as the three craft went past, one by one. Each set up a wave which gently rocked *'Encounter Group.'*

"Relax... enjoy yourself," said Wayne as he acknowledged the third boat that passed them with a wave.

Marcus became aware that he was clinging tightly to a rail, not daring to move. He felt self-conscious as the only person on the boat wearing a life jacket, but he knew he was the only one onboard who could not swim.

'Encounter Group' and crew were soon in a wide stretch of the Broads with few other boats in sight. There was a gentle breeze, the afternoon sun reflected on the swirling, moving water and the only noise was the regular hum of the engine.

"Here, mate, you take over for a minute," Wayne said jumping from his seat. Before Marcus had a chance to protest Wayne was gone.

"Man, get back here," bellowed Marcus but his friend had disappeared into their cabin. Marcus readjusted his life jacket so he could move into the bridge seat and took control of the wheel.

It seemed relatively easy to keep *'Encounter Group'* between the two banks; there was plenty of water on each side. Marcus was furious that Wayne had left him to take charge but he was powerless not to allow the boat its own fate. Like a mouse, Wayne crept back up to the upper deck. He had changed into a pair of burnt orange shorts, a smart black T-shirt and navy-blue deck shoes. Silently, he had managed to stand behind Marcus without being detected.

"I love Frida," he shouted at the top of his voice. Marcus, startled, was not impressed. He turned to see his friend carrying a large, white plastic bag. Wayne began pulling out a cassette recorder.

"Why man, have you lost your marbles, or what," Marcus demanded to know.

"Or what," replied Wayne smiling, "Abba ... Frida, from Abba. She's the pretty, dark-haired, quiet one."

"So unlike you then," Marcus quipped. Wayne was oblivious. The tape in the cassette was turning and Abba's 'Dancing Queen' blasted out at near full volume.

Wayne demonstrated his love of Abba by rhythmically swaying to the music. When the track was over, he switched off the cassette and pulled out two dark bottles from the plastic bag, gingerly handing one to Marcus.

"Newcastle Brown Ale," said Wayne, "I know you like it." Marcus moved over to let Wayne take control of the boat again. His irritation with Wayne had quickly disappeared. 'How could you be angry with a clown,' he said to himself as he gulped the warm beer.

"Why don't you become a singing telegram," said Marcus smiling and looking at his animated friend.

"Ah, 'The China Syndrome' film," muttered Wayne. Marcus wondered what he was talking about.

"They had that in the opening shot of the film of that name," explained Malcolm who had appeared on the upper deck to see what all the noise was about.

"Correct," said Wayne'

Oliver was keen to join the group and appeared wearing Speedos, an England rugby shirt and designer sunglasses.

"Very nice," commented Wayne as he handed a beer from a cardboard box he had brought to the open deck, "Anyone got a camera."

Malcolm had briefly gone down to sort out his clothes and toiletries in the cabin but came back for some fresh air. He was also anxious to point out the time.

"It's almost six," he said, glancing at his gold Rolex watch. Wayne's skill was keeping the boat at a gentle four knots. The captain was daydreaming and did not hear Malcolm until he repeated it, standing right beside him.

"Okay, I'll find a suitable mooring," responded Wayne, "even if it's between two trees." Oliver and Malcolm looked at one another. Marcus silently thought that was what Wayne would do, and he was correct. Wayne skilfully overshot the mooring and then allowed the tidal flow to manoeuvre 'Encounter Group' carefully beside the bank between two water leaning willows.

"Nice bit of parking," exclaimed Oliver.

134

"It's just like parking a mini on a motorway," Wayne bragged.

--o--

It was now almost eight o'clock and the four part-time sailors were sitting at a small table trying to play dominoes, whilst discussing politics. The washing up from the meal they had just eaten was still left on the side.

"There won't be any industry left the way we're going," said Wayne, "Nothing for real men."

"I know what you mean," chipped in Malcolm, "Did you hear about Corby? It's now a ghost town after they closed the steel works. You can buy a decent semi-detached house for £4,500." There were some 'tuts' and then Wayne put down a double three.

"Hey, where did that come from," said Oliver. Wayne seemed to have only a few dominoes left but kept some hidden under his hand. Malcolm put down a piece, followed by Marcus.

"There's a place in south Norfolk with an eight-acre mere," said Oliver, changing the subject, "and it's fed by seven underground streams." Wayne said he had been there to buy some books.

"Ah, seven streams," exclaimed Malcolm. The players looked up. "When people use the number seven it usually signifies an ancient site that has been Christianised," he continued.

"Uncle knows a lot about ancient history," said Oliver grinning. Marcus also admitted to knowing of the town, which he thought he had read somewhere that it had been named after Heathen water spirits. With that Wayne put down his last domino, winning the game.

"Fancy a stroll out," he enquired, leaping from his seat, "It's still a cracking night." Malcolm said that he wanted to catch up with some reading but the other sailors were keen to get away from the confines of the boat.

The three friends were soon striding along the river bank, pausing only to push small tree branches out of their pathway.

"Where did you two meet," enquired Oliver. Wayne explained that Marcus was in a trade union boxing bout and he volunteered to act as a ringside assistant. "It's like you seem to have known each other for years," he continued, feeling slightly confused. Wayne agreed that it did feel like a lifetime, explaining that they had just 'hit it off' from the beginning.

"Get walking you big Jessie," said Marcus pushing Wayne in the back.

The gentle movement of the water made a tune combining with the sound of the wind through the trees. It was the soul melody of the Broads. Oliver was keen to talk. He wanted to explain about the conversion of the space above his uncle's garage to a gym.

"Uncle agreed this area would make a better place for you both, compared to the basement," he stated, "But some of the work took longer than he imagined."

Marcus and Wayne both thought the new home for Hadrian's Gym sounded better than the dark, cold area they had looked at before.

"It's not just for us two," said Marcus, "I was hoping quite a few people could use it... yourself included." Oliver acknowledged Marcus's words without committing himself to anything. Marcus sensed that Wayne could not wait to move in.

"Wow, did you see that," said Marcus looking out over the water. The others wondered what Marcus had noticed. He explained he had seen an eerie flash of light in the water. Wayne thought it must have been a large group of fish catching the moonlight as they turned.

"Moon wane," he explained. Marcus looked perplexed.

"Shush... stop," Oliver said, putting out his left arm, "can you hear singing, or music, or something." The group came to an abrupt halt. Marcus thought he could hear a male voice somewhere ahead of them. The three friends decided on move on, along the bank, in the general direction of the sound. It was not long before the undergrowth thinned out and a small distant fire, with shadowy figures of people around it, came into view.

It was then that Wayne and Marcus simultaneously realised that they were looking towards a group of half a dozen naked figures.

Oliver was still striding forward; seemingly oblivious to what was going on ahead. Marcus moved quickly to catch him up, pulling on his arm.

"They haven't got any clothes on, Oliver," said Marcus in hushed tones as Wayne joined them.

The music had stopped but all three could vaguely hear a woman's voice, as if playing a leading part in a Shakespearian play. Wayne led the way as they edged nearer the glow of the fire.

"Stop giggling, Oliver," whispered Marcus, "I'm sure they can hear us."

The music had started again. Wayne could recognise a guitar being played, and the deep sound of drums beating a rhythm was obvious to all three. After a while there was only silence. An owl hooted from some unseen tree that made Oliver jump. He was feeling anxious that they were in the wrong place. As Marcus pondered returning to the boat, a young woman dressed in a flowing green robe, and wearing a garland of wild flowers in her hair, approached.

"Was that your music we heard earlier," asked Wayne, taking the initiative, as she neared him.

"Yes, we were singing to celebrate the seasons of nature and the spirits of water," she replied. Marcus and Oliver glanced at one another. Both had the same thought.

"It's Wayne, by the way," he said awaiting another response.

"Felicity... and friends," the young woman replied with a comforting smile. Wayne was not the only one to notice that Felicity was bare-footed, and wearing a gold ankle chain.

"Hi, I'm Peter," said a man coming forward, "You can stay and join us if you wish, we've got some food drink to share."

Oliver silently nudged Marcus indicating that he was going to walk back to the boat. He felt uneasy in the company of strangers. Turning, he disappeared into the darkness leaving Wayne and Marcus with the group of eccentric midnight revellers.

"So, what is it, exactly, you are doing," asked Wayne.

"Are you open-minded and truly curious to know," Peter replied.

"Yes, yes, of course," said Wayne. Peter looked at Marcus for his response.

"And me," he replied.

Felicity stepped forward and explained that her group were pagans who were holding a ritual to celebrate the power and

137

influence of the full moon. She waved her hand as if throwing invisible glitter into the air, indicating the way a circle was symbolically made on the ground to create a sacred space for the group.

"You have entered our loving space; Ingvi's Grove. It's a beautiful healing site," declared Felicity, "I hope you can feel it." Wayne nodded. "We believe in the power of the goddess," she continued, realising that the two amazed onlookers were of no threat to her or her group.

"I play the part of the god," added Peter, taking his lead from Felicity.

"Here," said Felicity holding out a piece of paper with large typed words on it, "Read this later. This is our story." Wayne took the paper, folding it so that he could slide it carefully into his back pocket.

"Much appreciated," he said, "but I think it's time for us to head back to our little boat."

"Ah, cruising the Broads," said Peter, holding out his right hand, "Now it all makes sense." After shaking hands, the two friends started to silently make their way back to *'Encounter Group.'*

--o--

Wayne awoke at dawn. Unlike the cockerel in the far distance, it was far too early to do anything. Even thinking was muffled. Wayne decided to lie in for another hour before getting up. He was vaguely aware that his cabin mate had not had a good night's rest. Wayne pondered on whether to ask his friend if he suffered from vivid dreams, or nightmares. He glanced over to Marcus, who appeared still asleep, and decided not to wake him.

The self-appointed captain was now sitting on the edge of the bed wearing his black jeans from the night before. He had noticed that there were many little green seed pods attached to the bottom of the legs, a legacy from walking through the thick undergrowth.

"Damn things," he muttered as he tried picking them off, one by one. Marcus was still under the covers. The task completed

Wayne slid his hand into his back pocket and pulled out the sheet of folded paper from the night before.

"Is that a note from your girlfriend," teased Marcus as he tried to grasp the sheet from Wayne's hand. He was perfectly aware of where the note came from. Wayne quickly made a dive to the left allowing Marcus to snatch only the air. "Give it over, man," demanded Marcus as he grabbed his friend's forearm. Changing tactics, Marcus put Wayne in a headlock, pulling him backwards on to the bed.

"Get dressed, you tart," laughed Wayne, "You're not meant to be teaching me wrestling on day two of our cruise." Marcus had not managed to see what was written on the paper but Wayne relented and decided to read it out loud.

"We all come from the goddess, and to her we shall return, like a drop of rain..." Marcus looked surprised.

"Wow", he said, "I didn't expect that. I thought it might be an invite to the next gathering." Wayne agreed. He thought it sounded like a chant for the ritual.

"Wicca," said Malcolm from outside their open cabin door. He had been attracted to the larger cabin by the sound of the horseplay and found a space to add his own thoughts. Wayne and Marcus looked at one another, not knowing what to say. Wayne was feeling embarrassed, but he did not know why. "Anyway," continued Malcolm, "I've come to tell you breakfast is prepared."

The crew of 'Encounter Group' just managed to all fit around a small table as they feasted on cereal with thick marmalade and partly burnt toast.

"This is one of my all-time favourites," announced Wayne, holding aloft a cassette tape in his right hand. He slid it into the machine balanced on his lap and pressed the play button.

"Ah, Gerry Rafferty...," said Malcolm. Wayne put his finger to his lips indicating he did not want anyone to speak whilst 'Baker Street' was playing. Wayne seemed to be in a world of his own; tightly wrapped in the music like a baby in a shawl. As the track ended and Wayne pressed the stop button it was Malcolm who first ventured to break the silence.

"I'm right with you there, Wayne," he said, "that was brilliant.... really special. That solo saxophone piece sends a shiver down my spine."

Wayne pointed out the irony of 'Baker Street' reflecting Gerry Rafferty's disillusionment with fame and the music business whilst making him more famous.

"It just shows you that if you have a passion for something it'll generally lead somewhere," pondered Malcolm.

"I would hate to be famous," said Marcus. Wayne turned to look at him.

"Really," his friend enquired.

"Yes, really," Marcus replied.

--o--

Malcolm had given Wayne some instructions, suggesting they visit a village fete that he had read about the week before. It was approaching mid-day and Wayne had seen a good place to tie the boat for the next stop. He pointed the area out to Oliver, who had come to take a look. Both agreed that there was ample room alongside a strengthened area of bank in front of a vast area of cut grass. In the distance stood a thatched building which Wayne cunningly guessed by the painted sign, was a village pub.

"Hey, Marcus ... Marcus," shouted Wayne, hoping to catch his friend's attention, "Can you come here and help with the docking." Marcus slammed the small toilet door behind him and raced past the table, leaving his life-jacket on it. He had not noticed the bulky brightly coloured life saver in his hurry to assist his friend. Marcus just wanted to prove to all on board that he could be of use on the boat.

He emerged beside Wayne who was carefully steering the boat nearer the bank. It was only a few yards away from some cut grass and the familiarity of land. Marcus went out onto the edge of the boat. He was aware that Oliver was behind him, holding a rope, his gaze fixed on the bank that was gradually moving closer. Marcus slowly edged forward and grabbed the other coiled rope. He got himself ready to tie the front in place the minute that *'Encounter Group'* touched the side.

The Broads seemed tranquil, almost hypnotically calm. There was a faint sound of voices coming from the direction of the village. Malcolm had chosen the site as he had read that Oggsby was holding their annual early summer fate on the day. Marcus was thinking that the village had been chosen well; the weather was perfect for outdoor activities and general fun and merrymaking.

"Bloody idiots," came an indignant shout from what Wayne called 'the bridge.'

Marcus went to turn back to see if Wayne needed help but in that moment of thought a tidal surge hit *'Encounter Group'* full on and with one powerful movement Marcus had been tossed into the water like a discarded apple core.

"Marcus's is in the water," shouted Oliver, hoping Wayne had heard over the hum of the engine.

'Encounter Group' continued to rock in the swell created by another, faster moving boat that had passed, music blaring out loud. Oliver saw the incident unfolding as if in slow motion. He had noted Marcus's last position between the boat and the bank.

Oliver pulled off his T-shirt with one quick motion and dived straight into the murky water, causing more turbulence. Wayne had not noticed Marcus's fall but saw Oliver dive in. He knew something unplanned had happened and left his seat to get a better view.

"Stay with the steering," said Malcolm, touching Wayne on the shoulder, "Oliver will get him out."

Wayne hesitated. The realisation of what was unfolding hit him, but his training kicked in and he was soon in full control of *'Encounter Group'* once more.

Marcus found himself trapped in the murky depths of the water. His eyes were open but he could see only a few inches in front of him. He felt oppressive water pressing on him from all sides. Panic gripped him like a vice. At one point he thought he had knocked into something solid but he could neither touch nor see anything. His head was spinning. Beautiful, constantly moving, translucent colours were swimming in front of him like a kaleidoscope.

The water between the boat and the bank swirled with a vortex of bubbles, weed and floating leaves and then Oliver's head appeared. He gulped the clean air and dived back down again. Eventually two heads could be seen above water. Marcus was fighting for oxygen, spitting out the muddy water that he had ingested; disorientated, and feeling as if he wanted to vomit.

Marcus experienced relief when he was suddenly on to the firmness of the grassy land. Wayne had seen most of the rescue and was now positioning *'Encounter Group'* slowly alongside the bank with short bursts of engine power. Once level he jumped off, not even thinking about securing the boat. His only thought was his drenched, exhausted friend. Malcolm made sure *'Encounter Group'* was tied up before Oliver stepped back on board, still dripping with muddy water and weed.

"Oliver, you'll have to get those wet clothes off pretty quick," said Malcolm, still shocked at what he had witnessed, "else they will dry on you like glue."

Malcolm was surprised to see that his nephew had a tattoo. Oliver went below deck and walked to the tiny shower to get rid of the smell of the rotting river vegetation that was his new deodorant. As he shut the door, he heard Malcolm ask something.

"Does your mother know you've got a tattoo," was the question.

Oliver smiled and turned on the stream of tepid water allowing it to run through his matted bleached streaked hair. Wayne caught up with Marcus in their cabin.

"Are you okay, me old mate," he enquired as he sat beside his friend on the bed. Marcus did not answer but simply continued drying himself with a towel. Wayne had seen Marcus leave the shower cubicle just before Oliver had used it.

"Yeah, don't worry yourself, man," Marcus eventually replied.

"But I *do*," responded Wayne, not sure what action to take after the main drama had played itself out. He felt guilty that it was not he who dived into the murky waters to rescue his friend, but knew Malcolm was correct in telling him to remain with the craft. Wayne left the cabin but soon returned with two steaming coffees.

"Put a drop of Jameson whiskey in mine," quipped Marcus, knowing that Wayne had no quick access to his favourite drink.

"If only I could …," responded Wayne, "It seems that's something we forgot."

--o--

Hours later Marcus and Wayne drifted ever deeper in conversation. They were now the only two on the boat. A pair of coffee-stained mugs had been put aside. The drinks had long since been drunk and the sun was slowly setting in the west. *'Encounter Group'* swayed with the moving water beneath them. Marcus, away in thought, turned to darker times.

"I want to tell you something," said Marcus, "no doubt triggered by me nearly drowning earlier." Marcus's thoughts went back to teenage years; the era he shared with a Tyneside family.

Marcus thought it was time he revealed more about his earlier years. He hoped his friend would accept it without being too shocked and without going into his default 'drama queen' mode. 'After all,' he thought, he had vividly spoken about incidences of past abuse to Malcolm, so 'why not Wayne?' He hoped, like Malcolm, Wayne would not judge him in any negative way.

For over half an hour Marcus talked passionately about the time he was at the approved school, and afterwards the gym. He disclosed how he was subjected to regular physical punishments that also contained more than a degree of sadistic humiliation.

Wayne listened to his friend describing how he sometimes got the taws on various parts of his body. Marcus described in detail how he had to do sit ups over the edge of a pool until he thought he would end up drowned. In hindsight he wondered if any of the observers had paid to see a 'show.'

Marcus was not sure why he felt the requirement to go into so much detail but, somehow, he needed to be honest about his past; he needed to unload.

"Terrible," said Wayne, shaking his head in disbelief, "I don't know what to say."

"Sorry… didn't mean to burden you like that," said Marcus, "I guess I'm recalling it after what happened earlier. I thought I might drown then too."

Wayne moved closer to his friend and offered a hug. Marcus said was not the 'touchy, feely type.'

"I'm sorry mate… I just thought…," apologised Wayne. Before Marcus could tell his friend not to worry about it. Wayne was out of the cabin and making his way to the upper deck. Marcus wondered what he should do. He waited a few moments before going up to the deck himself.

He got to the bridge but Wayne was nowhere to be seen. It was now too dark to see anything. Marcus looked out but still could not see his friend. He looked to the side again, across the bank to a group of bushes and thought he saw a figure near a tree. Wayne looked up as the sound of Marcus approaching focussed his thoughts.

"What's up," asked Marcus. "Nothing," his friend replied.

"Well, man, it doesn't look like nothing to me," said Marcus, "Come on …" Marcus offered a hand. "Boxing buddies," he said. Wayne took Marcus's hand and disclosed that the comment meant a lot to him.

"Jas and Ali, you called them … Jas and Ali …, pondered Wayne, "How could they do that to someone so vulnerable?"

"Look at it as strict boxing training," responded Marcus. Wayne sat in silence, sharing at the patchy grass below. Marcus apologised if he had disclosed too much. Wayne shook his head.

"I can never be as strong as you are," he murmured. Marcus told him that he needed to be that strong if he intended to box, pointing out that the world of boxing was tough and corrupt. Both sat under the tree in silence watching the moon rise. A sudden gust of wind rustled nearby ranches, and then calmness engulfed the Broads again. After a while Marcus spoke.

"I'm not good with intimacy," he declared, getting up from the cold ground.

"Not only you ...," Wayne replied.

"But you're married," said Marcus, perplexed.

"Yeah, state the obvious, why don't you," retorted Wayne as he too stood up. "Come on, it's cold outside," he continued. The two friends made their way back to the tethered boat and their accommodation.

--o--

Morning had long broken. It was time to leave the boat. Oliver was the first to leap off *'Encounter Group'* straight on to the grass that was the edge of Oggsby's huge village green.

"Let's see what's doing," he said, encouraging the others to follow him. All four crew were now off the boat and heading for the music and the babble of the crowds ahead. It was a warm, sunny day; perfect for the village fate Malcolm had suggested.

"So, Oliver, what were you up to last night," asked Wayne.

"Not much," he replied, not giving much away.

As they got nearer the stalls Wayne noticed that someone had set up a piece of equipment named 'Strongman.' He eagerly paid his pound to swing the hammer on to the metal target at the base.

"Come on Wayne," Malcolm shouted as he held the hammer high before crashing it down on the target. The line moved upwards but not enough the ring the bell at the very top.

"Damn, damn," said Wayne in frustration, "I'll have another go."

As he prepared his second attempt a few more onlookers were gathering to watch. The hammer fell with a loud thud once more but the line did not reach the top. Wayne was sweating with the heat and the effort he had put into wielding a heavy hammer. He paid another pound for his third attempt and psyched himself up.

"Imagine you are the mighty Thor," suggested Marcus.

Wayne's wet hands were losing grip on the handle. He put the hammer down and removed his T-shirt to grip his version of Mjollnir.

"I guess that's alright," enquired Wayne of the stall owner who just nodded his acceptance.

Wayne held the hammer with two hands and sent it crashing on to the target. It was clear that this was his best effort and the bell rang in confirmation.

"Well done that man," said the owner, "Here's your fiver." Wayne took a bow and thankfully accepted his winnings.

"That's me up on the day," he chuckled. Marcus and Malcolm turned for the beer tent but Oliver was hesitant, not knowing what to do next.

"You seem quite fit," he said glancing at his colleague. Wayne loved compliments but turned it back on Oliver.

"Well, I've been training a lot of late – how about you?" As Wayne and Oliver slowly walked towards the beer tent the conversation turned to the gym that had been set up at Malcolm's home.

"So, will we see you at our new Hadrian's Gym," Wayne enquired, gripping Oliver by the upper arm. "Don't be shy, everyone's now seen your little tattoo," he jested.

Oliver attempted to explain that he was not a great fan of boxing but might occasionally call in. Wayne assured him that was fine.

"I didn't have you down as the boxing type anyway, but you could pop in and build up those pecs," he suggested, pushing Oliver forward.

Oliver recovered from a stumble and pushed Wayne back. As the two got into a mock fight Marcus's gaze was drawn to a figure in the far distance near a white van. He was sure it looked like Sean.

"Carry on boys," said Marcus as he took the opportunity to break away, and was quickly walking towards the van.

As he drew nearer, he immediately recognised the lonely looking figure. It *was* Sean.

"Hey," said Marcus, "what are you doing?" Sean looked a little nervous before he replied.

"My folks are here with the fair," he said, mumbling.

Marcus was looking Sean over. He stood a pathetic figure with uncombed hair, dirty hands and fingernails, and a jumper with two large holes in it exposing bits of unwashed torso.

"I need to get away Mister Marcus, I'm not joking with you," Sean said, speaking a bit louder.

Marcus told him that he was on holiday, on the river, and could not help him. Sean's gaze dipped to the ground and at that moment Marcus was aware that he felt sorry for Sean, despite him once trying to steal his friend's hub caps. As if reading Marcus's mind Sean moved the subject on.

"I saw your friend using the hammer earlier," said Sean, "Is he a boxer?"

Marcus explained that he was in training to box, just to get fit. Marcus wanted to know if Sean had been following the group

146

around but Sean said it was just a co-incidence that he had seen the group that day.

"Well, Mister Marcus," said Sean, "I know you have no time for me so I'll be getting out of your hair..."

Marcus looked at Sean and thought he detected some sadness in Sean's eyes. With a tentative half-hug, Marcus said that Sean could contact him in a week's time and scribbled the communal phone number on an old receipt that he found in his pocket.

"Mister, you're a diamond," said Sean as the two started to go in different directions.

With a sprint Marcus raced back towards the beer tent where he guessed the others would be. He pushed through the crowded entrance and quickly joined a short queue at the bar, hoping not to be noticed until he had ordered a drink. Marcus felt a slap on the back.

"Where were you a minute ago," Wayne enquired. "Oh, I just popped out to have a look at something," he sheepishly replied, turning round to look for Oliver and Malcolm.

"I'll have half a pint of cider," said Marcus as the barman took his order.

Wayne sternly pointed out that he had not been in the beer tent in the first place.

"Why aye man, I know," replied Marcus, drink in hand.

He wondered what was best to tell Wayne, who had a look of disbelief on his face. Malcolm beckoned the two to come over to a table near the back of the tent.

"I'm just having the one," said Malcolm, grinning, with an almost finished pint in hand. "We had a lot to drink yesterday after that incident," he explained.

Malcolm sensed that Marcus and Wayne had some business to attend to.

"Come on Oliver. Drink up. I need your help on the boat," he said.

Oliver dutifully obeyed his uncle but wondered why the rush to get back so soon. It was unusual, he thought, for his uncle to be so direct with him. As Oliver and Malcolm left the tent the atmosphere turned heavier. Wayne had an uncharacteristically angry look about him.

147

"I saw you earlier," said Wayne bluntly, "talking with that gypsy kid." Marcus turned to Wayne pointing out that Sean had a name.

"Why, man, don't you start telling me who I can and can't talk to," quickly came Marcus's response. Wayne looked contemptuous.

"And you can take that look off your face, else we'll end up falling out," he continued, trying to get the upper hand.

Wayne said nothing. Marcus thought that he had control. The words had pierced Wayne's very soul and he felt anxious. Wayne was petrified of losing a friend and he knew deep inside himself that he would do anything to stop that happening.

"Okay, okay," said Wayne giving himself space to think. The two drifted out of the beer tent and stood near the white canvas door. A sudden gust ruffled the sides of the structure making a strange flapping noise. Wayne got a brief glimpse of Oliver and his uncle walking into the distance, merging with the crowds at the fate.

"You, man, are one insecure person," retorted Marcus, "and that'll be the undoing of you, mark my words."

Wayne denied the allegation but deep inside himself he knew that it contained more than a grain of truth. He feared losing his friend to the very person who had tried to steal his hub caps. Wayne felt hurt and betrayed but could not put his feelings into a meaningful sentence. The two friends started back to the boat in silence. Marcus was starting to feel sorry for his friend and sought to give him some reassurance.

"Nice move back there when you rang the bell," he said. Wayne nodded.

"I could have done that first time, a few years ago," he pondered.

"Yeah, right," was Marcus's immediate response.

The sun was still beating down. It was a hot day despite an occasional breeze, which allowed a clump of reeds to slowly wave. Wayne slipped off his T-shirt and sat down under an ancient willow tree.

"Man, you're not so bad for your age," jested Marcus looking down at his friend, "Didn't Oliver say the same?"

Wayne was deep in thought. When he did say something, it was subdued and made little sense to Marcus.

"My life's a sham... a sham," Wayne mumbled.

"What do you mean your life's a shame," demanded Marcus. He paused before saying, "You had a good life in the Royal Navy, you got married and now you are captaining a cruiser on the Broads."

Wayne said that he wished he could go back in time and lead his life a different way. It was evident to Marcus that Wayne loved being part of naval life. He wondered if it was something to do with the close community that he had read about.

"If you had taken a different course, we wouldn't be speaking together now," continued Marcus.

"I know, I know," Wayne answered looking at his friend.

Marcus thought he had caught Wayne at his lowest ebb. The two sat closely together looking out at the ever-changing patterns in the sky. Marcus eventually broke the silence.

"For a navy man you never got any tattoos done," he said.

"Don't like them," reflected his friend.

"Nor me," replied Marcus.

--o--

It was soon time to turn *'Encounter Group'* around as the midpoint of the cruise had been reached. Wayne found a wide stretch of water and easily pointed the craft in the opposite direction. It was an uneventful trip back to the marina. Wayne looked dejected. All on board seemed to think the return journey was quicker than the other way around.

"I don't really get that," said Wayne, "I'm gutted that we are returning home so soon."

As the boat edged gently towards its final moorings Wayne shouted for Marcus to join him at the front.

"Nearly back," he commented, his voice tinged with sadness.

Marcus stood beside his friend as the boat's speed gradually reduced below one knot. *'Encounter Group'* seemed to drift on miniature waves of water dancing to the tune of the early summer sun, it not wanting to make contact with the side of the marina.

Everything was eerily still, apart from the sound of low flying geese nearby. Marcus opened his mouth but no words came out. Swallowing hard, he tried again but Wayne held up a hand in a gesture that said 'stop.'

"Just listen," said Wayne, "Just listen."

With that he pressed the play button on his cassette recorder which Marcus had just caught sight of. After a two second pause Chicago's 'If you leave me now' started.

"Don't give up on me," whispered Wayne as he edged the boat within inches of the bank.

Marcus was silent, deep in thought, not understanding what Wayne meant. Marcus felt confused; too confused even to ask. 'Encounter Group' swung around and gently backed into a space between two other similar cruisers. As if by magic, Chicago's tune ended as Wayne switched off the engine for the last time.

"Synchronicity," exclaimed Malcolm breaking the magic, before leaving to fetch his belongings up from below.

Wayne went down again to take the last look at the floating bedroom. Everything was now ready to offload from the boat. Oliver jumped off the back and received the items of baggage, one by one, from his uncle. Marcus was putting his life jacket away. He would not have a use for it again.

"Back then," shouted Ivan as he hurried along the marina to meet 'Encounter Group.'

Wayne conveyed that they had a memorable time on the water, speaking at length about Marcus falling in.

"Just goes to prove," said Ivan, "that you should always wear safety equipment provided... right?"

Marcus looked on in embarrassment before putting the last piece of luggage into the Volkswagen. Holiday over, he just wanted to leave the marina.

Wayne was about to climb into his allocated seat when, out of the corner of his eye, saw a dark figure furiously pedalling towards him. He was surprised to see Reece at the marina but it reminded him that the break was now merely a collection of memories, and that he would soon be back at work on the council estates.

"You'll have to sort it," said Reece, dropping his cycle to the ground near Marcus.

It just missed his foot.

"They are going to kick us out," he continued.

Wayne soon worked out that Reece's mother had gone into rent arrears on her tenancy. Malcolm moved away. He decided to check the tyres. Marcus was fixated, wondering who Wayne's friend could be.

"Nice to see you too," Wayne eventually replied.

Reece was feeling more agitated, believing that Wayne was not taking the situation seriously enough. Wayne tried to calm him by putting his hand on the youngster's shoulder but Reece shrugged it off. Marcus looked on, watching Reece's body language, and thinking a fight was about to break out. Sensing that Marcus could become involved, Wayne was keen to contain the situation.

"I'll deal with him, Marcus," he said firmly, "Don't worry. Get in the van."

Oliver was already seated, and after Marcus joined him, the door was slid closed. It did not take long for Wayne to return, this time sitting in the front beside Malcolm. With a flick of the ignition the minibus was slowly moving along the rutted track away from the marina.

"Don't ask," sighed Wayne, "Just don't ask."

"Seat belt," instructed Malcolm glancing to his left.

Chapter 9

GLASTONBURY CALLS

Sean scurried out of the first-floor bathroom clutching two of Marcus's best white Egyptian towels to hide his nakedness. He was not seen by any of the other residents before he got back to flat 5.

"You dry yourself off," instructed Marcus, "I'll clean out the bath."

As Marcus passed Sean, heading for the bathroom, he playfully gave him a quick slap on the buttocks. Grinning to himself, Marcus entered the small space and picked up an old blue sponge. After a few minutes of cleaning away a dirt ring he was back inside his flat. It was his domain; he was in charge. Marcus informed Sean that he had put all of his dirty clothes in a black bag.

"Throw the towels on the floor and let's take a look at you," he demanded. Sean complied but put his hands across his genitals to shield them from view.

"Shy, are we," taunted Marcus. He did not expect an answer.

Marcus was judging Sean as he would a boxing opponent. He noted that Sean was around the same height as himself but slimmer and without his tone. Like Marcus, Sean lacked chest hair. Sean had blond hair with blue eyes and had an innocence, or naivety, about him. Marcus thought that Sean's facial expression would let him off any charge, including murder.

"Turn around," instructed Marcus.

Sean complied and it was then that Marcus realised that his companion had some bruising on his back. He judged that his guest had been given a beating by one of his relatives. Seeing Sean's back send Marcus's thoughts back to the time when he had to endure physical punishments at the gym. He sometimes had bruises on his back. Marcus refocussed on the present; he was pleased that Sean was now safe.

Another direct instruction saw Sean walk into Marcus's bedroom and lie face down on his bed. Marcus followed. He had every right to view Sean as the 'bad boy,' but somehow, he saw him as angelic.

"What are you going to do to me, Mister Marcus," asked Sean.

"You'll find out soon enough," was Marcus's deliberately vague response. A side drawer pulled open; Marcus was searching for some Aconite ointment. He eventually found it hidden away in a second drawer. Marcus unscrewed the cap and moved in closer to Sean, rubbing the cold balm into his back. It smelt good.

"It'll help with the bruising," explained Marcus.

He thought it about time a confused Sean got an explanation. At the same time, he did not want to question Sean regarding his torso. Marcus concentrated his hands on the areas that showed the most bruising, and then let his thumb slowly ride down his patient's spine.

"Okay," said Marcus, "turn over, on your back."

"Please, Mister Marcus, let me put something on first," was Sean's nervous plea.

"I can see why your folks beat you," retorted Marcus, "Man you're an awkward sod."

As soon as he had said these words Marcus wished that he could take them back. He paused then quietly slid open another drawer and pulled out a pair of his red y-fronts. He dropped them near Sean's face, and then briefly left the room.

"I knew you were a good man," said Sean, as Marcus came back.

"A good man with a wicked sense of humour," he quipped. Marcus rearranged Sean's arms symmetrically, pulling both outwards, before applying some ointment to another of the bruises on his side. Marcus now had a different type of balm in his hand. It was based on strong smelling Eucalyptus. Sean wriggled, and moved, then chuckled, as the refreshing balm was applied to his chest.

"Are you ticklish," asked Marcus.

"I should really be giving you more bruises for trying to steal my friend, Wayne's, hubcaps," Marcus jested.

"Sure, it's punishment enough being like this in front of you," Sean replied. On hearing that Marcus's mischievous side kicked in, and he decided to keep his guest in just his y-fronts for a bit longer.

"I'm going to cook us spaghetti bolognaise. Then I might sort you out a few of my older clothes," said Marcus. Sean swung himself into a sitting position on the edge of the bed. Marcus suggested Sean go into the lounge and watch some television whilst he prepared the food. It was not long before the two meals were put on the table.

"Am I going to eat dressed like this," asked Sean. Marcus confirmed he was. Sean gave him a pleading glance but Marcus was not about to give in.

"Maybe I could fit you with a leather collar and a lead and then you could eat like a dog," he said.

After the meal was consumed Marcus took the dirty plates and cutlery back into the small galley kitchen. It was space enough for him; Marcus did not usually entertain.

"I'm going to have to ask you to get dressed," said Marcus, playfully, as he left to get some of his clothes.

First, Marcus handed his visitor a pair of socks, followed by one of his old pairs of blue jeans. A pair of shoes followed.

"See, there you go, man," commented Marcus, "it all fits you perfectly..." Sean was wondering what was to follow.

"I prefer you like that," continued Marcus, "but the hostel manager might get the wrong impression of you."

"Or of you, Mister Marcus," came Sean's quick-witted response. Marcus threw Sean a faded denim shirt to wear, plus one of his old knitted jumpers.

Marcus located the completed application forms for Sean's placement at the hostel. It was only a twenty-minute walk away to the new accommodation. The manager, who Marcus spoke to earlier over the 'phone, indicated that they were willing to grant Sean an emergency placement whilst they assessed his needs. He knew in his heart this was the time when Sean really needed some professional help. Marcus hoped the temporary room offer would become more permanent, and that there would not be a crisis whilst he was on holiday in Somerset.

Marcus knew Sean desperately needed a break, and he a break of a different sort away from the city.

It had been over two hours since the trusty Volkswagen had pulled out of the service station. Marcus was fidgeting in his seat, wondering how long before they would arrive at the camp site. He had left his mind in East Anglia and his thoughts kept going back to Sean. He hoped the hostel placement had turned out well for the lad.

Marcus wondered, too, if he could have done more, or whether it was unkind of him to keep his guest in a pair of his y-fronts for over an hour. Part of him feared that he was turning into a Stefan 'mark two' from his own dark past. Marcus eventually concluded that as Sean came from a family of travellers, he should be quite resilient – yet Marcus thought Sean was somehow 'different.' He deliberately forced his focus back to the enchanting Somerset countryside.

Wayne looked bored.

"Over there!" exclaimed Marcus, pointing across at an angle.

The distinctive profile of Glastonbury Tor greeted them from afar. Wayne sighed before putting the vehicle into a lower gear. The road had become hilly, with many twists and turns. He was able to glance to his right to get a view of the Tor, and the sheep in the fields that surrounded the road.

"Make a wish," said Marcus, "It's a tradition when an outsider sees the Tor."

"I'm certainly that," muttered Wayne. Both pilgrims concentrated on the road ahead, knowing that they were nearing the end of a long journey. Wayne suddenly took one hand off the steering wheel as if gesturing.

"I now feel like a traveller," he chuckled. Marcus was relied that his friend's sense of humour had returned, but wondered what had been troubling him.

"It's been a fair old drive," commented Marcus, thinking that Wayne was becoming tired.

He realised that Malcolm's 'hippy' minibus was probably a lot different to handle compared with Wayne's family saloon. With that thought still in mind, Marcus's attention was drawn to something fluttering in the distance. As the minibus drew nearer to a bend it was evident that the fluttering was a long line of small but colourful flags, arranged like bunting.

"Slow down a bit," he instructed Wayne, "that looks interesting." As they approached, the minibus was parallel to a gap in a long hawthorn hedge.

"That's it," said Wayne as he put the minibus into reverse, then turned into a large field. The sign for the Golden Pentacle campsite was now clearly visible.

There was a hut and what looked like a shower block up ahead. Wayne turned towards that area; it looked promising. The whole site seemed to buzz with the energy of the campers. It had been a sweltering drive from east to west, and the temperature outside was still that of an unusually hot summer's day. They passed dozens of tents pitched in all parts of the site. People were walking around or just sitting outside their temporary homes, trying to get a bit of shade. Ahead, a group of lads with long hair and wearing faded jeans were throwing a Frisbee back and forth. Wayne leaned out of his side window.

"Excuse me, mate, is that the booking office ahead," he shouted.

The lads nodded before resuming their game. One, with much shorter hair, came to the side of the minibus and asked if they were booking for the festival. Wayne replied that they did not know a festival was on.

"Sunstead Season," the lad announced, "It's actually more like a moot."

"A moot ...oh, right ...mate," Wayne said, not really understanding.

His mind was unfocussed; still on the road. He put the minibus into gear, pulling up near the hut. Wayne was curious to know where Marcus had found the site.

"It was an ad in a Sunday newspaper, I think," he said, scratching his head, "I didn't know there was a festival on."

Wayne looked perplexed. Marcus got out and went into the hut. It had an overly large wooden office sign on the door. Having confirmed the booking, and been told the two could pitch their tent almost anywhere, the minibus was moving again along a central track.

"Do you want to be near the middle, or on the edge," asked Marcus. Wayne thought an edge near a small grouping of trees looked just fine.

That is where Wayne parked the minibus before having a walk around to inspect the ground. Wayne grabbed the dark green, four-person tent and laid it on the ground.

"It should be okay here," he said. Marcus had no reason to disagree; the site looked perfect.

The two pulled and stretched the base of the tent, making sure the entrance part was facing the main site. Marcus was tasked with assembling the tubular frame whilst Wayne began banging in the tent pegs. The tent still lacked form but Wayne decided to crawl inside to check the base was precisely how he wanted it. The heat was intense inside the flattened structure. Wayne was finding it difficult to find the entrance. As a joke on his friend, Marcus had zipped it closed.

Wayne finally found the collapsed entrance and came out, slipping off his T-shirt before standing. As he pulled himself up, he bumped straight into the lad who he had spoken to not forty minutes beforehand.

"Just came to see how you were getting on," he said, "I'm Gwydion by the way."

Wayne acknowledged him, but looked flustered. He was now using his T-shirt like a towel.

"Who's your friend," Gwydion wanted to know.

Marcus walked across and explained who he was and where they had journeyed from. Wayne guessed Marcus had zipped him inside but Gwydion's presence was now a lucky distraction. Gwydion said his friends liked the minibus.

"But then, they are much hippier than me," he explained.

Marcus thought Gwydion was trying to say he had different interests compared to his friends. Wayne did not pick up on the cue, but commented on Gwydion's summer tan.

"Yeah, it has been baking hot all week," he replied, Maybe I did over do it."

"Want a hand with those, Marcus," said Gwydion reaching for a set of poles.

Marcus nodded and let him get on with it, before handing two of the main poles to Wayne. The roof of the cavernous tent was being pushed up as Wayne located the holes where the ends of the poles sat. It was now beginning to look like a usable abode, albeit quite dark inside. Marcus pushed a few more poles into the tent whilst Gwydion was pulling out some guide ropes to create stability.

"Have you got a mallet," asked Gwydion.

Marcus threw one across to him. After about ten more minutes the structure was fully up. It only left Wayne to start loading some home comforts into the tent from the minibus.

Wayne beckoned his two helpers inside.

"What do you think," he asked. Gwydion thought it cave like, but Wayne pointed out he could set up a light from the ceiling.

"Just for night," he explained.

Even Marcus was now finding a bit hot inside the tent and also slipped off his shirt. The gloom obscured any shyness, and he quite forgot that he was now the only one inside.

"Marcus, come out," shouted Gwydion.

In response, Marcus crawled to the entrance and looked out. Gwydion was staring from afar with Wayne nearby setting up a camping stove. Gwydion moved over to the tent and helped Marcus out. Wayne looked perplexed.

"Are you going to stay for the whole festival," enquired Wayne.

He was secretly hoping Gwydion was planning to leave, feeling unhappy with the stranger around. Gwydion said he would definitely be staying for the coal walking in a few hours' time.

"We've got to do it," said Marcus.

His friend nodded, but then rolled his eyes, before sorting through the cans of food they had brought with them. As Wayne was pretending to be occupied, Gwydion suddenly announced he would return to see what his friends were doing. Wayne was relieved and fell back onto the grass

"I can't make him out," said Marcus, after Gwydion disappeared into the distance, "but I don't think he's a bad lad."

Wayne disclosed that he felt a sense of unease when Gwydion was present, but could not explain why.

"I guess he's a bit full on," admitted Marcus.

A few hours later and Marcus and Wayne had eaten, and drunk a bit of farm cider bought on the way. It was getting darker and Marcus thought it time to wander into the middle of the camp site to see what was going on. They could see the glow of the embers as they approached, with a couple of men using rakes to distribute the hot coals.

"You're here," said Gwydion as he touched Marcus on the shoulder.

Wayne's facial expression said everything; he was not amused.

"It won't be long now and then people will be walking the coals bare foot," Gwydion said.

He reminded the two that they must roll up their trouser legs to save the bottoms getting burnt. Marcus started to adjust his trousers and Wayne followed. All three were now bare footed as they moved to the starting point of the walk.

"Marcus, why don't you walk beside me, and your friend can follow," suggested Gwydion.

Wayne said he had not decided whether he was doing it or not but Marcus coaxed him into agreeing.

"Now that we have got here, we might as well join in," said Marcus, "besides which you look funny walking around with your trousers like that."

As Gwydion had participated in festival walks before, he decided to step on to the coals first. He appeared confident, faced front, and was soon walking quickly towards the other end. Marcus was the next to go, followed by Wayne, who was still unsure whether it was a good idea. Marcus could feel the heat of the coals underfoot and decided to walk faster. He was soon parallel with Gwydion.

Looking around, the coals gave an eerie glow and contrasted with the darkness of the summer night. An orange moon was rising slowly behind a group of sombre oak trees. The smell of the burning coals reminded Marcus of fires in his first home. Long haired hippy types were playing flutes and banging drums along the route to encourage the walkers. A huge bonfire, surrounded by revellers, meant the end was in sight.

"I told you it was safe and that we could all do it," remarked Gwydion with a smile, "and you've both got strong feet."

He turned to Marcus and gave him a hug. It was all over too soon.

Wayne reluctantly agreed that he had enjoyed the coals walk. It had given him a boost of energy at the very time he needed it, but he but silently wished Gwydion would return to his hippy friends.

"Let's wander back to the tent... I need a drink," said Wayne, as he brushed some sweat off his brow. He looked distracted.

Marcus thought it a good idea, despite some bands playing rock music near the middle of the site. He turned and noticed Gwydion looking on as if lost in time and space. He suddenly felt the odd one out with both Wayne and Gwydion appearing 'strange.'

"What are your friends doing," Marcus enquired.

"Not sure," Gwydion replied.

Wayne looked at Marcus, silently willing him to tell Gwydion to leave. Marcus started to walk in the general direction of the tent but was aware Gwydion was still nearby.

"Gwydion," said Marcus, "Why don't you join us. We've got some cider."

Wayne was not happy but felt he could not openly protest. Wayne and Gwydion sat outside the tent, separated by the entrance whilst Marcus dived inside to find some mugs and two bottles of farm cider.

"Sorry," shouted Wayne, "I haven't set up the light."

"So, Gwydion," said Marcus emerging from the darkness, "What do you do for a living?"

Gwydion said he was currently in catering but had done other jobs such as labouring and working at an airport.

"We've got an airport near us, haven't we Wayne," Marcus suddenly exclaimed.

"Yeah," came his stilted reply, "There are airports everywhere."

Wayne was more interested in looking at the hundreds of stars in the clear night sky.

"You and Gwydion can stay and chat," said Wayne, as he suddenly got up, "but I want to be alone with the stars."

With that he wandered off. Marcus noticed he was not wearing any shoes.

"Is Wayne married," asked Gwydion, after a few minutes.

Marcus acknowledged that his friend was, indeed, married. He wanted to know why Gwydion has asked the question, but his companion just lay back on the grass and pointed out a constellation overhead.

--o--

Marcus awoke at just after nine. He could smell cooking coming from outside the tent and he guessed, rightly, that Wayne was making breakfast. He stuck his head out of the tent to attract Wayne's attention.

"Why man, it's really warm," he commented, crawling a bit further into the outside world.

Wayne said the breakfast was ready and Marcus should not wait to get dressed. As Marcus hit the warm air in his black y-fronts, Wayne handed his friend a plate of camper's food, consisting of beans, sausage and tomatoes. Marcus took it and sat down in one of the portable camouflaged canvas chairs they had brought.

"Not bad," said Marcus, "Not bad at all." With that Wayne handed Marcus a mug of hot coffee.

"I've already done my teeth and had a shower," Wayne disclosed. "Why don't you just get dressed and we can go," he continued.

Marcus wondered why all the hurry, after all they were in sleepy Somerset, but Wayne was keen to visit the Tor. Marcus decided to run to the shower block and back, which he did in little under ten minutes.

"Hurry, up," said Wayne as Marcus scrambled back into the tent.

As Marcus got dressed, he still wondered why the panic to leave the site.

"Right," stated Marcus, "We can go then..."

Wayne had been studying an Ordnance Survey map of the area but he said he had memorised it, so did not need it to find all the nearby places they could visit. Marcus grabbed a small canvas bag in case he bought something in town.

The initial part of the route involved walking along the main road. Marcus let Wayne take the lead whilst he dropped back a few paces. Every time a vehicle passed, they had to hug the thick hawthorn hedge. It was not long before they could head into the safety of a field, away from the traffic and the noise.

"That's more like it," said Wayne as he picked up the footpath ahead.

Marcus asked his guide how he knew the footpath was where it was. Wayne gave an honest response.

"I saw the sign for it, me old mate," he grinned.

Marcus chuckled. It was a pleasant walk through open fields and meadows, and the gradient was definitely getting steeper by the minute. A group of crows took off from a large sycamore tree ahead and began circling noisily. They eventually flew off into the distance.

"I can see a hedge ahead with a gap in it," said Wayne, "That's the bit where we come out into the road."

Wayne paused a moment to take off his T-shirt. He was starting to feel the fierce morning heat but liked the sun on his bare skin. Marcus always thought his friend ought to have been born in somewhere like Verona. The two were soon out and across the road and starting off across another meadow. Rustic foxgloves seemed to be everywhere around. The bees could not get enough of them.

A man and a woman in their fifties were moving towards them, having already experienced the Tor. Wayne acknowledged them with a smile.

"Not too far now," the man shouted.

Just when things were getting a little bit boring the two trekkers saw the shadow of the Tor. That spurred them on. Wayne, leading, redoubled his pace.

"Wow, it's windy up here," he said, putting on his T-shirt back on.

Marcus pointed out that he had begun boxing training so should not always take the easy option if things got a little uncomfortable. Wayne sensed his friend was correct but did not know what to do. He secretly wondered if he could commit to the training without faltering and giving up.

Marcus was drawn to the strange whirring sound of a bullroarer. He moved over to take a closer look. A guy in bright clothing and with 'Afro' hair extensions was skilfully working the device on a long cord. It seemed to Marcus to be the ideal spot to work a bullroarer.

Wayne joined his friend. He had been looking at the ruined tower of the former church on the site.

"Not much of the church left," said Wayne.

Marcus thought the church had been toppled in a rare British earthquake. Wayne was becoming fascinated by the view and wanted to see the landscape from another angle.

"You can see for miles," he exclaimed, "I wonder where that is," pointing ahead. Before Marcus could say anything, another person answered.

"That's over towards Wells," came a strangely familiar voice.

It was Gwydion, who proceeded to slap Wayne on the back. He was furious, and walked off.

"How come you are up here," asked Marcus, who was genuinely interested.

He was thinking that Glastonbury was already turning out to be a very weird place. Gwydion replied that he knew the two would start off the day by visiting the Tor.

"I'm often up here," he said.

Gwydion pointed out a few more spots on the horizon and then enquired where Wayne had gone. Marcus, slightly embarrassed, had to admit his friend had got 'the hump' and wandered off to be on his own for a few minutes.

"You keep him under control for his own good," Gwydion replied.

Marcus secretly knew that was very wise counsel, and had been expressed before. With that, Gwydion said he had to depart the Tor to go to his job. Before leaving he advised Marcus to experience all of the high street, and pointed out the best descent path to get there.

Marcus now went to look for Wayne. He knew that so long as his friend was still on the Tor, he would not be too far away.

"There you are," said Marcus as he located Wayne sitting propped up against one of the tower's sturdy walls.

He immediately got to his feet. Wayne said he had been deep in thought but Marcus considered that he looked grumpy.

"Man, you need a serious talking to," said Marcus as he led Wayne away and sat down on to the west side of the hill out of the wind. It remained warm and sun soaked on that side.

"Take your training shoes and socks off, and your T-shirt," instructed Marcus.

He gathered them up and put them in the bag he was carrying. Wayne looked perplexed but he could tell that Marcus was going to say something profound.

"Save your anger for the ring," he said.

Wayne buried his head in his hands; he knew what was coming. Marcus paused until Wayne was sitting up straight again before giving him a lecture.

Marcus pointed out that Glastonbury was a fairly small town where everyone, apparently, knew everyone else. Gwydion was just trying to be friendly and that Wayne should not take this as a negative. Successful boxers were calm between bouts but could harness the energy of anger and use it skilfully in the ring, but nowhere else.

"I know, I know, mate," said Wayne, "You are right, as ever. I need telling ... I've messed up again."

Marcus said that Gwydion had given some useful advice on seeing the high street and that is what they should go and do. Wayne was looking at his friend, who was now standing up about to walk away from the Tor.

"You can walk like that," insisted Marcus, "It's your grounding punishment."

Wayne joked that he was not the only one on the Tor to be dressed informally.

Marcus was pleased that the points he had made had been correctly received by his friend, and they were soon setting out to the town centre on the path that Gwydion had pointed out. Some of the path had been well trodden causing Wayne to complain about the stones underfoot. He walked on the softer grass whenever possible.

A stile stood ahead as the next thing to negotiate. Marcus was the first to get to the other side, and another field of wild flowers. Wayne put one foot on the step but somehow managed to lose his balance, half crashing into his friend as he landed on the floor. Luckily, he fell on some long grass. Marcus laughed out loud but Wayne's angry expression spoke volumes.

"I'm not having a good time," resorted Wayne.

Marcus just looked on, trying not to grin.

"Here softie, take your shoes and socks back," said Marcus, "Put them on, man."

Wayne obeyed but looked miserable. The two moved further into the field and sat near some long grass.

"Anyway, what shoe size are you," asked Marcus.

Wayne said he was size seven but wondered why his friend had asked the question. Marcus said that most of his friends were either size seven or nine.

"We share the same size," Marcus pointed out.

Wayne's expression started to thaw. Marcus was now looking at his friends back.

"Why, soft lad, you've got a bit of a bruise coming on your shoulder," he commented.

Wayne looked miserable again saying that he was not having the best of luck and that the trip was meant to be a short holiday break.

Marcus started to massage Wayne's shoulders.

"I could get used to this," his friend said, "You've definitely got healing hands ... I'm not just saying that."

Wayne's thoughts went back to an aunt who worked for a spiritual healing charity and could get results by the laying on of hands.

"Her hands felt hot when she was healing," explained Wayne, "just like yours now."

It was not the first time someone had relayed this to Marcus, but he had never spoken about it for fear of ridicule. Marcus told Wayne to sit up straight whilst he held his hands over his friend's head. He moved them to the side, whilst not making physical contact.

"I've come over all goose bumps," said Wayne.

The two decided that they ought to make the most of their few days in Glastonbury, so decided to journey on down the well-worn path towards the high street. Wayne had not travelled a few feet when he found he had something sharp in his shoe.

"Bloody stone," he said before taking his shoe off and tipping it out.

"The universe is telling you that you should be walking bare foot at a sacred site such as this," commented Marcus. Wayne could detect a degree of sarcasm in his friend's voice.

"Yeah, yeah, whatever, me old mate," he retorted. Marcus had not expected Wayne to take his words literally but when he looked round, he saw that Wayne was carrying his shoes and socks.

It seemed as if time was at a premium so the two decided to walk quicker until they got to the high street. By the time they reached a pavement Wayne was fully dressed. Turning into a residential area with Victorian cottages on one side and the road sunken on the other changed their view. Everything seemed busier compared to the fields they had emerged from. As a huge lorry rushed by, Wayne assured his friend that the shops were not far away. As they walked on Marcus pointed to a long, tall stone wall that eventually had an entrance.

"Look at that house," exclaimed Marcus, staring down the drive. The two crossed the road to get a better view of the splendid early Victorian gentleman's residence.

"It's a retreat centre, me old mate," said Wayne, "I looked it up before coming."

Marcus was fascinated. The grand entrance seemed as if it was pulling him towards the building; he gazed on, spellbound. Marcus wondered what it would be like to be on a retreat in Glastonbury, as opposed to experiencing a steady stream of Wayne's dramas.

"Aha, we're here," said Wayne as they turned into the high street.

It felt so calm compared to the main road, yet it had an alluring buzz to it. Some of the buildings at the top of the high street appeared a bit 'run down.' Marcus was still thinking about his grand house and what a contrast there was now.

Wayne nudged his friend on the arm, pointing to an obvious 'new age' shop close by. The aroma of woody incense drifted out across the pavement, and they soon found themselves inside. It was an Aladdin's cave of spiritual objects ranging from small crystals to statues of the Herne the Hunter. Another section towards the rear catered for locals and pilgrims wanting a robe.

"Do you think I'd look good in a robe," Wayne suddenly asked.

"Why aye, man," Marcus replied, "Have they got a shocking pink one in your size?"

Wayne looked flushed and embarrassed. It did not help that, at just that point, a young female shop assistant asked if then pair were looking for anything in particular.

"My friend wants a long pink robe," laughed Marcus.

Wayne tried to justify himself being in *'The Green Experience'* by explaining that he knew a little bit about Wicca. His words became slightly jumbled. The shop assistant left the two to browse. Marcus found area of books and magazines for sale and soon was drawn to a 'how to' booklet on runes. It brought his thoughts back to the rune woman who once sat with him beside the river. He decided to purchase it along with a pack of *'Sunwheel'* branded joss sticks.

"Maybe we should look for a café and get something to eat," Wayne suggested.

Marcus thought that a sensible idea as it was approaching one o'clock. He pointed across the road to a café called *'Tanha Bite.'* Wayne thought it had an odd sounding name but the facade was bright and inviting with rows of small orange and blue flags fluttering over the door and window. It was a great spot to watch the world go by, being situated on a corner at the end of the high street.

The two travellers entered the café as a group were leaving. Wayne suggested he grab the recently vacated table by the window, whilst Marcus picked up a menu. They soon agreed that they both wanted a pizza with salad, plus some bottled cider. Wayne ordered from the counter area and returned to join his friend. Marcus was gazing out of the window.

"It's a strange town," he said, "but there's something enchanting about it."

"Yes, I can see why it's long been a place of pilgrimage," added Wayne.

The two were looking out onto the street, half discussing what they would do with their afternoon. The ruined abbey was mentioned, plus visiting a bookshop and some craft shops.

Suddenly a server was upon them with an extended arm placing their order on the varnished wooden table.

"Enjoy," came a familiar voice.

Marcus and Wayne looked up, and then glanced at each other. They could hardly believe they were being served by Gwydion. Before anyone could say anything, he had vanished into the back of the shop.

"I ... I don't believe it," said Wayne.

Marcus pointed out that Gwydion had said he now worked in catering.

"Well, the cheeky ... chappie," commented Wayne.

He held back saying more, remembering only an hour prior he had been lectured by Marcus on not taking issue with the locals. Wayne gulped a mouthful of cider, and then leaned back in his seat. He looked slightly confused.

"You seemed to take an instant dislike to Gwydion the minute you set eyes on him," commented Marcus.

Wayne admitted it was true but did not know why. He speculated that it was as a result of him being tired and 'on edge' after the long drive in an unfamiliar vehicle. Yet Wayne speculated that it did not feel the complete answer.

"Maybe you thought Gwydion was a bit over friendly," suggested Marcus, "Sort of imposing himself on others."

Wayne had to admit this insight was nearer the mark. Marcus saw himself on a bit of a roll and ventured to suggest his friend was also like that. Wayne listened with increasing interest.

"You took an instant dislike to Gwydion as he subconsciously reminded you of yourself," Marcus continued. Wayne said he would have to think more about the theory, but felt somehow it was true.

By now the meals had been eaten, leaving only empty plates and almost empty glasses in front of them. Gwydion suddenly appeared again moving rapidly from the back of the shop and removed their plates in a whirlwind of activity. Before the two had a chance to speak he was back with more ciders.

"They're on me," he said, leaving the friends in astonishment.

"Why did he do that," asked Wayne.

Marcus referred to an earlier conversation painting the locals as friendly, saying this was just an example of what he was trying to convey to his friend.

"You are right," sighed Wayne. He knew when he had been beaten.

--o--

It had been several hours since Marcus and Wayne had returned from the high street. They managed to get to see the ruined abbey and some more of the 'new age' shops. Surprisingly, Wayne had purchased a dark blue cloak. Marcus wondered what he would use it for. It was still light; a warm evening and many festival goers were walking around, drinking or listening to the bands on the elevated stage.

The sun was slowly descending and Heavy Metal music drifted through the warm air. Wayne was pleased they had seemingly picked the perfect spot to put up the tent. It was quiet enough to talk, but they could hear the festivities in the background and felt part of the Sunstead Season vibe.

"If our visitor comes across, we'll have to offer him some drink," said Marcus.

Wayne agreed; he readily acknowledged that he had undergone a change of mind concerning Gwydion. Initially, Wayne thought Gwydion intrusive, but now saw him as a friendly local.

"Here, take some of this," said Wayne handing him a bowl of soup he had just prepared on the cooking stove.

Marcus took the bowl and grabbed a hunk of bread to dip in.

"You're ruining your clothes," exclaimed Wayne in frustration, as his friend dripped tomato soup over his T-shirt, "Take it off."

"Only if you do first," quipped Marcus.

Wayne gave his friend a sideways look. He often did not know if Marcus was joking, or saying something serious. Soon the pair were enjoying their basic meal bare-chested. Marcus suggested Wayne take an early morning run to the Tor the next day.

"Do it shirtless," added Marcus," Make it part of you boxing training." Wayne nodded.

Marcus pulled open the tent flap and crawled in to get some cider. He came out with a bottle, plus two white enamel camping mugs.

"I wonder if we'll see Gwydion," commented Wayne as he grabbed a mug.

He could not wait to receive the locally brewed liquid gold. Marcus took a mouthful of his cider and sat on the grass outside the tent. Wayne looked across awaiting words of wisdom from his mentor.

"I don't know," was Marcus's considered response.

Wayne relaxed, taking in more of the campsite atmosphere. It did not concern him that the future was a mystery. The sun was setting, a warm breeze blew and the sound of Heavy Metal music was the backdrop. Marcus could see that his friend was, at last, settling into the mini holiday.

--o--

Marcus woke up to the sound of pigeons cooing. As he came to his senses, he was suddenly aware that he was the only one in the tent. The entrance flap was half open allowing a cool morning breeze to drift in. He could hear the faint sound of voices and a car pulling away in the distance. Marcus had no idea of the time but assumed Wayne had gone for his morning run to the Tor.

"Not up yet," shouted Wayne as he lifted the tent flap. Marcus pulled the blankets closer and rearranged his pillow.

"I'm enjoying myself," he mumbled, "chill out." Wayne was outside preparing some toast and coffee and seemed in an unusually buoyant mood.

"I know I can do it," explained Wayne as he stuck a mug of dark coffee just inside the entrance of the tent.

Marcus crawled over to take it. He was wearing nothing but a green woolly jumper that stunk of many past bonfires. Marcus decided that he needed to position himself nearer the tent entrance to understand what his friend was saying. Wayne said that he had taken Marcus's advice and gone for the run, bare-chested. As he set off, he immediately noticed a buzzard circling overhead.

"The funny thing is, me old mate," explained Wayne, "as I ran on it was always just in front of me – like urging me on." Wayne thought it must be his totem animal and that it was with him on the run for a reason.

"Man, you've lost me a bit," said Marcus. He was trying to re-orientate himself to the new Wayne. "What is it you can do," he asked.

"Box," replied Wayne, looking surprised. "I now know I'm ready to box," he declared. Marcus was still trying to take everything in. He wondered if he had drunk too much cider the night before, but was pleased by the invigorated Wayne, who seemed much happier. Marcus decided to test his friend by explaining that he had befriended Sean just before coming on the Glastonbury trip.

"You remember Sean, don't you," he asked, staring straight at his camping companion.

Marcus was scanning Wayne's facial expressions to gauge what he was really thinking. Wayne acknowledged that he did, indeed, remember Sean.

"I decided to help him with an application for his own accommodation," said Marcus. He awaited a response.

"Okay," said Wayne, "Well, let's hope he gets it then. I guess you being good with forms made a credible case for him."

Marcus was surprised his friend did not react badly; something inside Wayne had changed. He decided to drop the conversation whilst he was ahead.

"Why don't we go into town again," suggested Wayne.

Marcus agreed that it was a good idea but said he needed to go to the shower block first.

"I'm going to look at some stalls near the gate," said Wayne, "They are selling wooden crafted items." Marcus shouted back his approval.

Wayne walked over to the stalls. There were four in a row but one looked particularly interesting. A man in his thirties, and dressed in authentic Viking period costume, was behind a table draped with a thick, dark blue cotton covering. A large, embroidered gold Heathen Mjollnir sign hung low at the front and moved gently with the breeze. It was the unique display of many hand-crafted Norse items. Wayne picked up a drinking horn.

"There's a knack to it," said the stall holder.

He beckoned Wayne to hand it to him. The stall holder then slowly filled the horn with water.

"See if you can do it," he said. Wayne, eager as ever, put the horn against his lips, tipping it back at the same time. A sudden wave of water soon slopped over his chin, dripping on to his T-shirt.

"Let's have a go," said a refreshed Marcus, who had crept up on his friend and observed everything from behind.

Marcus knew that it would be easier as half of the water had been slopped out. He took the horn and held it at an angle, tipping the contents very slowly.

"That's a bit better," said the stall holder as Marcus managed to get most of the water down his throat.

"How long are you here," asked Wayne.

"At least a few hours," came the reply. Wayne explained that they were off to look around the high street, but he was keen to buy a few items.

"Andrew," said the stall holder, thrusting his hand forwards.

As Wayne shook his hand, he said that he could do a special deal; he would charge a tenner for two horns. Marcus urged Wayne to agree, and a deal was quickly completed.

--o--

The end of the break was all too soon upon the two campers. Everything had been put inside the Volkswagen save for the tent, which was still on the grass, folded.

"Help us get this in somewhere," instructed Wayne as he started to lift the temporary home.

"I could get used to Somerset," Marcus remarked as the tent was pulled into the back of the vehicle.

"Me too, mate," pondered Wayne, "Me too. This place has really changed me." Marcus looked on.

"Ah, I forgot to tell you ..," said Wayne, changing the subject, "I was speaking to Ian and he said that Dominic has now got a job in a café in the city."

Marcus pondered if it was one of the newer, trendy cafés that were springing up, especially near the waterfront. He was pleased that Dominic seemed to be getting on with his life despite his earlier injuries.

"It's a shame that he can't box again," said Marcus, "I could tell he was really into sports."

Wayne agreed and thought Dominic would have been a good travelling companion on the Glastonbury trip. Marcus added that he would have also have liked to have invited Oliver.

"Agreed," said Wayne, "Glastonbury has focussed the mind," he continued.

The two campers recognised that Glastonbury had a strange 'pull' for them; they did not really want to leave. Both could imagine living in the area.

As the minibus exited the camp site gate for the long journey home Marcus and Wayne pledged that, one day, they would return – perhaps with a larger group.

Chapter 10

WAYNE'S OPPORTUNITY

Marcus used his 'gifted' key to open Malcolm's front door. It was a strange feeling going into someone else's home when they were not in, even though they had given their unrestricted permission. Marcus pondered on Malcolm trusting him enough to give him the freedom of his home. He wondered if Malcolm was a naturally trusting person, or whether he saw something particularly safe in him. Marcus felt privileged.

As he passed through the long hallway, he was aware that the only noises were coming from him and the house itself; the faint ticking of an antique clock somewhere, the groan of wood underfoot and a squeak from a flexing shoe. The house smelled Edwardian. No sooner was Marcus at the end of the hallway the piercing sound of the door bell sounded.

"Just typical," grunted Marcus as he headed back to open the front door. He was expecting his friend, who barged in as if fleeing a pack of hungry wolves.

"You're keen," said Marcus looking at Wayne.

"Yeah, got all me training gear with me," his friend replied.

As they walked through the house and into the garden Marcus told Wayne to expect a tough session. The work, on what had been dubbed 'Hadrian's Gym,' had been completed creating a large, airy space above Malcolm's generous garage complex. The entrance to the gym was up a flight of metal stairs at the side and then through a wooden door.

"It's turned out good," said Wayne looking at his new home, "lovely space ... great..." Marcus was examining a punch bag.

"Yes, I forgot you hadn't seen it before," replied Marcus.

Wayne left to get changed. He quickly reappeared in the gym hall wearing shorts, a T-shirt and training shoes and eager to begin his session.

"What do you want me to do first," he asked. Wayne, as ever, was keen to please his mentor.

"Let's work on your upper body," replied Marcus.

Wayne moved over to one end of the cavernous area and gripped a sturdy metal bar. He pulled himself up using his arms in a controlled manner.

"See if you can do twenty," instructed Marcus, observing from a distance.

Wayne soon went through a dozen chin-ups but started to strain.

"Put more effort into it," shouted Marcus.

Wayne was able to do seventeen full chin-ups before struggling and dropping to the floor.

"Sorry, mate," he said drawing breath.

Marcus was swiftly arranging the next part of the training. First the dumb-bells followed by press ups and then more attempts at chin-ups. Wayne was not permitted a break, save Marcus looking for a key to open a cupboard; his friend pointing out the chin-ups 'failure.'

Marcus soon appeared carrying a brand new Bullworker. His trainee moved closer to him to take the exercise machine.

"T-shirt off first," he insisted.

Wayne slipped off his blue 'Fly Navy' top and obediently awaited the next, ever difficult, task. He was aware that he was sweating. Moving over to his sports bag Wayne took out a towel and started drying his upper body.

"Who gave you permission to do that," asked Marcus glaring at his friend.

"Sorry, mate," came the reply.

"Punishment," barked Marcus, "see how many chin-ups you can do."

Wayne was forced abandon the Bullworker for more chin-ups. He could not match his earlier score. Marcus offered Wayne a mug of water which only served to make Wayne sweat more.

"Now you can do ten minutes with the Bullworker," said Marcus.

Wayne gripped each end of the exerciser and pushed hard, creating a painful pressure. Marcus was observing his friend's efforts at resilience and muscle building.

Almost an hour had elapsed since the two had entered the building. Marcus called a pause to the intensive training. He instructed Wayne to lie face down on a mat, put his hands behind his head and bend backwards. Marcus, kneeling down beside Wayne, explained that boxers who win bouts are agile and supple. Wayne felt Marcus's hands moving up and down his back in a firm but comforting way. He finished by pulling Wayne's arms from behind creating a curve to the spine.

"I really needed that," replied his friend.

"I know," said Marcus in hushed tones, "but we are not finished yet."

Marcus and Wayne sat on the mat and ran through the programme for the next day. The idea was to invite Reece over for some training.

"I've told him to come here at eleven," explained Wayne, "I hope he's got the bottle to do it." Marcus nodded.

"Yes, but we will just have to see," concluded Marcus.

As Wayne rested, Marcus jumped up to get a pair of boxing gloves.

"Shoes off," said Marcus, thrusting the red gloves towards Wayne.

Marcus directed Wayne to the brand-new hanging punch bag. His friend was still keen to please and accepted the last challenge of the workout.

"I might show you how it's done tomorrow," said Marcus as he brought the training to a close.

All that was left for Wayne was to experience one of the small showers that had been installed on the ground floor. Marcus explained to his friend how to locate them.

"I bet it's like a ship's shower," quipped Wayne.

"Well, that should suit," his friend replied.

--o--

The next day was a typically lazy Sunday. Wayne and Marcus met at Hadrian's Gym for another workout. Malcolm was still abroad visiting friends in Switzerland, so the house was empty.

"What time did you tell Reece to call round," asked Marcus, looking at his friend.

"About eleven," Wayne replied, "but you know what these kids are like... never get out of bed until midday."

Wayne went on to explain that he had to get up, wash and get dressed at all hours when he was part of the Royal Navy. Marcus detected that Wayne wanted to reminisce so suggested going into the house to make coffee.

"I've only got a key to the front," said Marcus, "so we will have to walk round."

It seemed strangely empty without Malcolm. Even with two people inside the feeling was slightly 'unlived in.' Wayne had just finished rinsing his mug in the kitchen sink when the doorbell rang. He hurried towards the hallway, knocking Marcus on the way.

"So, you found the place alright," said Wayne as he greeted Reece.

Wayne explained that they had just finished coffee and wondered if Reece wanted anything to drink. He declined. Wayne detected that Reece looked nervous.

"We've got to go out of the front to get into the back," explained Marcus as they left Saxon Lodge.

As the three entered the gym from the back garden Marcus took Wayne aside and told him to set a good example by changing down to his boxing shorts.

"Whatever you say, me old mate," came the reply, You're the expert in all this."

Whilst Wayne disappeared to get changed Marcus showed Reece around the open space pointing out some of the equipment that Malcolm had generously donated. Reece looked overwhelmed, as if it were his first day at 'big school.'

"Don't worry," said Marcus, touching Reece's arm, "Relax and you'll be fine."

Reece nodded and tried to justify his presence. He gave a long explanation about how Wayne had suggested boxing as a way of controlling his sudden bursts of anger that were getting him detentions at school.

"His mum agrees," interrupted Wayne as he suddenly appeared, wearing a pair of black shorts.

"Make sure you cut out the price tag," quipped Marcus as he pulled the elastic on Wayne's shorts.

Reece at first looked confused, but was soon smiling.

"I only ever see him in his caretaker uniform," admitted Reece.

"What do you think of him now," asked Marcus provocatively.

"Okay," came the muted reply.

Marcus and Wayne briefly made eye contact before Marcus got his friend started on his training. As Wayne began hitting the punch bag Marcus returned to Reece and took him aside. He hoped that some of the youngster's nervousness was dispersing.

"Have you brought along any sports gear," asked Marcus. Reece shook his head. "That's no problem," continued Marcus, "We have spare gloves, but you'll need to be bare-chested."

Reece hesitated as if thinking, but then removed his top clothes in front of Marcus's gaze. Marcus asked him what he did in P.E. lessons at school but Reece replied that he usually got out of them by feigning a dubious illness.

"How old are you," asked Marcus abruptly. Reece said that he was 16. "That's a good age to start," said Marcus looking at his newest recruit.

He noted that Reece was quite slim, even for a sixteen year-old, but stood with a straight back. Marcus saw potential in Reece and hoped that he would commit to the discipline of the gym. He found a spare pair of boxing gloves and thrust them towards Reece, who unexpectedly turned away. Reece had tears flowing from his eyes. Marcus led him into a side enclave and attempted to discover what was wrong.

"Sorry, sorry…. I just don't know," said Reece using his arm to hide the tears. He started to shake. Marcus suggested it might all be too much for him at his stage of life.

"I'm alright now," muttered Reece.

"I think we'll have your shoes and socks off too," said Marcus feeling more directive.

He led Reece back to the punch bag where Wayne had been working for over ten minutes. He was now pacing himself.

"Show Reece how it's done," instructed Marcus, "and you can go slow at first and then build up the tempo."

As Wayne began mentoring Reece, Marcus quietly slipped away like a farm cat on a mission.

He soon returned in his shorts, and wearing Wayne's Fly Navy T-shirt as if it were his own.

"Move aside," said Marcus, "see how the pros do it." Wayne was transfixed by Marcus's rapid and powerful bursts against the punch bag.

"You haven't lost your touch, mate," said Wayne looking on.

As if a point had been made, Marcus moved away and instructed Wayne to use the dumb bells and bench. He walked over to a cupboard and took out a Bullworker, leading Reece to the other end of the gym. Marcus slowly slipped off his T-shirt and began to show Reece the usefulness of the Bullworker exerciser.

"Now put your hand here, said Marcus, "and as I push the bars together feel how the muscle tenses." Reece felt a little uneasy as he touched Marcus's torso.

"Okay, let's catch up with Wayne and you can try the Bullworker yourself," said Marcus. Wayne looked around and stopped what he was doing.

"Twenty press ups," demanded Marcus as he glared at Wayne.

It was almost midday when Wayne said he wanted to end the training session as he had to get back home.

"Lunch with the other half," he joked.

Wayne was soon showered, dried and dressed. Marcus left him his blue T-shirt. With a wave he descended the staircase and out into the fresh air. Marcus watched him leave through a small window.

"You see how many press ups and sit ups you can do," said Marcus as he left to get changed.

He was soon in the gym space again.

Marcus was keen to learn from Reece what he thought of Hadrian's Gym and the equipment.

"You both treated me like an adult," said Reece. Marcus replied that he *was* an adult.

"And I know Wayne thinks the same," said Marcus.

Reece went on to explain that he got so frustrated at home when his mother restricted his movements and treated him like a little child.

"Maybe that's why you get angry sometimes," pondered Marcus, "I know you're a good kid." Reece nodded.

"Plus ... she doesn't want me to join the Paras, but I will," said Reece.

Marcus was beginning to understand a bit more about Reece's world. He wondered if he should bring up the knife incident Wayne talked of but decided it no longer seemed so important.

"What did you think of Wayne's efforts?" asked Marcus. Reece said he was impressed with all that he did.

"He's fit," he continued.

"I bet you didn't expect to see Wayne in a pair of shorts," Marcus joked.

Reece shook his head and laughed nervously. He indicated that he would be back for more training. Marcus looked smug.

"I can get you ready for the 'forces," he said, "but did will be tough. Are you man enough to take it?" Reece affirmed that he most certainly was.

"Why not come back in the afternoon. Just the two of us," suggested Marcus.

Reece said that he would do that.

--o--

Marcus was sitting in Saxon Lodge's impressive library room, waiting for Reece to ring the front door bell. He had taken the liberty of eating some of Malcolm's bourbon biscuits. His gaze was now drawn to a section containing several hardbacks on the Second World War when the door bell sounded.

"So, you decided to come back," he said, "I'm pleased. You made the right decision."

Marcus went on to say that he thought Reece showed courage and that would be good for him in the Paras. Reece admitted to nearly turning back on the journey but decided against it.

"Anyway," he said, "I got my return bus ticket by then." Marcus grinned.

"We all have choices in life," said Marcus. He felt himself slipping into lecture mode. "Not choosing something is also a choice," he continued.

He found it easy to support Reece's desire to join the armed forces but guessed his mother had a different opinion.

"Do it for *you*," emphasised Marcus, "If you want it, you'll achieve it, but you'll have to get really fit."

Marcus asked Reece if he thought he was committed enough to engage with regular training. Reece agreed to put his faith in Marcus and a tough training programme, and the two left the house through the front door for the gym.

"Did you get any shorts," asked Marcus.

Reece said that he had forgotten to bring his school shorts. Marcus told Reece to change down to his y-fronts. Sheepishly, Reece emerged from a more secluded part of the gym space. Marcus pointed to a mat and Reece moved across the floor.

"Flex," instructed Marcus. Reece hesitated. He looked confused.

"When I say flex, you do this," said Marcus, demonstrating. "It shows off your muscles, if you have any," he continued.

"When I say flex, you do it for me. Okay," barked Marcus, taking the part of a Territorial Army P.T. instructor. Reece obliged, bringing his arms up in front of his trainer.

"You'll have to bulk up," Marcus commented.

Reece's trainer now disclosed that he knew the lad had drawn a knife in the presence of his friend.

"Use your anger to power your training," shouted Marcus, as if the session had moved to Colchester Barracks, and then left to get changed.

He soon returned wearing only a pair of black shorts and instructed Reece to bring out all the spare mats to create a square, a couple of mats deep. Both moved on to the springy, rubberised surface. Marcus left the improvised ring and returned with two sets of boxing gloves. Once on, without warning Marcus landed a punch full on Reece's abdomen. He crumpled with the blow on to the mats.

"Fight back ... fight back," shouted Marcus, becoming more agitated.

Reece was on all fours like a wounded animal. He was confused as well as winded. Marcus kicked Reece hard on the backside. He repeated the blows until he saw Reece finally make an attempt to stand.

181

"Ready to use your anger," asked Marcus taunting the lesser fighter.

Reece was half way to standing but Marcus pushed him back on to the rubberised surface again.

"Where's your little knife now, boy," Marcus taunted.

Reece, angered, finally stood up and tried to land a punch on Marcus but he missed, only hitting the air as his trainer moved back. Marcus seized his opportunity, raining blows on Reece's torso.

"Aarh, stop, I give in" cried Reece as he crumpled back on to the mats, "I give in... I give in," begged Reece, looking like a wet mouse in the gaze of a tom cat.

Reece was looking for mercy but Marcus knew what he had to do to bring his protégé on. He walked away, quickly returning with some punch pads.

"Get ready," demanded Marcus before leaving Reece and then returning with a mug of water.

Marcus offered his trainee a sip but then threw the cold liquid at Reece's face. As Reece's anger rose again Marcus quickly put on the pads and absorbed the full force of his opponent's red rage. Blow after blow landed on the pads as Marcus moved from position to position.

"Good... good," came Marcus's encouragement. "Nice and powerful," he continued, "Great work."

--o--

Wayne and Marcus arrived at a café in the heart of the city almost at the same time. Neither had been to 'The River View' before. It was a new venture in an area of run down warehousing and abandoned factories, but had the water nearby. The government had been generous enough to allocate huge sums of money to regenerate the area with ambitious plans for shops, housing, bars and restaurants.

"Haven't been to this bit for ages," said Wayne as he greeted his friend just inside the entrance, "It looks all different."

It had a busy atmosphere for an otherwise remote site.

"Yeah, looks okay," Marcus replied, "They've done a lot of building work around here."

Some red brick Victorian factories were boarded up; others were half demolished creating a fascinating wilderness. Self-seeded buddleia bushes were growing everywhere.

Marcus strolled up to the counter. A group of women had just taken their orders back to a table. As he looked ahead of him, he was perplexed to see such a range of coffees available. He did not recognise most of the names on the board. Smartly dressed staff were working stainless steel machines; pulling levers, boiling pots of hot milk and using what appeared to be concentrated steam.

"Reminds me of the Flying Scotsman," joked Wayne.

"What would you like," asked an eager young man as Marcus composed his thoughts.

"Two coffees," he replied.

"We don't do ordinary coffee," came the response.

Marcus looked embarrassed but glanced towards the board again.

"Okay, two cappuccinos then," he said hoping to get something drinkable back.

After a few minutes the two took their small, fluffy headed drinks to a wooden table.

"I thought I saw Reece yesterday," said Wayne, "on one of my estates. But maybe it wasn't him." Wayne said that the lad who looked like Reece did not react to him sounding his van's horn, or to him shouting his name.

"Doesn't sound like it was him then," said Marcus who went on to disclose that he had invited the lad back to Hadrian's Gym after Wayne had left. Wayne looked perplexed.

"Why," he asked putting down his cup at an angle to the saucer.

"He seems keen, so I pushed him further," explained Marcus.

"I'm keen too," said Wayne waiting for an explanation.

"I know, but Reece wants to join the 'forces," Marcus said.

"But I was in the Royal Navy," snapped Wayne.

"It's not a bloody competition," Marcus retorted, "You are so impossible to deal with."

The two friends sat in silence sipping their exotic coffee. Wayne was staring out of the window. He could just about make out the tops of the boats drifting past. It reminded him of the

Broads holiday and his youth on board naval frigates in hotter climes.

"I was thinking that Sean could be your boxing buddy," said Marcus deliberately breaking an awkward silence.

Wayne suddenly came out of his distant daze and was paying attention again. Marcus shocked his friend by suggesting that Sean could train at the gym. Wayne shook his head.

"No ... No way," he said.

"Come on it could be fun," continued Marcus, grinning.

"I'd thrash him good and proper," replied Wayne.

His loudness was attracting attention from a group of young women sitting nearby. They started chatting and giggling amongst themselves, occasionally looking over. Wayne had not noticed that he was now centre stage.

"Sean is not as bad as you think," said Marcus, "and I'll prove it to you."

Wayne said it was about time he was leaving for home. The two got up, their coffee cups long since cold.

As Wayne walked down the street, he could feel his anger building. It seemed to him to be a mixture of frustration and annoyance but he could not work out what was behind it. His pace was picking up. He slowed briefly to kick a can across the street. It felt good. He longed for another ninety-nine cans to kick.

Jogging along the road, Wayne thought he could smell smoke. He dismissed it, saying to himself it must have been people smoking in 'The River View' and it had got into his clothes. River view, smoky view; Wayne's sense of humour was starting to return. He jogged on with a grin on his face. Wayne wished that he was now in the gym using the punch bag to better ground himself.

He punched the air as if in a real bout. Then it came to him like a knock-out blow; he could see Marcus training Reece, or worse Sean, to fight before he had the chance to prove himself in the ring. He knew then that he had to arrange something himself, and wondered if he could find Max's telephone number at home.

As he rounded the corner he was confronted by a scene of panic. A woman in her thirties was at her front gate in a distressed state. Wayne could see smoke billowing from inside her house; a few people were standing around.

"Please help me, please ...," she begged Wayne, "My little girl's asleep upstairs."

"Where upstairs," shouted Wayne, "where?"

His military training was kicking in and he had to know precisely where to go. She pointed to the box room at the front of the house. Wayne could hear distant sirens. He guessed that someone had called the fire brigade but was determined to go in first.

"What's your girl's name? said Wayne.

"Emily... Emily..." was the frightened response.

Wayne took off his coat, putting it over his head and instructed Emily's mother not to follow him inside.

"Emily," shouted Wayne as he raced up the stairs, his voice being muffled by the coat partially over his head.

He hurried towards the small box room and, lifting the coat, shouted for Emily again. There was smoke everywhere but Wayne could not detect a fire. He shouted the little girl's name over and over, stopping to feel under the bed. Wayne was fighting nausea and giddiness but did not want to give up. He heard a siren and observed blue flashing lights outside. As he turned to go out, he saw the outline of a small child, crouching.

Instinctively he grabbed Emily under his arm and started running down the stairs. Choking, he stumbled straight into the first fireman to attempt a rescue. As the child was lifted away Wayne collapsed in a heap in the front garden.

"Get some oxygen over here," said a fireman waving his arm, "Quick."

As a face mask was applied Wayne was aware of the chaos unfolding all around him, but he could see that Emily had been reunited with her mother. He felt himself passing out.

--o--

Marcus and Wayne had arranged to meet at Hadrian's Gym on Thursday evening. Wayne was keen to resume training and Marcus keen to teach, but his mentor had heard about the fire incident. It had been all over the local media.

185

"Well, look at you, mister hero," was Marcus's greeting.

Wayne felt embarrassed by the fuss saying that anyone would have done the same in the circumstances and he was pleased no one lost their life. He was touched by a 'thank you' message received through the newspaper from Emily's mother.

"Apparently it was a malfunctioning electric blanked," said Wayne. "But I'm here to resume training," he continued.

Marcus wondered if his friend was up to training but handed him a pair of small black trunks and instructed him to get changed. Wayne looked bemused but knew not to question his mentor. He soon returned wearing the Speedos.

"How did you know my size," asked Wayne

Marcus quipped that boxing trainers know everything about their trainees, but he was keen to get Wayne's confidence back.

Wayne wanted to know what progress Reece had made in his one-to-one session earlier.

"I tortured him," said Marcus.

"Okay," replied Wayne. It was not the reaction Marcus was anticipating.

"Didn't you hear what I said," continued Marcus.

Wayne turned towards Marcus with a perplexed 'whatever' expression on his face. Marcus was intrigued.

"Don't worry," he said, "I'm not going to torture you as you need to get back to training slowly."

Marcus was well aware of the effects of smoke inhalation and wanted to see if Wayne's stamina had been diminished.

"I'm almost naked, mate," laughed Wayne nervously, as he was given another instruction.

Marcus started by getting his friend to jog to one end of the gym, and then sprint back. This was repeated several times until Wayne began to flag.

"Can't hear any coughing or wheezing," said Marcus, "which is a good sign."

With that Wayne did start coughing, going red in the face until his mentor provided him with a mug of water.

"Trust you, drama queen," said Marcus, smiling.

After a short break Wayne was using a horizontal bar to practice some chin ups. He managed almost thirty and was happy with that.

"So, what do you think, me old mate," asked Wayne.

The question seemed deliberately open but Marcus commented on Wayne's physique complimenting him on the effort he had put in to get a good tone.

"That means a lot to me," said Wayne resting on a mat.

Wayne was now confident enough to broach the subject of him feeling ready to box in front of an audience. Marcus listened intently as his friend went through a list of reasons why he needed to try for a paid bout.

"I agree," said Marcus as he put a hand on Wayne's shoulder.

Marcus beckoned Wayne saying, "Let's discuss it in Malcolm's library. He's away on business." Wayne hesitated; he felt underdressed for the house.

Sensing the issue, Marcus turned and said, "Come like that. You are still in training."

Wayne did not think to question his mentor as they left the gym via the external staircase, but felt a refreshing breeze across his skin. It momentarily reminded him of being on Glastonbury Tor.

Wayne and Marcus sat opposite each other in identical dark green autumn patterned armchairs. Marcus leaned over to switch an electric fire on.

"I agree you are ready to box," Marcus said, "but it's not going to be all plain sailing."

Wayne asked why he was not allowed to change before leaving the gym and Marcus explained he was making the point that boxers are always in the limelight.

"If you feel uncomfortable now then maybe boxing is not your thing," said Marcus, "You will be closely observed by an audience. Sometimes it feels sadistic. "You will have to deal with a bit of voyeurism... like me watching you now... Do you understand what I'm saying?"

Wayne nodded, but quietly acknowledged to himself that he *did* feel uncomfortable.

"Listen, man, listen ... It's a bit like being a Roman Gladiator dying in front of a crowd. They prefer you to die slowly and stoically," said Marcus, "You'll get punished – it's not like messing about here in the gym."

"I know you've had a tough upbringing," replied Wayne. This time it was Marcus who nodded.

"I want to say something," said Marcus, "no doubt brought on by me thinking you are ready for a public bout."

Wayne looked surprised by the remark. Marcus spoke again about the time he was with a Tyneside family as a naive teenager.

"On the Broads trip I told you a bit about how I had to undergo physical ordeals," said Marcus.

"You did," replied Wayne, "That shocked, then angered, me."

Marcus reiterated that anger was a part of boxing culture, and that his trainee would have to learn to use it. He used the analogy of the U.S. Marines being trained.

"Not all get through," said Marcus, "Mainly the drop outs lack real aggression, or 'grit.'"

Wayne pondered on the subject and then remembered that his friend had said he regularly got the belt as a punishment.

"That's correct," said Marcus.

Wayne wanted to know what it was like, and if Marcus thought things like that still occurred.

"I'd say they still occur," came the considered reply.

Marcus said that the punishments were a regular part of his gym life. After refusing a water ordeal he was obliged to accept the belt on a number of occasions.

"That must have been hard," commented Wayne, desperate to learn a bit more.

Marcus said the punishments were a mix of physical pain and humiliation.

"Like I said before, they wanted to add in humiliation so an audience was often invited to watch," Marcus said. "When you sign up with one of these underground agents you don't know what you are letting yourself in for," he continued. Wayne nodded.

"Are you prepared for anything," Marcus asked.

Wayne said he thought he could cope with the training and the punishments dished out randomly for failure.

"I have to prove myself," said Wayne.

"It's not like me giving you some minor punishments," reiterated Marcus, "Their punishments could be akin to the ones I underwent."

188

"Maybe you need to step up the punishments," mumbled Wayne. Marcus's thoughts were interrupted by his friend speaking again.

"I've come over all goose pimples," he said, "But you believe I'm ready, don't you?"

Marcus told his friend to go back to the gym and get changed. Wayne stood up and made his way to the door. He was about to leave but hesitated.

"Marcus, me old mate," said Wayne, "I think the wife's having an affair with one of our neighbours.

Marcus said he was sorry to hear that.

"It's okay," Wayne replied, "It's like I don't care. I feel my destiny is somewhere else."

Marcus did not know what else to say, but he empathised.

"It's the loneliness of being oneself, me old mate," said Wayne, "If you understand what I mean?" "We had a sort of initiation club on Ajax," Wayne continued, "But the thing was I was too insular to get involved. I wish I could go back in time."

Marcus acknowledged that he knew *'Ajax'* was a Leander class frigate but his mind was no longer in the room. He was struggling to process his feelings and what his friend was saying; they seemed to be merging into one.

--o--

Reece turned the corner and could see Wayne already waiting outside the swimming baths. He hurried forward with a nervous smile on his face.

"Got all your gear then," Wayne asked, "else you'll be swimming in your y-fronts.".

Reece nodded and put his blue back-pack on the ground beside him. Several people were going through the grand entrance to the Victorian baths with its fussy red brickwork and dark green tiles. Reece was wondering why both of them were just standing outside.

"I've got to wait for someone else," said Wayne.

Reece wanted to know if they were waiting for Marcus. Wayne shook his head. He explained that Marcus was not a swimmer.

189

"What do you think of Marcus, then," enquired Wayne, breaking the silence. Reece gave his friend a sideways look.

"You can say," continued Wayne, trying to get an answer.

"He's okay ... he's quite tough ... the training is tough," Reece replied, wondering if he had said the right thing.

"If you are going into the armed forces the training will be tough," said Wayne, "Stick with Marcus and you'll be thanking him one day." Reece started to relax.

"Well, fancy that," said Max as he hugged Wayne.

He had suddenly come upon Wayne whilst he was distracted. Max was dressed in a long sheepskin coat and was holding a large cigar. The air was suddenly full of Havana. Max assumed Reece was Wayne's his son but Wayne explained he was the son of someone he knew.

"Oooh, if you say so," said Max, laughing.

Wayne had forgotten how flamboyant the boxing arranger was, but was both unnerved and pleased to see him again. As the three moved towards the entrance, Max said he would pay for all the tickets but he would observe from the spectators' gallery.

"Thanks, me old mate," said Wayne as they parted ways within the building.

Wayne and Reece headed towards the changing cubicles.

The small boxes looked as if they had not been painted since the 1940s. They were the original Victorian woodwork; an impressively sturdy structure. Wayne stepped inside and slid his metal catch closed. He wondered how many swimmers had been 'trapped' inside cubicles by tight latches, which brought on a mischievous smile.

It did not take him long to change down into the pair of Speedos Marcus had donated. As he adjusted them, he found himself thinking that Marcus was very intuitive of his needs, and was pleased he had him as a friend. Reece's earlier description of 'tough' seemed to resonate. Wayne was still saying the word to himself when he slid the door catch back and stepped outside. Reece was soon beside him.

"Feeling cold," asked Wayne.

He could see that Reece had his arms protectively across his chest.

"Come on then Reece," said Wayne as they headed for the warm slipper bath and then the main pool.

The air smelled strongly of chlorine. Wayne was straight in with a dive but Reece decided it was safer to climb down the metal steps into the unforgiving chill. Wayne was treading water, watching Reece. He had no idea of how good a swimmer he was. Wayne then caught a glimpse of Max higher up and wondered if he too was being observed. Marcus's words from a week earlier still rang in his ears.

Wayne felt he *was* being watched, and judged, and the thought of that momentarily brought on a wave of anxiety. As he started to wonder if wearing Speedos was a good idea, he suddenly thought that everyone was watching everyone else.

"Hey," shouted Wayne after a spray of water hit him full in the face.

Reece swam off laughing like a naughty nine-year old. Wayne filled his lungs and dived below the surface, twisting his body to swim in the vague direction of where he had last seen Reece. After a few seconds he surfaced for air, looking for Reece at the same time. Another underwater glide allowed him to come up just behind the younger swimmer. He pulled his colleague from behind but was aware that the pool life guard was glancing over; about to say something. 'The look says it all,' thought Wayne as he composed himself.

"I'll race you to the end of the pool," said Reece, wondering what trick Wayne was about to play on him.

The two spent about twenty minutes swimming lengths or just going across the shallow end. It was evident to Wayne that Reece was a proficient swimmer once he found his confidence. Wayne moved himself to the shallow end corner, near the steps. He was looking at some of the fathers with their children and wondered what it would have been like to have kids of his own. He knew that his wife did not want children, so it was never discussed. He was distracted by Reece joining him.

"Did Marcus buy you those trunks," asked Reece, looking below the waterline.

Wayne felt himself getting flushed. He dipped under the chlorinated water to save himself.

"Yes," he said as he surfaced, confirming that they *were* a gift from Marcus.

With a thud and a splash both swimmers unexpectedly got a soaking as a young man jumped straight off the side near them. Wayne was curious to know why Reece had asked his question but he declined to say what was on his mind.

"I'm meeting Max in the café after we get out. I'm going to see if I can get a boxing contract from him," said Wayne, bringing the subject back to his agenda.

"Will you get hurt boxing," asked Reece.

Wayne shook his head and explained with good training and paced stamina, injuries would be kept to a minimum. He said that he appreciated the faith Marcus put in him and all that his friend was doing for him.

"Reece, we're lucky to have Marcus, and he recently told me I was ready for a proper, paid bout," explained Wayne, "In addition Malcolm is fantastic in providing the gym space free of charge."

Reece's gaze was still on the colours the water was making on Wayne's lower body. He seemed deep in thought.

"Has Marcus ever hurt you," Reece enquired.

"No, what on earth makes you ask that, me old mate," Wayne responded.

Reece was quiet, peering into the water and still wondering about Wayne's gift.

"In fact, Reece," said Wayne, "I wish Marcus would punish me more, just to toughen me up."

Wayne gripped Reece around the torso and pulled him under the water, immediately releasing him. Wayne was soon at the edge of the pool.

"Time to go," he said with a pull on to the third step out. The two were on firm ground again.

"We need to get this chlorine off ourselves," said Wayne as he beckoned Reece towards the showers.

"Freezing," Reece gasped, as he stepped under the cold water.

The two agreed that they were not going to stay under for long and were soon inside the cubicles getting dried off and dressed. As a fully clothed Reece started to walk away Wayne took him aside and tried to explain again why he wanted to meet up with Max.

"I just need to prove myself, maybe like you do," he said. Reece looked on knowingly. "You can go home now," Wayne continued, "and I'll catch up with Max in the café."

Reece nodded and the two went their separate ways.

--o--

"Well, hello there, Charles Atlas," said Max as he greeted Wayne with a hug.

Wayne felt flushed again. He could feel his face going red and realised that he felt uncomfortable in the presence of Max but he did not entirely understand why. He thought it might be because of Max's flamboyant style, and way of speaking. Wayne had spent most of his life trying to hide his insecurities.

It now felt like Max brought them to the surface so that the whole café could witness them. He was aware that he had kept his insecurities from his naval shipmates, and his wife. On the surface he was Wayne 'happy-go-lucky' but underneath he was Wayne who had to constantly prove he was a man.

Max beckoned Wayne to a table in the corner. There were already two mugs of coffee waiting.

"Oh, that was presumptuous of me," said Max, as Wayne was about to sit down, "You can have what you want."

Wayne replied that coffee was fine, but his eyes were more on the tempting cakes behind the glass counter.

"You're confident in the water," said Max.

Wayne agreed and explained it had been useful as his first career had been in the Royal Navy. Max's eyes seemed to light up as he spoke passionately of the need for discipline in the ring, adding that Wayne must already know that.

"Yes," replied Wayne "but I think I need more discipline in my life – that's what is attracting me to boxing." Wayne was still feeling nervous but he knew deep inside that if he did not commit himself now, the moment would be lost forever.

"I've seen you in the water. I know you are fit enough to box," said Max, "but there will be hurdles to overcome."

He outlined his plan for Wayne. Max stated that the next stage would be a medical and for him to see how well he sparred. Wayne said he was keen to get involved and felt committed.

"Assuming you pass all of that, and still want to continue," said Max, "the next bit would be getting you a trainer."

Wayne said he thought it would be Max that would be training him but his colleague pointed out he was more of a manger than trainer. Wayne found himself feeling relieved that someone other than Max would train him. He did not know why.

"Some people find being allocated to a new manager a bit daunting," said Max.

Max attempted to convey that it was a bit like a 'meat market.' He said he would probably be in a room with up to three or four prospective trainers who would grill him, look him over physically and maybe want to see him use the boxing equipment.

"Some people don't like the limelight so drop out at that point," explained Max.

Wayne replied that his friend, Marcus, had said the same thing.

"Clever lad," came Max's quick response.

Wayne was confused as to who Max was referring to – himself or Marcus.

"Anything else you want to ask or say," enquired Max.

Wayne's head was spinning. He had not realised the full emotional impact on him hearing that he could soon be boxing in front of an audience. Wayne shook his head.

"Good lad," said Max, "Now I want to say a bit more."

Wayne finished the last mouthful of coffee and sat back in his chair, eager to take in the next piece of information.

"Wayne, some of your potential trainers are involved with bouts that, shall we say, are more Spartan," continued Max. He looked perplexed.

"Spartan," Wayne asked.

Max went to explain that some boxers fight naked, similar to ancient times. Before Wayne could take it all in Max was saying that these bouts pay more. He felt himself getting hotter and was sure his face was turning red.

"What do you say," asked Max.

Wayne found his voice faltering but could muster enough words to indicate he would think about it. Max suggested that Marcus could help his friend with the correct decision.

With that Max stood up to leave. Wayne copied.

"I'll give you a call soon," said Max.

After a hand-shake both were making their way out of the swimming baths. As Wayne walked back to his car, he knew he felt a mixture elation and trepidation, in equal measures. It was similar to when he opened his letter telling him that he had been accepted into the Royal Navy. As he put the key into the ignition, he reassured himself that everything would be fine.

Wayne had only been driving for a few minutes when he spotted a red telephone box ahead. He parked the car just as a previous user was leaving. Wayne put his hand into his pocket to confirm he had enough loose change to feed into the box on the assumption his friend was at home. He was.

"I've been accepted, mate," said Wayne, almost shouting down the phone.

Marcus told him to calm down and asked what he had been accepted into.

"Max is going to arrange a boxing contract," Wayne replied "You remember Max, don't you," he continued.

Marcus acknowledged he did recall Max, and then went on to congratulating his friend. He pointed out that the work had only just started.

"You'll have to use the gym more," said his mentor.

"Yes, yes, I know...," said Wayne, "I'm definitely up for it." Marcus enquired what the next stage would be.

"I think it's a medical, and then getting allocated to a trainer. Well at least I think that's what Max said," Wayne explained.

He still sounded excited as he put his hand in his pocket for another 10p coin. Wayne brought up the suggestion that some boxers fight naked. He wanted to hear what Marcus thought of that.

"If you are up for it, you get paid more," said Marcus. He went on to explain that some audiences wanted to see people box that way.

"Think of the ancient Greek lifestyle," said Marcus sarcastically as he attempted to bring the call to a close.

Chapter 11

ACCEPTANCE AND CONTROL

Wayne turned off Hagham Road into the spacious car park of Featherstone Hall. There were numerous spaces to choose from. He decided on an area of the car park with no other vehicles nearby, and positioned his car between the faded white lines marking the bays.

No sooner had he turned off the Marina's ignition then another car parked beside him. 'Isn't that typical,' he muttered to himself, 'Of all the places ...' He looked over into the next car and saw what he assumed to be another potential boxing candidate inside. He was not wrong.

"Hi, mate," said Wayne as he squeezed out of his car, holding on to the door. "Are you here for the boxing assessment," he continued.

"Yes, I am... I'm David by the way," said the stranger.

Wayne introduced himself as he went to the boot of his car to find his sports bag. David looked a few years younger than Wayne and appeared confident. Wayne wondered if the confidence was a 'front' and, like him, David felt anxious but would not allow himself to show it.

As the two walked into the community hall carrying their sports kit, Wayne asked David if he had come far. Before he could answer someone else spoke.

"Well, greetings boys," boomed a familiar voice from the stairwell. It was Max.

He explained he would introduce both candidates to the trainers waiting upstairs and then leave for another appointment. The three walked up the stairs and then into a small hall laid out with various bits of gym equipment. Wayne momentarily felt a rush of anxiety but tried to hide it, thinking of the talks Marcus had given him over the past few months.

Three trainers introduced themselves and there was a flurry of hand shaking. Wayne forgot their names as soon as they had been voiced, but he held on to the safety of knowing Max and David.

"We have some good trainers here," stated Max in a firm voice, "but you have to prove yourself to them over the next hour or so." He cleared his throat.

"They are looking for new talent but they don't have to take anyone here. Oh yes, we are expecting another guy to arrive," he continued.

Just as he had finished speaking a young man, carrying a branded sports bag, came through the door. Then another round of hand shaking took place. This time Wayne remembered the names, Mark, Alan, James and last boxer Christopher by repeating them over in his head.

The three candidates were instructed to change into their shorts, then return and put on a pair of boxing gloves, which Wayne could see on a side table. He sensed that it was a case of 'every man for himself' from now on. Wayne took the initiative by getting undressed quickly and coming straight out and heading for the gloves. They were soon on.

"Well done that man," shouted Alan.

Wayne was soon followed by the other two. He glanced over, mentally comparing himself to David and Christopher as Marcus had taught him; wondering how good they would be. He also found himself judging Christopher's choice in shorts – pale blue with floral patterns. Wayne felt himself more professional in black shorts.

"David, you start on the punch bag, and Wayne and Christopher in the middle, here," instructed Mark.

Wayne took a deep breath and awaited the order to fight. He was correct, and the two commenced boxing in front of the trainers. It seemed that Christopher was holding back and there followed a few minutes of gentle sparring. Wayne was wondering how much experience Christopher had in the ring. He was the youngest of the group.

"Get stuck in there," shouted James.

Wayne did not know who his comments were aimed at but redoubled his efforts and landed a punch squarely on Christopher's jaw. The blow sent his opponent staggering backwards but Christopher managed not to fall. Alan stopped the bout and all three candidates were instructed to swap around with Wayne now facing David in the middle of the room.

As the second session commenced Wayne told himself he was lucky to be boxing twice in a row. He sensed David had more focus, so was determined not to let his concentration drop away. After nearly five minutes of intense boxing Mark put his hand up to end the fight. He had two chairs ready and said they would have a short break and go into another round.

"In the middle," shouted Mark, as he beckoned the two to stand up. This was the cue for the second round.

As Wayne weaved in and out of David's space, dancing around his opponent, he briefly caught a glimpse of Christopher. He was standing gloveless and watching the action unfold.

"And stop," said Alan, holding his hand up.

All three trainers offered a few tips to both Wayne and David before instructing them to remove their gloves. Wayne returned to the table but was aware that Christopher was now missing from the hall. He ventured to ask.

"We've had to let Christopher go," explained James, "He's a good candidate, but not quite ready."

Wayne felt sorry for the lad and hoped he had not taken it too hard. He was keenly aware of his part in Christopher's downfall but could 'hear' the nagging voice of Marcus telling him to 'man up.' Wayne knew he only had one chance to prove himself.

The two candidates were introduced to the gym equipment. Wayne started off with the dumb bells. He was used to these, and working hard with them did not faze him. He made sure he was facing the trainers. In his mind Wayne believe he had the edge over David's physique, which, he thought, was more akin to a rugby player.

During the next twenty minutes or so both candidates swopped around, practising press-ups, chin-ups, using weights and a medicine ball. They were also required to sprint from one end of the room to the other. Finally, first David, and then Wayne had to use a Bullworker exerciser.

Alan pointed out that Max had left jugs of water in the kitchen area that the two could use. Wayne decided to hold back and let David go in. He was soon in the main room again drenched in sweat. James brought the two together in the middle of the space.

"Would any of you two box like the ancient Greeks – naked," came his unexpected question.

Wayne felt himself getting hot and he looked at the floor. He was glad that he did not take any of the water on offer. It seemed an alarming question to have to deal with, but he had been warned about such things by Marcus. An uneasy silence was broken when David declined. The trainers were looking at Wayne for an answer and he eventually felt he had to reply.

"I guess so," he said.

"That sounds a bit half-hearted," said one of the trainers but Wayne could not recognise who had voiced it.

David was instructed to get changed and leave the building. Wayne felt it would soon be the defining moment to prove himself worthy.

"Slip off your shorts, Wayne, and go over and use the punch bag," instructed James.

Wayne knew he must comply but found it difficult to slip off his shorts wearing boxing gloves. As he tried to work down the elasticated waist, he realised he was getting nowhere fast.

"Okay, Wayne, you could have asked for help," said James, "but you'll do a forfeit instead."

As he looked around the room Wayne noticed that Alan and Mark had gone. Wayne turned to face James.

"That's right it's just the two of us now," said his potential new trainer.

James helped Wayne off with his gloves and then headed for the kitchen. He came back holding a mug of water. Wayne wondered what his forfeit would be.

"Drink this," he said, offering it up to Wayne.

He was sweating as much as David had been earlier, which told him he had put a lot of effort into the earlier gym work. James threw him a towel, but he wished his tormentor had thrown him back his shorts.

"You can walk away now with your head held high or submit to the forfeit, said James."

Wayne felt he had come too far to turn back so agreed to his final ordeal of the day.

"Okay, kneel down, lean slightly back and grip your ankles," instructed James.

Wayne felt very exposed by this but turned his thoughts to Marcus. James was missing from the room but soon came back with an apple threaded with a long string. James dangled near Wayne's mouth telling him to take a bite. Wayne knew it was a bobbin apple; always impossible to bite.

Wayne moved backwards and forwards, right and left but could not get a bite from the apple. He was feeling both frustrated and humiliated, wondering why he had allowed himself to be put in such a position. Suddenly James handed Wayne the apple, telling him to go and get changed. As Wayne stood up James explained that he was seriously considering taking him on.

"I have a few doubts," he confessed, "But I'm almost there."

Wayne felt he was on the cusp of something life changing and desperately wanted to hear a definite 'yes' from James.

"Do you want me to start on the naked punch bag now," asked Wayne.

James touched him on the shoulder and told him to get dressed. Wayne wondered what that meant. He felt deflated, like a balloon with most of the air taken out of it. As he wearily put his clothes back on, he was convincing himself he had failed. He wondered if James thought his physique was not up to his standard.

Wayne looked dejected as he came back to the middle of the room. He slung his sports bag over his shoulder and was about to leave when he heard that he would be taken on.

"But I thought ...," said Wayne in amazement.

James asked him what was on his mind. Wayne replied that he thought he was too old for a boxing contract or that his physique needed more work. James laughed.

"You are not too old and you should be proud of your physique," James replied, "I can see you've put in a great deal of hard work and training to get to this stage. Max was right in recommending you."

"Thanks, mate, I won't let you down," said Wayne as the two went their separate ways out of the building.

Wayne's mood bounced back like a child being given his favourite toy; he now felt elated. As he left the hall, he was struck how the weather had changed. The champion felt the cooling of drizzle on his face as he walked to his car. Wayne put his key into the lock, twisted it, and pulled up the boot. His sports bag was soon inside.

The car park was eerily empty, the silence only broken by the car boot slamming shut. As Wayne walked around to get in to the driver's seat, he was aware of someone getting out of one of the few cars still left in the car park. It was David. He had moved his car nearer the exit but seemed anxious to talk.

"How did it go," he asked as soon as he was in range of hearing.

"Great, me old mate, just great. I got through," Wayne replied.

"So glad to hear that," said David, thrusting out his right hand.

He thought that he had 'mucked up big time,' but Wayne assured him he had done well. The two stood in the drizzle, slowly getting wetter, until David suggested they sit in his car. Wayne was keen to see what the inside of a new Volkswagen Golf was like.

"No metal dashboard then," said Wayne, "It would look good in blue."

"I'm sorry mate," said Wayne, "I'm getting your seat a bit damp."

David did not seem the least concerned. He was curious to know what occurred after he left the room, and whether Wayne did present himself naked.

"Yes," said Wayne.

He paused to reflect on what had happened in front of James.

"Sorry. just curious," added David.

Wayne acknowledged this and described what had happened.

"I'm all mixed up and my head is in a fog," he continued.

David said that he desperately wanted to be able to go naked but nagging fears stopped him at the last moment.

"I'm still regretting my decision," he pondered, "I've lost my best chance to box."

Wayne agreed that his thoughts were similar, and that eventually led him to undertake the forfeit, despite his embarrassment.

"It felt humiliating," added Wayne, glancing at David, "A bit sadistic, as my mate Marcus hinted it might be."

201

Wayne talked more about Marcus saying that his friend had got him so far but he still was unsure whether he could box naked in front of an audience. David was intrigued about Wayne's relationship with Marcus.

"I'd like to meet him," said David, "You talk of him as if he's some sort of guru."

Wayne was looking straight out of the half open window, still processing the day.

--o--

Wafting tobacco smoke reminded Marcus of the first time he had met Malcolm. He reflected on how everyone's lives had changed over the course of just a year. The atmosphere in the agricultural venue remained electric, and Phil Collins's 'In the Air Tonight' started to play through the sound system. Marcus thought the music an appropriate build up to the finale.

"Here it is," said David, turning towards Marcus.

David had seen the compare step into the middle of ring. Marcus could hardly wait to witness his friend's first paid fight.

"I just hope he wins this one," David exclaimed, "He's almost obsessed with it all." Marcus nodded.

As he looked around in the half-light it seemed there was still a large crowd of spectators awaiting the final bout of the evening. The compare took the microphone as the last two fighters nimbly entered the ring, and was soon confidently announcing their names and how many fights they had. Marcus could see that Wayne had a big grin on his face, and was pleased that he had not lost his confidence.

"In the red corner give a warm welcome to new kid Wayne Bradshaw, and in the blue corner welcome back Joshua Ellis."

Each boxer flexed in turn in a ritual to Zeus going back the first Olympic games. There were cheers and applause, with a few indistinguishable comments all jumbled in a melting pot of babbling testosterone sound.

"You can tell Wayne has really put in the training," said David.

Marcus agreed and explained that his friend had used the gym almost every day during the build up to the fight.

"You gave him a good talking to that evening we were all at that pub," David observed.

Before anyone could say anything else, the audience were on their feet shouting encouragement and whistling their near exhausted enthusiasm. It was too noisy to conduct a conversation. The old barn seemed to be alive to the sounds of the men who were expecting sweat, if not blood. Marcus had to pause as he could not make himself heard. He glanced to his right and saw that Oliver was fully engaged with the moment.

"They look reasonably well matched," commented Oliver as he spoke directly into Marcus's ear. He got a nod back.

"Seconds out, round one," announced the compare as the bell rang to formally start the fight.

Wayne showed that he could take the initiative from the off, but as Marcus silently observed his friend he wondered if he was being too enthusiastic. He hoped Wayne had heeded his advice to pace every round.

In the initial seconds Wayne was able to get a few punches onto his opponent's torso. He went in hard. Half way through the round the more experienced Joshua was able to land a punch on Wayne's jaw. He stumbled back, but quickly recovered. Three minutes were up; it was the end of the first round.

"Pace yourself, man," shouted Marcus.

He was not sure if Wayne had caught his advice in the noise and confusion.

"The crowd's so loud," commented Oliver. He wanted an explanation from Marcus.

Marcus thought the onlookers expected the virgin to lose spectacularly. Marcus's eyes were fixed on Wayne as the second round got off to a slower start. Perhaps his protégé had heard him shouting advice above the screaming crowd, he pondered. To Marcus's trained eye both boxers now seemed evenly matched and the fight was proceeding in a more thoughtful way. The audience was quieter, with only a few comments along the lines of 'get stuck in.' It was now Marcus's time to grin.

As the second round came to a close Marcus turned to Oliver with, "So far, so good."

"Yeah, he's holding up well for the newbie," Oliver replied.

Wayne was in his corner being fussed over, but it was soon the start of the third round.

Marcus wondered why the group had sat so far from the front; so far from the action. There was an element of Wayne's first paid bout being something of an anti-climax. Marcus had been a big part of his friend's training but felt somehow disconnected. He cleared his mind by looking ahead to the ring. He considered Wayne looked determined enough to go on despite a slight swelling to his upper lip.

"He's taken a lot of punches," observed a concerned Oliver.

Marcus assured him that Wayne would be fine.

"I've instilled grit into him," Marcus commented.

Yet deep down Marcus was troubled. He could see that Wayne's body was being pummelled by the more experienced boxer. Marcus was all too aware that he had encouraged Wayne to embark on a boxing career. As the bell for the ending of the third round sounded Marcus realised that he had not been concentrating on the fight, but on his own thoughts.

"You look miles away – everything alright," asked Oliver, touching Marcus on the shoulder

Marcus nodded incongruently.

The fourth round was now underway. Despite a swollen lip Wayne seemed to be gathering his 'second wind.' Two upper cuts in quick succession sent Wayne's opponent stumbling backwards. The crowd was getting louder with lots of shouts all jumbled into one melee of testosterone fuelled contradictory sound. Marcus's head was equally confused. He was no longer looking at the ring.

"Aah," exclaimed David.

The crowd were in uproar again. Marcus looked up. He could see Joshua on the canvass being counted out.

"A knockout," said Oliver.

Marcus was now standing, partially to get a better view and partially in unison with the crowd.

"Wicked …," shouted David, waving his fist.

The bout had come to an unexpected end and Wayne had won his first paid fight. From afar, he looked pleased with himself. Joshua managed to regain his senses as he stood in line with Wayne, the referee holding up the grinning victor's left arm. As the spectators started to disperse Marcus wondered if the fight had been 'all too easy.' He had not come to terms with what had just happened; it felt surreal.

Oliver and David had things to do, so decided to leave with the majority of the crowd as ABBA's 'Super Trouper' played. Marcus shook their hands and thanked them for coming.

"I wish it could have been me in the ring," commented David, "but I'd have to have had you as my trainer."

With that Marcus found himself on his own wondering how long Wayne would be before leaving the venue. Marcus was not wearing a watch so lost track of time. The whole venue seemed eerily quiet; a contrast to what had occurred just twenty minutes prior.

Marcus decided his best option was to try to follow any sounds. He moved closer to where the thought he heard people speaking. It was when he was close to a doorway which led to a dimly lit area, that he caught a glimpse of a naked Wayne in the distance.

"Are you looking for someone," came a voice from behind.

Marcus turned around to see a casually dressed man who seemed part of the boxing management team."

Just waiting for one of the last boxers to come out. Wayne Bradshaw is his name," he replied.

"Down here," came a vaguely familiar voice.

Marcus looked down a corridor to see Max, wearing his trade mark sheepskin coat, beckoning him forward. Marcus approached the two and was wondering why Wayne had still not got dressed. He was sensitive to his friend's embarrassment but could do little about it.

"A slight problem," said Max.

Marcus tried to focus on his face to avoid embarrassing Wayne.

"In here," said Max, pointing to a side room, "It's a lot more private."

Max pulled out three grimy plastic stacking chairs and arranged them in a circle. Wayne was the first to sit down, leaning forward. Marcus noticed he had some redness around his upper body, and parts of his face, but seemed largely unscathed.

"The thing is," said Max, "it was a bit embarrassing Wayne winning the bout. Good on him, but it wasn't really meant to happen. Now I've got the bookies complaining." He turned to Marcus.

"I need a favour from Wayne," he continued, "You know exactly what I mean, don't you Marcus?"

Marcus nodded; he understood all too well what had just occurred.

Max suggested it was time Wayne signed up to a naked bout. Marcus thought back to the time he had warned Wayne about such shows and wondered if he had sufficiently prepared his friend for the real world of underground boxing. He also wondered if he had made a mistake in encouraging his friend to get involved in the first place. After all, he thought, he had himself been through some terribly abusive episodes during his time as a boxer.

"Sit up straight, Wayne," snapped Max, "Stop slouching."

Wayne moved back in the chair as if he had been given an electric shock. It was impossible for Marcus not to notice all of Wayne's naked body a few feet in front of him. He felt a deep empathy for his friend.

Max and Marcus were talking about Wayne as if he were not in the room. When asked directly, Wayne could not commit to a naked bout. Marcus tried to gently persuade him. He felt it was the more preferable option.

"Well," said Max, turning to Marcus, "you know exactly what needs to happen. Let's hope that you *can* make it happen."

There were tones of velvet menace in his voice. Max got up and said he would leave Marcus and Wayne alone to come to the 'correct' decision. As soon as Max had left the room Marcus stood up and stacked the two redundant plastic chairs back in the corner.

He beckoned Wayne to stand up. Now all the chairs had been put away. Wayne said that he assumed everyone would be proud of him, achieving a win on his first paid bout. He was beginning to see that the dark world of boxing was not like that.

"Man, you've got yourself in a fix and the only way out is to agree to what Max wants," insisted Marcus, "Can't you understand?"

Wayne felt exposed. Marcus detected that Wayne was still procrastinating; still wondering what best to do. He was becoming impatient and feared Max would soon return.

"Do you want to be Max's slave," asked a frustrated Marcus. "I'd rather be your slave, me old mate," Wayne sarcastically replied, with a grin.

Marcus felt his frustration rising, he still was not sure Wayne was taking the whole situation seriously.

"Well," said Marcus. "if you are my slave, I'm ordering you to agree to the naked bout."

Wayne shook his head, saying he had to think about it. With that Marcus sprung forward like a wild cat. He pushed Wayne hard against the wall and with his right hand gently grasped his friend's testicles.

"What… what are you doing, me old mate," Wayne grunted.

"Agree," responded Marcus, giving them a prolonged squeeze.

"Arrh … okay, okay," grunted Wayne.

Marcus loosened his grip as Wayne relented. Wayne was standing with his hands protecting his genitals when the door opened. It was Max.

"I see you've got your friend firmly in hand," he said, "That's the way to handle him... nice and firm."

Marcus thought he must have been listening all along, just the other side of the door. Max knew Wayne would enter his first naked bout. Finally, the victorious boxer was allowed to get dressed.

--o--

Wayne parked his car in Albert Drive and the two were soon out and crunching up the driveway to the house where Marcus had his rented flat. The approach was dark, with old yews crowding in. Something unseen scurried in the undergrowth. Marcus put his key into the solid Victorian front door and swung it open, stepping inside the musty hall.

"Get yourself in, you tart," he quipped, turning to his friend behind him.

They were soon walking up the tatty staircase towards flat 5. Marcus remained silent until he entered his flat. He did not want his neighbours to hear any bickering between friends. Marcus stepped inside, letting out a sigh, followed by Wayne.

"Sit on that chair," said Marcus pointing forward, "I'll get some ointment."

He explained to his friend that he would put some anti-bruising balm on his friend's face, and then leave him to do his own chest and arms. The idea was for Wayne to stay overnight. Marcus switched his television on. An episode of 'Columbo' was half way through. As the one-eyed detective analysed the evidence concealed from him, Marcus was in position applying the healing ointment to his friends bruised face.

"If your other half could see you now," Marcus joked.

Wayne did not think it so funny. Marcus suggested his friend go in to the guest bedroom and apply some of the ointment to his torso. Wayne took the glass container and walked through.

"I'm going to put a pizza in the oven," shouted Marcus as he turned up the heat.

The fridge was the next place to look for some bits of salad. Marcus was no cook, preferring to drink rather than eat, but he felt obliged to be the good host whilst Wayne was staying.

"What do you think," asked Wayne as he remerged into the lounge.

"Nice arms," replied Marcus, trying to be provocative. He achieved his aim of making Wayne blush.

"I don't know why you are blushing," Marcus continued, "as I've seen *all* of you now."

"And virtually handled all of me too," quipped Wayne, grinning.

Marcus pondered on whether he had been too harsh in persuading his friend that he had to agree to Max's agenda, but he did not detect any bad feelings.

Wayne wondered if a whiskey was on offer. Marcus explained he could only have a very watered-down mix.

He handed the glass to his friend with, "In case you have received a head injury." Marcus's own drink was stronger.

"Mind you," said Marcus after taking a mouthful of alcohol, "anyone would think you did have a head injury the way you acted in that room with Max and me."

"If you had not agreed to the naked bout, I'm sure Max would have forced me to take part instead," he snapped.

Wayne said he did not think of that; he was still high on ego, confusion and adrenalin.

"People make money," said Marcus, "Don't ever try to cut their supply of money off."

Wayne was slumped in an armchair, slowing sipping his watered-down drink. The message was beginning to take hold.

"Yeah, you're right as usual," Wayne admitted.

Some of his earlier energy had dissipated, and seemed to be drifting into a more philosophical mood. Marcus asked his friend if he was tired. He shook his head, and took a sip of his drink. The smaller bedroom would be Wayne's for the night. Marcus did not want to keep him up if he wanted to rest.

"Do you believe in reincarnation," asked Wayne.

Marcus thought it a strange question, seemingly coming from nowhere. He felt obliged to answer honestly.

"Yes," he replied, awaiting more detail.

Wayne said he was convinced that he was a sailor on a ship in either the eighteen or nineteenth centuries. He said he really did believe it, and occasionally had dreams about it.

"You see," said Wayne, "I got it a bit wrong then too."

Marcus wanted to know what he meant by this.

"I think I was cheeky to some of the officers and didn't do something," Wayne continued.

Marcus rolled his eyes, thinking of what had occurred earlier in the day.

"I was a bit of a know-it-all and that led me to getting the lash," Wayne said.

"That makes sense," replied Marcus sipping his drink.

Marcus saw his friend looking over at the bottle of Jameson.

"You can have a little bit more," said Marcus, "But remember why, and what I told you."

Wayne moved forward and poured his own measure, adding some water to disguise the mix. Marcus was well aware of what had just occurred, and the look said everything.

"That's the thing," said Wayne, responding with words, as he sat back in his chair, "I keep doing wrong... I *do* need punishing, just like earlier."

Marcus pondered on what his friend was really saying. He thought Wayne had been punished enough for one day, despite him winning his maiden public fight.

"I would submit to the lash again," said Wayne, "if it cured me of my darker traits."

Marcus moved the conversation on to the Victorian navy and naval discipline. He pondered if Wayne really wanted to be whipped, seemingly for his own good, but he only saw an already battered torso in front of him; he shied away from asking him directly. Marcus thought about putting on the television but decided that watching 'Dads' Army' would be a diversion. He had to tackle the issue of the physical punishment head on.

"Would you want to be whipped now," Marcus asked. Wayne's face was turning red with embarrassment.

"Not sure, me old mate ... ," he replied, "Really not sure."

Marcus suggested Wayne was bruised enough and that extra bruising on his back would arouse suspicions from his wife.

"I've finally left Sandra," said Wayne.

Marcus was shocked, and said so. Wayne related that they had been on different 'pages' for at least two years. Their views about starting a family differed. She wanted more commitment, whilst he wanted more freedom.

"I've felt hemmed in for ages," admitted Wayne, "and I never felt that way out at sea on a small ship."

Marcus could understand that.

"In some ways I'm shocked," pondered Marcus, "but in other ways, I'm not. I know you don't do a lot together."

Marcus decided it was time to go to bed. "I'm off," he said as he walked into the main bedroom.

Wayne sneaked in one more 'secret' drink before also deciding to get some sleep. He stood up, switched off the light and made his way towards the second bedroom in the dark, stumbling on a poorly placed box as he entered. Marcus came into Wayne's room to see what had happened.

"It's okay, mate, I just tripped on something," explained Wayne, as he settled himself into bed.

"I see," Marcus replied.

--o--

Just over three weeks had passed since Wayne had won his first paid bout. Marcus had used the time to make arrangements for Wayne, Sean and himself to meet at the gym. Sean was not getting on well at his accommodation, although Marcus did not fully understand what the issue was. In truth, Marcus had always felt sorry for the traveller and had said he could move in with him on one condition – that he let Wayne give him a thrashing for his attempt to steal his friend's hub caps.

Everyone had been briefed and agreed to Marcus's unconventional plan. Sean had consented to be given a beating. He had a long-held desire to move in with Marcus. Wayne had gone along with his friend's suggestion of Sean receiving the belt.

Marcus felt powerful, but he wondered if Wayne would go ahead with the punishment when they finally met up at the gym. Wayne had spoken of wanting to be whipped but never of whipping another. Now the day had arrived.

When Wayne entered the gym, Marcus and Sean had been there for a good twenty minutes. Sean was wearing a pair of grey tracksuit bottoms and one of Marcus's old, faded, blue denim shirts. Marcus was determined to control the environment. He could see Wayne was glaring at Sean, so beckoned him across.

"Shake," instructed Marcus.

Wayne complied in a tokenistic way, bringing his hand down sharply within a millisecond. Marcus instructed his friend to strip to the waist. Wayne compiled and was soon bare-chested. Marcus pulled Sean towards him and started to unbutton his shirt. After the first three buttons had been undone Sean tried to unbutton the next.

"No," shouted Marcus, slapping Sean's hand away.

Wayne looked on in astonishment as Marcus continued his work. Sean was now shirtless.

"Face Wayne and flex," Marcus barked at Sean.

He half-heartedly raised his arms, but this only served to infuriate Marcus. Wayne wanted to say something but felt confused and powerless. Marcus moved over to a table, where an array of punishment tools had been carefully laid out in a neat row, and picked up a riding crop.

"Flex... flex," demanded Marcus as he whipped the traveller across the bare back. Sean felt embarrassed to be showing his clean torso to Wayne but the pain forced him to obey Marcus's commands.

"That's more like it," said Marcus, looking across to Wayne.

"Marcus... ," said Wayne, his voice trailing off.

Marcus momentarily left the space, quickly returning dressed in an identical pair of grey tracksuit bottoms, similar to Sean's.

"What do you want us to do," asked Marcus.

Wayne was confused and enquired who the 'us' referred to.

"Me and Sean," came the quick reply.

Wayne stepped back, looking equally confused. Sean was hoping that Marcus would allow him to get dressed and leave the gym.

"Not sure, me old mate ... not sure," Wayne eventually replied.

"Well, we're both standing here in front of you," came Marcus's response. This remark did not do anything to clarify Wayne's state of mind.

"Do you think Sean looks a bit skinny compared to me," enquired Marcus.

Wayne naturally agreed. Marcus suggested that Sean should do some physical exercises, as he was in a gym and they had all the equipment.

"Why not use the rowing machine," he said.

Marcus and Wayne lifted the machine from one corner and put it down the middle of the space.

"Put your shoes on and sit here, instructed Marcus, pointing to the rowing machine. Sean quickly returned with his shoes on.

"Slave ship punishment ... I'll leave him to you," was Marcus's next remark, as he left the gym.

Sean apologised to Wayne for trying to steal his hub caps but said that his family pressurised him into doing such things, albeit he knew it was wrong. Sean was still talking as Wayne was looking at the possible punishment tools laid out in front of him on the table. He chose a flexible leather belt, tapping it rhythmically into the palm of his hand.

"Only four strokes," he said, "For the four hub caps."

Wayne instructed Sean to start rowing. Once he got into a good rhythm the first lash hit his back, followed by a second and third. Wayne paused before giving Sean the final stroke, which was delivered more forcefully.

"Uh," exclaimed Sean, "… that hurt." Wayne responded by saying it was meant to, and that he could have easily given more strokes.

"You're too kind for your own good," Sean responded.

--o--

It had been over a fortnight since Sean had been at Hadrian's Gym for his punishment. Not a word had been spoken about it since.

Sean had now moved in with Marcus, shifting what little possessions he owned into Marcus's second bedroom. Sean's worldly goods comprised mainly of a few clothes, which were now neatly folded in a plain 1950s chest of drawers. Marcus had donated some of his 'cast offs' to boost Sean's wardrobe. His coat had its allocated place; it was hanging on the back of an old wooden kitchen chair, painted sky blue.

"Marcus, when is Wayne coming round," enquired Sean.

Marcus thought that it would be sometime after nine. He had to get through his first naked bout, get dressed, receive some feedback and then drive over. Marcus hoped that Wayne had learned his lesson and would either lose the bout, or draw. He anticipated Wayne rushing in, full of energy, 'giving it large,' as his friend would say. He also wondered what was in Sean's mind when he posed the question.

"Have you thought about what I said about you changing your name," Marcus asked.

Sean said he was not against the idea but Marcus would have to help him with the paperwork.

"William Thurston would suit you," chuckled Marcus.

He was not sure where he had got the name from, but it felt right. Sean wondered if Marcus was being serious. Marcus realised, too, that everything would have to be legally correct through a Deed. He was desperate for Sean to start a new life and get away from his unfulfilling past.

"We need to get a drink in before Wayne comes round," said Marcus unexpectedly.

He hurried to get two whiskey glasses and some Jameson. Once on the table Marcus looked for some soda water in the fridge. He explained to Sean that Wayne should not drink after a bout, but that he was unlikely to listen.

"You understand why, don't you Sean," said Marcus.

Sean said he did. Marcus filled the glasses with a generous amount of whisky in each. He had not asked Sean if he wanted an alcoholic drink.

"You put your own soda water in," he insisted.

Marcus sank back in a chair, drink in hand. He seemed pleased with himself, but found his thoughts drifting.

"When Wayne comes round," said Marcus, "I want you to go into the bedroom and change down into just those grey tracksuit bottoms I got you."

Sean indicated he understood what was being asked of him but did not understand why. He could not refuse as he was living under Marcus's roof. Sean looked across at Marcus for something more.

"I want you to show Wayne what progress you've been making with the dumb bells," he explained. Sean looked a bit deflated and sipped more of his drink.

The sound of the front door ringing alerted Marcus to what he had to do next. He quickly sprung out of his chair like a startled cat, tidying the alcohol away in the fridge whilst shouting at Sean to go to his bedroom and get changed. Sean thought his flatmate sounded unusually anxious. Marcus was soon at the front door and opened it to see a grinning Wayne. He embraced Marcus before his friend beckoned him inside and led him upstairs to his flat.

"I did it, me old mate," explained Wayne, "I did it."

Marcus let Wayne speak without interruption. He explained that just before getting into the ring he almost lost his nerve and thought of backing out.

"I took a deep breath, thought of my naval training, and just went for it," he said.

"It was still difficult at first," explained Wayne, "but during the rounds I just forgot I was naked."

Marcus suggested that was because he dropped his thinking mind at that point.

Wayne agreed and added, "I just thought, what's the worst thing that can happen? Marcus coming into the ring and grabbing me by the balls, that that made me laugh."

"So, I was with you in the ring even thought I was at home," said Marcus.

"Yes, that's right, me old mate, you were in my head," Wayne conceded, "In fact you're always in my head."

Marcus grinned but did not speak. Wayne said that the bout ended in a draw, and that the officials were happy with that.

"I've learned a lot, and a lot about myself," he said.

As Wayne was speaking about his experience in the ring, Marcus was pulling open cupboard doors and taking out some half-used candles. He spread them out on the living room table and went back into the kitchen to look for some matches.

Marcus lit each of the large, white candles in turn carefully moving along the row until each was glowing and wavering in the gentle air currents. It seemed like a sacred act. Having completed his solum task, he turned to Wayne to give him his full attention.

"So, who was your opponent; what was he like," asked Marcus enthusiastically.

"They called him Tygo the tiger," said Wayne, who went on to point out that this was his real first name.

Wayne explained that he was Dutch and come over from Holland for the bout as nothing like that existed in his home country.

"He even lives on a boat in Amsterdam," Wayne continued.

"He seems a soul mate of the water," Marcus suggested.

Wayne agreed, and said that both boxers had exchanged addresses and would write to each other.

"Tygo's a bit younger than me, and I'd say more athletic," explained Wayne, "and I'd also say doesn't have a problem with being seen naked."

"Speaking of which, do you want to use our bath," Marcus asked.

Wayne responded by saying he would be going back to Malcolm's house, and would think about it there. Marcus looked perplexed.

"I'm staying there for it a bit ... yes," said Wayne.

He suddenly looked distant; deep in contemplation. Marcus tried to ascertain what was going on so asked a direst question of his friend.

"Have you and Sandra really broken up?" Wayne nodded.

Marcus knew that things had been strained for a while but was surprised to hear about a formal break.

"Malcom's good," said Wayne, "He's allowing me to stay for ... well, for as long as I want."

"At least Sandra won't see your beautifully bruised body," quipped Marcus, trying to lift the mood, "but it looks like neither will I."

That seemed to be the signal for Sean to come into the lounge, carrying a pair of dumb bells. It was clear by Wayne's expression that he was not expecting to see Sean in Marcus's flat, let alone sporting the same grey tracksuit bottoms he wore at the gym.

"Show Wayne what you can do with the dumb bells," instructed Marcus, "and give him a flex before you start."

Sean duly obliged. Marcus pointed out to Wayne that Sean was staying with him, "just as you are doing with Malcolm."

Wayne wondered if the two things were really that similar.

"What are you going to do with your life from now on," enquired Marcus.

"Mate, I really don't know," his friend replied.

Wayne said that he had certainly gone through two linked things that had come in quick succession.

"A paid bout and then the naked bout," enquired Marcus.

Wayne confirmed this, but was thinking that just as that had happened, his wife and he had parted for good.

"Everything has a time," muttered Marcus.

Sean had paused his exercising but resumed the dumb bells for a minute or so. He then turned to face Wayne.

"Let me ask you a question mister Wayne, if you don't mind," he said, "Are you looking for some-*one*, or some-*thing*?"

Wayne ignored the question.

"Anyway, I think it's time for me to go," said Wayne, "Got to check in at Saxon Lodge bed and breakfast."

Marcus said he understood and escorted his friend to the front door of the converted house.

"Sean's too clever for his own good," commented Wayne as Marcus opened the heavy door with its dirty Victorian stained-glass panels.

"I'll give him a slap when you've gone," laughed Marcus.

Wayne did not know whether to take the remark seriously. As he went to close the door, Marcus noticed a spider in its web in the corner of the porch. It brought his thoughts back to the time when he observed a spider making a web outside his office window. That was just before his boss showed him the union literature asking for boxers to come forward.

Marcus hurried up the stairs and re-entered his flat. He checked the rows of candles, which were now hot enough for drips of wax to run down the sides, making small pools.

"What are you going to do with those," asked Sean"

"It's for your initiation," Marcus responded, "Go and lay down on the bed facing up."

Sean obliged, slipping off his track suit bottoms before getting into position.

As Marcus came into the room carrying the two largest candles Sean said, "I thought you'd prefer me like this."

"Why, yes," replied Marcus, his solemn expression dissolving into a grin. "You're learning fast," he continued, "Get ready."

Sean relaxed and mentally prepared himself to became the bruised initiate.

Printed in Great Britain
by Amazon

80195891R00124